Praise for the *New Yo*
Paws & Claws

## *The Ghost and Mrs. Mewer*

"[A] hit! [Davis] has created a pet owner's utopia in her series . . . An intriguing mystery that keeps you guessing right up to the end . . . Absolutely fabulous."

—Open Book Society

"Engaging and entertaining . . . [Davis] always writes a delightfully charming tale that is hard to put down . . . I tend to forsake chores to get to the end of her stories."

—Dru's Book Musings

"If such a town as Wagtail really existed I would move there in a heartbeat . . . Atmospheric and chilling . . . [A] wonderful story filled with fur and frights!"

—Melissa's Mochas, Mysteries & Meows

"[A] beautifully written, cleverly crafted mystery sure to please pet-lovers and fair-play-mystery fans alike. The swift pace, engaging narration, and strong sense of place make it very easy to lose yourself in *The Ghost and Mrs. Mewer*."

—Smitten by Books

## *Murder, She Barked*

"Krista Davis has created another charming series with a unique setting, an engaging heroine in Holly Miller and her furry sidekick, Trixie, and a wonderfully quirky supporting cast of characters—two- and four-legged. I'm looking forward to my next visit to the Sugar Maple Inn."

—Sofie Kelly, *New York Times* bestselling author of the Magical Cats Mysteries

*continued . . .*

"Krista Davis has penned a doggone great new mystery series featuring witty, spirited Holly Miller and her endearing canine sidekick, Trixie. The adorable, pet-friendly setting of Wagtail Mountain will appeal to animal lovers and mystery lovers alike, and the intriguing plot twists will keep you guessing to the very last page."

—Kate Carlisle, *New York Times* bestselling author of the Bibliophile Mysteries

"Krista Davis has created a town that any pet would love—as much as their owners do. And they won't let a little thing like murder spoil their enjoyment."

—Sheila Connolly, *New York Times* bestselling author of the County Cork Mysteries, Museum Mysteries, and Orchard Mysteries

"A charming blend of small-town eccentrics and big-city greed, *Murder, She Barked* touches all the bases of the cozy mystery—including a bit of romance—and does so with style." —*Richmond Times-Dispatch*

"Well-written dialogue, fun characters, and romantic complications that never go as the characters—or the readers—expect . . . Readers will enjoy this skillfully plotted mystery and its biting humor." —Kings River Life Magazine

"[A] fun, fast-paced read. The plotting is top-notch, and I love the quirky characters. I could not put this book down. The story will keep you guessing until you find out whodunit. The author has plenty of dogs . . . I mean red herrings to keep you turning those pages. I am looking forward to reading more books in this delightful new series." —MyShelf.com

*Berkley Prime Crime titles by Krista Davis*

*Domestic Diva Mysteries*

THE DIVA RUNS OUT OF THYME
THE DIVA TAKES THE CAKE
THE DIVA PAINTS THE TOWN
THE DIVA COOKS A GOOSE
THE DIVA HAUNTS THE HOUSE
THE DIVA DIGS UP THE DIRT
THE DIVA FROSTS A CUPCAKE
THE DIVA WRAPS IT UP
THE DIVA STEALS A CHOCOLATE KISS

*Paws & Claws Mysteries*

MURDER, SHE BARKED
THE GHOST AND MRS. MEWER
MURDER MOST HOWL

# Murder Most Howl

Krista Davis

BERKLEY PRIME CRIME, NEW YORK

**An imprint of Penguin Random House LLC**
**375 Hudson Street, New York, New York 10014**

MURDER MOST HOWL

A Berkley Prime Crime Book / published by arrangement with the author



ISBN: 978-0-425-26257-3

PUBLISHING HISTORY
Berkley Prime Crime mass-market edition / December 2015

PRINTED IN THE UNITED STATES OF AMERICA

10 9 8 7 6 5 4 3 2 1

Cover illustration by Mary Ann Lasher.
Cover design by Diana Kolsky.
Cover logo by Alpimages/Shutterstock.
Interior text design by Kelly Lipovich.



Penguin
Random
House

*For Dr. Jonel Nightingale, DVM, and Kyle Monger,*
*veterinary assistant, who went above and beyond*
*to save the life of my beloved Mochie*

# Acknowledgments

One of the problems with writing mysteries set in a wonderful place like Wagtail is the high number of homicides that must occur in such a lovely town—an issue affectionately known as the Cabot Cove Syndrome. I considered moving this story forward in time to help solve that problem but found too many things remained unanswered from the previous books. Did Oma ever take her cruise? Did Holmes get married? What happened with Ben? In the end, I decided to move the calendar only slightly. After all, these are mysteries, and a murder or two are part of a mystery. I beg your forbearance on this subject since we all know that a town as delightful as Wagtail would surely have no murders at all.

Several of the animals in this book are modeled after real dogs and cats. With heartfelt apologies for omitting a mention in the acknowledgments in *The Ghost and Mrs. Mewer*, I have to thank Paige Bennett for allowing me to use her sweet Yorkshire terrier, GloryB, who, as it turned out, now lives in Wagtail and also makes an appearance in this book. Funny Ella Mae is modeled after Sue Ross's min pin and rat terrier mix, whom she describes as ten pounds of terror. And Leo is based on a real cat by the same name, who belonged to Amy McClung. At an auction benefiting the Thomas Jefferson Center for the Protection of Free Expression, Amy won the opportunity to have the pet of her choice in one of my books. When Amy sent along the information about Leo, I was taken by her loving memories of him. I hope I have done justice to this kitty who was such a vivid character in real life. Thanks to Josh Wheeler, director of the Thomas Jefferson Center, for making the arrangements.

Special thanks go to Betsy Strickland for naming the book club The Thursday Night Cloak and Dagger Club! As always, I appreciate the support and encouragement of my friends, online and off.

I am so grateful for the eagle eye of my editor, Sandra Harding. Over the years, I have learned to always take her sage advice. Sadly, this is the last book Sandy will edit for me, as she has moved on. I am blessed to have had Sandy as my editor and thank her from the bottom of my heart for everything she has done for me.

Very special thanks to my new editor, Julie Mianecki, who stepped in without missing a beat. I look forward to writing more books with Julie.

My delightful agent, Jessica Faust, wears many hats on my behalf: business manager; negotiator; advisor; contract interpreter; and the one I love the most, friend.

Most of all, I have to thank my readers. I cherish every note and message. I feel like I have gotten to know so many of you. And for each one of you who has reached out to me in some way, I know there are more who also dream of a place like Wagtail.

*You ask of my companions. Hills, sir, and the sundown, and a dog as large as myself that my father bought me. They are better than human beings, because they know but do not tell.*

—Emily Dickinson

**MURDER MYSTERY WEEKEND PARTICIPANTS**

Ian Tredwell and Blanche Wimmer Tredwell
Geoffrey and Charlotte Tredwell, and Ella Mae, a miniature pinscher and rat terrier mix
Robin Jarvis
Sylvie Porter
Myrtle McGuire
Weegie Anderson and Puddin', an apricot poodle
The Baron von Rottweiler, victim

**SUGAR MAPLE INN STAFF**

Holly Miller
Mr. Huckle
Shelley Dixon
Zelda York and Leo, a large tabby
Trixie, a Jack Russell terrier
Twinkletoes, a calico, feline ambassador of the inn
Gingersnap, a golden retriever, canine ambassador of the inn

**RESIDENTS OF WAGTAIL AND HOLLY'S FRIENDS**

Val Kowalchuk, owner of the Hair of the Dog Pub
Norm Wilson, a local businessman
Savannah Wilson, Norm's wife, and Bingo, a Corgi
Aunt Birdie DuPuy, Holly's aunt
Max Hemmerich, owner of Tall Tails Bookstore
Shadow Hobbs, handyman
Hollis Hobbs, Shadow's father
Holmes Richardson, Holly's childhood friend
Ben Hathaway, Holly's former boyfriend

"These are the murder weapons." Val Kowalchuk reached into the chestnut leather tote she had brought with her and pulled out a pearl-handled pistol.

The new owner of the popular Wagtail pub, Hair of the Dog, Val was brimming with clever ideas to bring tourists to Wagtail, our pet-themed town nestled in the mountains of western Virginia. Enthusiastic and hardworking, she was quickly becoming a good friend.

We were on our way to Café Chat for brunch to finalize some details about Murder Most Howl, Wagtail's murder mystery weekend, when Val pulled the pistol from her purse. I stopped dead. "That looks real!"

Val twirled it on her forefinger with alarming ease. With her short, dark brown hair, sparkling brown eyes, and the pistol dangling from her finger, I was tempted to nickname her Calamity Val.

"Amazing, isn't it?"

We walked on. "Frightening. Someone could mistake it for a real gun."

Val snorted. "Wouldn't do them much good. It's made of wood."

We reached the double arched doors of the restaurant. Over top of the entrance were the words *Café Chat*. Sleek stylized cats curved to create the capital *C*'s. The name was a bilingual double entendre, because *Chat* meant cat in French.

But when we turned to enter, Trixie, my Jack Russell terrier, took off. I no longer used a leash to walk her around town. We had been practicing coming when called and most of the time she listened to me, but she still had a mind of her own and sometimes followed her nose elsewhere. I knew where she was headed this time, though, straight to the doggy play area. "I'll meet you inside," I said to Val.

Trixie sped across the green, the park in the middle of Wagtail's pedestrian zone. When I caught up to her, she was politely sniffing a corgi who ran loose.

An attractive blonde woman bundled in a puffy purple jacket and faux fur boots was talking on the phone. Although I didn't know who she was, I'd seen her around town before and thought the corgi belonged to her.

I looked up at the silvery gray sky. Even though it was ten in the morning, and other people walked dogs, there was a silence in the air. A peaceful stillness that meant snow was on the way.

The woman on the phone whispered, but it was so quiet that she might as well have come right up to me and spoken aloud.

"Blanche is in town." She paused. "That's what I thought, too." She sucked in a deep breath of the cold air. "I'm finally going to do it. I can't go on like this."

I gave Trixie a few minutes to run with the corgi. She would behave better at Café Chat if she burned off some energy. I felt a little bit guilty about listening to the woman's phone call, but good grief, if she was going to have a private conversation in public, what did she expect?

"Of course I'm nervous! Why do you think I've put it off

for so long?" She smiled at me in spite of eyes rimmed in red from crying.

I dug in my pocket for a treat, held it out, and called to Trixie. She gave the corgi one last look and evidently decided that a cookie was more enticing. As Trixie and I walked away, I heard the woman say, "This weekend. The sooner the better."

Trixie scampered into Café Chat, probably as relieved as I was to be out of the cold. I helped her out of her plush pink coat and hung it on the rack with my own boring winter white jacket.

Zelda York and Shelley Dixon spied me and waved their hands in the air. Val sat with them at a table next to the window.

Zelda and Shelley worked at the Sugar Maple Inn with me. In her spare time, Zelda was building a pet psychic business. I wasn't sure that she could really read the minds of dogs and cats, but so far, she'd been fairly accurate.

Wagging her tail, Trixie darted between round-backed bistro chairs to greet half a dozen dog friends on the way to our table. My little girl with the black ears and spot on her rump had the good sense to approach Zelda's cat, Leo, cautiously. She stopped short of him and gently extended her nose toward his.

An extraordinarily confident cat, Leo stretched his white paws forward, showing off the blaze on his chest and demonstrating his total lack of concern about Trixie's presence. Everyone in town knew the large tiger-striped tabby with the characteristic *M* on his forehead.

I slid into the chair next to Val. White tablecloths and white toppers gave the casual bistro a slightly upscale feel.

Zelda, as full-figured as she was full of life, held a gold candlestick, turning it in her hands. She had braided strands of her long blonde hair on both sides and pulled back the braids. They hung like beautiful garlands on the sides of her head, reminding me of a Norse princess. "This is so cool. But I don't get it. Why only four weapons? Doesn't everyone get a weapon?"

I guessed the wicked meat cleaver Shelley held was also a

weapon. Shelley had cut her light brown hair and streaked it blonde to lighten it. It was a layered bob of large curls that I envied. My own straight brown hair would never cooperate in that kind of cut.

She wore Wagtail chic, a fisherman-style knit sweater in cream. Her bulky olive-colored jacket hung over the back of her chair. "You want me to hide this in—" Shelley tilted her head to read a note on the cleaver "—oh my word, it's a little rhyme!"

The waitress interrupted to take my order. I was so spoiled by the terrific breakfasts at the Sugar Maple Inn that I found it difficult to eat breakfast out. "Two eggs sunny-side up with roasted potatoes, and the same for Trixie. I'll have coffee, and she'll have water, please."

Zelda looked at Val with apologetic eyes. "I'm sorry I had to miss the last few meetings about the murder mystery weekend. Now I'm lost. This sounds like a scavenger hunt."

Val placed a gorgeous bottle on the table. About four inches high, it had been a painted metallic green that made it look like glass. On one side, it bore a skull and crossbones painted in silver on a red background. "Murder Most Howl is a cross between a scavenger hunt and a murder mystery game. The participants all play themselves. But each of them will have a secret from his or her past that ties them to the victim. For instance, there's a participant named Robin Jarvis. When she receives her secret at the initial meeting at Hair of the Dog tonight, Robin will find out that she's the sister of the victim's second wife. And that she came here to avenge her sister's death. But she doesn't have to wear a costume or be anyone but herself. Get it? She doesn't have to pretend she's a millionaire or a movie star. It's up to each player to decide whether to share the secret with anyone. The goal is to solve the mystery of who killed the victim. They have to figure out who the killer is, the motive, and how he or she murdered the victim."

"So each of the players has a reason to kill him? How do they figure out which one did it?" asked Zelda.

Val passed each of us a couple of bloodred envelopes. "These contain additional clues. The yellow sticky on each one is the rhyme they will receive to help them find it. Use that as your guide to hiding it. Where would you look if you read that rhyme?"

I started to look at mine, but she continued. "In the packets they'll receive tonight, each player will get a list of the rhymes. Some will lead to clues and some will lead to weapons. Everyone starts with the same basic information, but obviously, not everyone will find the same clues. Some of the clues will be red herrings that take them in the wrong direction. But there is one thread of clues that fits together to provide the identity of the killer, the motive, and the means."

Zelda waved the bottle at her. "Where do the weapons come in?"

"Three weapons will be hidden. They're sort of a bonus. If you're lucky enough to find one, you can use it to force competitors to share clues with you. Obviously, having a weapon is a big advantage, so they'll be trying to steal them from each other. The merchants around town know more clues, and that will draw people into stores, restaurants, and businesses to chat."

"You mean the merchants have more clues to hand out?" asked Shelley.

"No. They know gossip about the victim. Just like real life. Residents of Wagtail are always gossiping. This is no different."

"That's so clever," said Shelley. "A really great way to get people out and about in Wagtail."

"Each of you will hide one weapon. All the players will have the same opportunity to discover them—so make them a little bit difficult to find, okay? The first victim will be killed by poison, so I'm keeping the bottle." Val handed me the candlestick.

"It's so light! This could actually be used as a candlestick."

Val grinned. "They're hand-carved. That's real gold leaf covering the candlestick."

The waitress delivered our food and set two small dishes on the floor, along with water bowls for Trixie and Leo.

I glanced at Zelda. "I hope Leo is hungry. Trixie might try to eat his food."

Zelda laughed. "Are you kidding? Look how big Leo is. It's Trixie's food that might be in danger."

I kept an eye on Trixie anyway. She had been homeless and scrabbling for food before she adopted me. I assumed her insatiable hunger was a result of that terrible time.

Val was drinking coffee, staring off toward the door, when she groaned. "Not Norm Wilson, please," she whispered. "He's been such a pill."

I glanced up to see him heading our way. Norm had a round face and a rounder belly. I imagined that he looked much like he had as a young man, except heavier. The buttons on his blue Oxford cloth shirt strained against the fabric, threatening to reveal all. He wore khaki pants, loafers, and no socks despite the cold weather—a Southern male affectation that I had never quite understood. His fair hair was sparse but a bit of it hung over his forehead.

"Look at this, the four prettiest ladies in all of Wagtail."

I thought Val might spew her coffee.

The rest of us politely murmured greetings.

He spied the pistol. "Who's packin'? Is it legal to have a gun in a restaurant?"

"That one is perfectly legal," said Val, a bit testy.

He took in the clue envelopes and the candlestick. "Oh, I get it. You're meeting about Murder Most Howl. Mind if I pull up a chair? You should have notified everyone if you were going to have a meeting."

Was Val holding her breath?

I smiled at him. "I think Val has everything under control, Norm. But it's kind of you to offer."

"Always happy to pitch in." He thumped the table. "Y'all just give me a call if you run into trouble." He ambled away muttering to himself, but I was pretty certain he said, "And you will."

I leaned toward Val and spoke softly. "What was that about?"

She looked around at us, her brown eyes sincere. "I know I'm new to Wagtail, so don't think poorly of me. I just detest that man."

Shelley picked up a piece of toast. "What did he ever do to you?"

The corner of Val's mouth twitched. "I don't really want to tell you. You'll think I'm a petty and horrible person." She paused. "You know what? I shouldn't say anything."

Zelda grinned. "Now we'll be thinking the worst. Spill, girl!"

Val heaved a sigh. "I bought the pub at auction, and Norm was such a jerk. He kept bidding it up and up. Honestly, I don't think he wanted it. I truly think he did it just to jerk me around."

Shelley's eyes met mine. "I don't know, Val. That would have been an expensive mess for him if you had stopped bidding."

"Tell me this, then. If he wanted a pub so badly, why didn't he take some of that money and open one across town somewhere?" She shook her head. "Nope. I paid much more than I should have because he was getting a kick out of it."

"It was nice of him to offer to help with the mystery weekend," said Shelley.

Val's hands curled into fists on the table. "Are you kidding? I wouldn't be surprised if he sabotaged it. Norm was against this mystery weekend as soon as Hollis Hobbs tried to limit Norm's involvement. Hollis hates him, too. Norm is not the sweet, amiable guy you might think."

Zelda set her coffee cup down. "Everyone I talked to was excited about the mystery weekend."

"Everyone else has been so generous and helpful. The grand prize is a week at the Sugar Maple Inn, thanks to a certain Holly Miller and her grandmother." Val grinned at me.

"Plus a host of free meals at restaurants and cafés, and massages, beds, and food for dogs and cats, not to mention gift certificates to spend at some of the stores. Runners-up will win gift certificates for stores and services, like the zip line and pet grooming."

"So they just run around looking for weapons and clues?" asked Zelda.

Val swallowed her last bite of eggs Benedict. "No. It's quite interactive. People can play by themselves or in teams. Just you wait. They'll tell lies to throw one another off the track of the murderer. I hear people get very competitive in these types of games."

"So who is the killer?" asked Zelda.

"I'm the only one, besides the killer and victim, of course, who knows who they are."

"Aww, c'mon. Let us in on the secret," Zelda begged.

"Okay," said Val, looking altogether too mischievous, "the victim is the Baron von Rottweiler, a resident of Wagtail."

Shelley, Zelda, and I exchanged glances.

"I've never heard of him," said Shelley. "And I've lived here forever."

Val laughed. "Well, you'd better meet him soon because someone is about to do in the poor fellow."

Zelda scowled at Val. "That's not fair. At least tell us who the killer is!" She leaned forward, gleeful.

Val tilted her head at us. "No way. I'm not having you supply additional clues to someone just because you like him or her."

"You don't trust us!" said Shelley.

"Isn't that always the first rule of a murder?" asked Val. "Trust no one."

"Let me get this straight," said Zelda. "All the players get the rhyme that's on the outside of the envelope. That's the scavenger part? It leads them to the envelope?"

"Right. Each player gets a list of the rhymes in the packet they'll receive tonight." Val nodded her head. "Then, whoever is the first to find an envelope gets the clue inside about the murder. And that person is the only one who knows that fact."

Our waitress had just brought our check when Zelda grabbed my arm. "Don't look now, but isn't that Blanche Wimmer, the famous model?"

We all gazed out the window next to our table.

Zelda hissed, "I said, 'Don't look now'!"

"Please. Everyone knows that's the universal directive to look immediately." Shelley leaned back for a better view. "That is Blanche! Older, definitely heavier, but just as beautiful as ever. I can't believe she's here in Wagtail. How old do you think she is?"

"She has to be forty or forty-five," I said.

Val frowned and dug in her tote. She pulled out an iPad and flicked it on. "Could her name be Tredwell now? I have a bunch of Tredwells registered for the mystery game, and one of them has the first name of Blanche."

I turned to Val in amazement. "How cool is that? A celebrity is playing."

Val beamed. "We have to get some pictures. Hey! I could start a wall with signed photos of famous visitors at Hair of the Dog!"

"She does those infomercials now," Zelda whispered. "The kind they run on TV in the middle of the night. Men cannot resist Blanche. She could sell anything to my good-for-nothing ex-husband. He bought hundreds of dollars worth of makeup from her one night."

"He wore makeup?" asked Val.

"No. That's my point."

"Maybe it was for you?" asked Shelley.

"Like I needed ten eyelash curlers and a dozen lipsticks in the same color? I made him to take all that junk with him when I threw him out of the house."

I gazed at Blanche, trying not to be obvious. "If memory serves, she wasn't even eighteen when she became the *it* girl." She had graced the covers of countless magazines and tried acting in a few abysmal movies.

At the moment, she was turning the heads of people passing by her, and suddenly I felt sorry for her. It couldn't be easy being recognized everywhere she went.

Blonde hair rippled over the fluffy collar of her faux lynx jacket. Tight leggings clung to her long legs. Her face had filled out but her eyes were as big and stunning as when she was in her heyday. I guessed she was wearing ample makeup, including fake eyelashes to achieve that look, but from where I sat, she still looked like a star.

Blanche glanced around as though she was waiting for someone, then dodged into a store.

As we left Café Chat, snow drifted from the sky. Promising

Val we would hide our clues and weapons, we went our separate ways. Trixie and I headed back to the inn.

Snow had begun to lace the pines around Wagtail. The Sugar Maple Inn, which I thought was beautiful at any time of year, would be especially enchanting in the snow. Several owners had constructed additions built of locally mined stone, resulting in a sprawling building. The inn had been in my family since before my birth. And although I hadn't grown up in Wagtail, my parents had shipped me back every summer to spend time with my grandmother. To me, the Sugar Maple Inn was home.

A long porch full of rocking chairs spanned the front of the main building. In warmer weather, guests lounged there all day long with their dogs and cats. Not a soul was there now. Trixie and I cut around to the side entrance where guests checked in.

We shed our winter jackets in the office, and I read the clue for the candlestick aloud to Trixie.

*Outside of a dog, a book is man's best friend.*
*Inside of a dog, it's too dark to read.*

*—Groucho Marx*

Books and reading, eh? The players would surely be looking through Tall Tails, the bookstore, for the candlestick. "C'mon, Trixie. Val said to make it difficult to find the weapon." Trixie followed me to the inn library, which was loaded with my grandmother's favorite genre—mysteries!

Located in the newest addition, the library joined the cat wing to the main part of the inn. A cushy window seat begged to be lounged on, but the gas fireplace hadn't been turned on yet, and I felt a chill in the room. I flicked it on with the remote control.

Kneeling, I slipped the candlestick behind a group of Agatha Christie paperbacks on the lowest shelf. I stood up and examined it. Most people were taller than me. I couldn't tell that the books had been shoved forward to make room for something behind them. I doubted that anyone who wasn't looking for the weapon would notice.

"What do you think, Trixie?"

She wagged her tail, which I took as approval.

Back in the office, I nabbed packing tape, bundled Trixie in her plush pink coat, and pulled on my own puffy white jacket again.

When we stepped outside, I was glad I had dressed Trixie. A frigid breeze swept through town. The kind that chills a person to the bone.

My next clue made me laugh.

*The friendly cow, all red and white,*
*I love with all my heart:*
*She gives me cream with all her might,*
*To eat with apple-tart.*

*—Robert Louis Stevenson*

I jogged along the increasingly snowy path of the green to warm up. Trixie sped ahead of me, sniffing around trees. I cut to the right and hurried to the big two-dimensional cow outside of Moo La La, the ice cream shop. Not surprisingly, there was no long line of customers at the window today.

"Holly! Holly!" Jim Maybree, the handyman at the Sugar Maple Inn, waved at me and hurried in my direction. "I'm glad I ran into you. I was on my way to the inn. I don't know how to tell you this, so I guess I'll just blurt it out. I finally got a job as a ski instructor over on Snowball Mountain!"

"Congratulations!" I said cheerfully, but as I spoke it dawned on me that this might be very bad news for the inn. "That's great, Jim."

"It's my dream come true. I've been trying for years and was beginning to think it might never happen. I can hardly believe that I finally landed that job." His face fell. "But it means I won't be able to work at the inn anymore."

He looked so sad that I hastened to reassure him even though it wasn't good news for me. "We're very happy for you. Just give us a little time to find a replacement?"

I thought he might be sick.

"I . . . I kind of told them I'd start tomorrow. That was wrong of me. I don't want to let you down. I can go back and tell them that—but then they might hire someone else . . ."

It was my turn to feel a little bit ill. No one to take care of pooper scooping, or to fix leaky faucets, or to bring in wood for the older fireplaces?

"I should have given you notice. I'll turn them down."

I shook off my queasiness. "Don't be silly. No one should ever pass up a dream job. It might not come your way again. I'll find someone else."

Jim almost crushed me in a bear hug. "Thanks, Holly!"

"Uh, Jim? You wouldn't know anyone who would like the job, would you?"

"I'll ask around and let you know. Thanks for being so nice about it. I think your grandmother might have given me a hard time for leaving her in the lurch."

She might have at that. My Oma, German for grandma, had taken me on as her partner at the Sugar Maple Inn. She was finally off to Hong Kong with her best friend, Rose, on a richly deserved two-week-long cruise.

I had been so pleased that Oma felt confident enough to leave me in charge of the Sugar Maple Inn. I was in my early thirties, so it wasn't as though it was my first job, but managing an inn was unique and sometimes posed unusual challenges. The inn was Oma's baby. She had worked long and hard to make it a success. It didn't surprise me one bit that she was reluctant to leave it in my hands. Anyone's hands! But I was glad she had.

At least, I'd been happy about it until I overheard her talking to my father, who had pointed out that January was always a sleepy, dead month in Wagtail when nothing happened. "A safe time to leave Holly in charge," he'd said. Oma agreed, deflating my ego considerably. I knew they meant well and hadn't intended to insult me, but it made me more determined than ever to prove that Oma could safely leave the inn in my hands. Now that I was her partner, she needed to have confidence in me.

I heaved a big sigh. It was okay, I told myself. Everything would be fine. By the time Oma returned from her trip, I would have a new handyman on staff, thus proving my competence to handle anything that came along.

The snow was coming down heavily now. I shivered in the cold. In a big hurry, I taped the clue on the back of the cow and rushed to leave the other clue taped to a park bench before hurrying home to the inn where chaos reigned.

Zelda was manning the reception desk. Dogs ran around the room, playing with Gingersnap, Oma's golden retriever, who was the Canine Ambassador and official tail-wagger and nose-kisser of the inn. A tiny black and cream dog raced in circles through Gingersnap's legs and around a bloodhound puppy, who seemed confused and apprehensive.

A large mixed breed with long yellow and white fur stood out of the way near the love seat. He took in the bedlam with worried eyes, and his tail wagged ever so tentatively.

"Are these the dogs for If the Dog Fits?" I asked. The Wagtail Shelter, a no-kill facility, had come up with an idea to match people to dogs. The idea was that the shelter would drop off a few appropriate dogs, and the participating person could select one to try out for the weekend. They would spend the weekend together, and hopefully fall in love and adopt.

"Now don't get mad at me," said Zelda. "I know they're supposed to be in crates but they all wanted out and promised me they would behave."

I had my doubts about Zelda's alleged animal psychic abilities. "Zelda, what dog wouldn't lie to get out of a crate?"

Zelda gasped. "Dogs never lie. They're more honest than any human I know."

"Uh-huh. Even the little black and cream tornado who is racing around getting everyone else riled up?"

"Ella Mae. Isn't she adorable?"

The automatic glass door slid open. Guests walked in with more dogs, who happily joined the fun. It was too late to corral them all. I shrugged off my bulky jacket, helped Trixie ditch her little coat, and tossed them into the office before I rushed to Zelda's aid.

One of the women had already snatched Ella Mae into her arms. She cooed at the little dog, who rewarded her with kisses.

Gingersnap trained her eyes on Ella Mae. The little dog's coloring resembled a miniature Doberman, black with cream that started on her paws and extended to her chest.

The woman clutched Ella Mae as though she feared Gingersnap might harm her.

"Don't worry about Gingersnap," I said. "She's very friendly."

"For Pete's sake, Charlotte, put that dog on the floor and let her play. Nothing is going to happen to her." The man who uttered those words was attractive in a friendly way with neatly trimmed hair brushed back off his face. A glimmer of gray had crept into it. One eyebrow was up a little higher than the other, imparting a slightly impish look that I bet extended to his character. He was reasonably trim, and looked like someone who probably had a responsible kind of job.

Charlotte held on to the dog and ignored him. "Charlotte and Geoffrey Tredwell," she said to Zelda, who glanced at me as soon as Charlotte said the name. "We're part of the If the Dog Fits weekend." She planted a smooch on the little dog's head.

Her husband quickly added, "We're also playing the Murder Most Howl game. Char, how about the big yellow dog?" He walked over to the timid dog, bent, and ruffled the dog's fur. "How about it, big boy? Would you like to be our dog? Do you like to run? I need a running companion."

"That's Rooster," said Zelda. "He doesn't like that name, though, and won't be upset if you change it."

The yellow dog wagged his tail, but Geof Tredwell gave Zelda a curious look. "Char, I bet Rooster is already house-broken. Look how friendly he is."

Char shook her head.

"Do you expect me to run with that little dog? People would laugh at me. He's smaller than a cat."

"Ella Mae is a girl, and she's adorable." Char held her up and cooed at her, which resulted in a dog kiss on Char's nose.

The Tredwells were our first guests to participate in the If the Dog Fits program. "Congratulations! So you and Ella Mae are spending the weekend together to see if you're a good fit?"

Geoffrey hacked and turned away coughing. When he recovered, he said, "Char. Be serious. We need a real dog, not one the size of a rat."

"Geof, if you say one more bad thing about this dog, you better hope they have an extra room. She's not a rat. She's part miniature pinscher and part rat terrier. It says so right here on the papers. I don't know anything about rat terriers, but I'm betting they hunted rats. Which is more than you can do." She glanced past him out the window. "Will you look at that snow? Ella Mae is going to need a coat."

Geof turned his eyes toward the ceiling. "Saints above, spare me! Now she's going to buy the dog a wardrobe."

Char demanded, "Which room is mine, please?"

I picked up her luggage.

Geof looked down at Rooster. "I'm sorry, fellow. Really and truly sorry."

Rooster's tail flicked in a sad wag. The bloodhound puppy who had been ignored by the Tredwells sat in a corner looking sad and bewildered. I wanted to adopt him!

I asked the Treadwells to follow me.

Geof trailed along behind us as we walked to the elevator.

"C'mon, Char," he said. "You know I'm not fond of tiny dogs that can fit in a purse. We should choose a real dog like Rooster."

"You better get another room if you don't want to sleep in the snow, Geof. I'm not putting up with disparaging remarks all weekend. I love this little doggy!"

Ella Mae's ears stood up straight. She turned her head, looking around and taking everything in with bright eyes. I wondered if she knew instinctively that Geof didn't care for her. Probably. Dogs were amazingly adept at picking up on emotions. If it bothered her, she didn't show any sign of it. Would she snap or growl if he tried to pet her?

Then again, Ella Mae had been cooped up at the shelter. She was probably thrilled to be out in the world. Maybe she would try to win him over.

I unlocked the door to Stay and swung it open. Char entered first, and I could hear her exclaiming about it.

Geof studied the word on the door. "Stay? Does that change to Leave when you're done with us?"

I laughed at his interpretation. "All the rooms are named after dog and cat activities. Sit, Stay, Fetch, Pounce . . ."

"Swell," he muttered unenthusiastically.

The room featured a bay window, from which we could see the snow falling. A stone fireplace in the corner was ready to be lighted. Silky curtains hung off the frame of a mahogany four-poster bed piled with inviting pillows. Their wildflower pattern matched the window seat cushions.

Two welcome baskets rested on a coffee table, one chock full of dog toys and goodies, the other loaded with wine and munchies for the Tredwells.

"Does the fireplace work?" asked Geof.

"It does. If you need help with it, just give us a shout."

His wife shot him a glance. I expected another retort about finding a room of his own, but she released Ella Mae, who ran around sniffing every corner, her tail curled over her back.

"The initial meeting for Murder Most Howl is at Hair of the Dog at seven thirty tonight. It's marked on the map Zelda gave you. Let me know if you need anything."

I walked out of the room wondering about them. I hoped that Ella Mae would win over Geof during the weekend.

When I returned to the registration lobby, fifteen women who couldn't stop talking about the murder mystery weekend crowded the registration lobby. Two had brought their dogs along and two held cat carriers. The dogs, a poodle and a basset hound, mingled with Gingersnap, Trixie, Rooster, and the poor bloodhound puppy who had been ignored by the Tredwells. All tails flew high with excitement.

From the chatter, I gathered the women were all part of the same book club, called The Thursday Night Cloak and Dagger Club. One even wore a Sherlock Holmes–type hat. Mostly in their forties and fifties, they seemed to be good-natured and spirited.

"My word, but it's cold here. I hope there are some nice stores in town. I didn't pack any long johns." The speaker held the leash of a miniature poodle, whose apricot coat very nearly matched her own hair in both color and curl.

"Honestly, Weegie," said a short woman who held herself very erect. "We're in the mountains, what did you expect?"

Weegie's expression showed polite disdain for her friend. "We're from North Carolina," she drawled to Zelda. "I can't recall when it was this cold at home, Myrtle."

Myrtle's jaw tightened. I guessed she had been a dark brunette, because her hair had turned silken gray with dark streaks. The set of her jaw made me think she was a no-nonsense type. She looked at a friend who had obviously anticipated the chilly weather, because she wore a black puffer jacket. "Sylvie," said Myrtle, "are you sure you won't room with Weegie?"

Sylvie chuckled in a good-natured way, revealing sweet dimples on her pudgy face. Her round cheeks pushed up the oval wire-rimmed glasses she wore. Sylvie edged near the registration desk and pulled off a cap, revealing super-short two-tone blonde hair. Blondish bangs hung at the top of her face but had been trimmed a good inch above her eyebrows.

Her hair grew darker in tone toward her ears and the nape of her neck.

"Honey, I'm a terrible roommate," she said. "Sometimes I wake in the middle of the night and flick on the TV or read."

"I should have booked a single room," Myrtle grumbled.

Weegie didn't bother turning around. "You know that I can hear you, right?"

Sylvie squealed when Leo jumped on the counter right next to her. She sucked in a deep breath and staggered back a step.

"I'm so sorry. Where did he come from?" I asked, lifting him off the registration desk.

Myrtle giggled at her friend's shock. "He followed us inside."

Leo didn't seem perturbed. He strolled to the small landing on the stairs and watched us.

"Would you like a Sugar Maple Inn GPS collar for your dog?" I asked Weegie.

"GPS? You mean it tracks her?"

"In case she gets lost. There's no charge for it. You just turn it in when you leave."

"Well sure, if it's free." She turned her head to face her dog. "Would you like that, Puddin'?"

Puddin' didn't seem to mind when I latched the collar on her.

I had just settled Myrtle, Weegie, and Puddin' the poodle in Swim and returned to the registration desk when Zelda handed me the phone with dread in her eyes. "It's not beginning well," she whispered.

I took the phone from her. It was Val. Her voice sounded oddly controlled, as though she was making an effort to be calm. "We have a problem. A tree fell on electrical wires and half of Wagtail has no electricity—including Hair of the Dog."

"That's terrible! Do you want to sleep over here tonight? You can stay in my spare room."

"Holly! You're not getting what I'm saying." Suddenly she sounded panicked. "We have to start Murder Most Howl at the Sugar Maple Inn tonight!"

# Three

"No problem," I said to Val. "We would be happy to have the initial meeting here. We'll just have to notify everyone. Put a sign on the door of the pub, and we'll give people an extra twenty minutes or so to walk over here. Does that sound okay?"

Zelda bit her upper lip and watched me. "This is going to be trouble," she hissed.

"Nonsense," I whispered. "Val, just let me know what you need." I hung up the phone. "It will be fine. We have enough room to accommodate everyone. You start calling our participating guests to let them know. I'll round up Mr. Huckle and Shelley, and they can help me get the Dogwood Room ready. No problem." I'd said that twice in just a few seconds. I hoped I wasn't saying it to convince myself.

I trudged up the stairs to Oma's apartment. I'd been resentful when she told me that Mr. Huckle would be staying there during her absence. I loved Mr. Huckle, but having him live in the inn to watch over me was the equivalent of having a babysitter. Formerly a butler for a wealthy family in Wagtail, he was ancient and proper in a way that made me want to pull my shoulders back and stand straighter, but he was a dear man. Oma claimed he lent a dignified air to the inn, which was undoubtedly true, but the reality was that she wanted to give him a job when he found himself unexpectedly unemployed.

I knocked on the door. The moment Mr. Huckle opened it, Trixie jumped up and placed her paws on his knees. He bent to pat her. I was surprised to see the wizened little man in the formal attire he favored for work. It was almost as though he'd been waiting for me.

Mr. Huckle jumped at the opportunity to help. I wasn't sure if it was just his nature or years of being a butler that made him eager to be of assistance. Whatever the reason, I was glad to have him around in spite of my initial resentment.

While we walked downstairs, I told Mr. Huckle about losing our handyman. "Know of anyone who might be interested in the job?" I asked.

Mr. Huckle took a beat too long to respond. "Perhaps that's something your grandmother would prefer to take up upon her return."

*Hmmpf.* I hadn't expected that response. We needed a handyman now. Besides, this was something I could handle. I was perfectly capable of hiring someone. I let the topic slide and moved on to the project of setting up chairs.

Mr. Huckle, Shelley, and I formed an assembly line of sorts to bring extra chairs up from the basement. I refrained from mentioning to Mr. Huckle that a handyman would have been helpful. In the basement, I hauled the chairs onto the elevator and pressed the button for the main floor. Shelley took them off the elevator and carried them to Mr. Huckle, who arranged them in the Dogwood Room and the adjoining lobby.

Once a grand home, the inn had been expanded and updated over the years. It was situated in a prime location between the end of Wagtail's pedestrian zone and Dogwood Lake. The original lobby and grand staircase faced a plaza and the green, where people strolled with their dogs and cats.

Each side of the green was lined with sidewalks, where most of the stores and restaurants were located.

Oma had renovated recently, moving the official reception lobby to a new addition on the west side of the inn. We'd discovered, though, that it was wiser to keep an eye on the front door of the old lobby because that was where most people came and went.

At my insistence, we had added an elegant concierge desk, where Mr. Huckle could take a load off his feet when he wasn't busy elsewhere. At night, we now locked the reception lobby on the side. The night manager worked at the desk in the old lobby. A buzzer at the reception door rang at the concierge desk if someone arrived after dark. So far it was working out fairly well.

I dusted off my jeans and joined Mr. Huckle, Shelley, and the cook in the Dogwood Room, which was open to the old lobby and the grand staircase. Outside the two-story windows, snow gently drifted through the air. A fire blazed and my calico kitten, Twinkletoes, who was getting bigger by the day and was more of an adolescent now, was curled up in front of it, snoozing with her black tail over her pink nose, the cat equivalent of a *Do Not Disturb* sign.

Trixie danced toward her carefully but had the good sense to leave the sleeping cat alone.

"Looks great!" I said.

The cook appraised our work. "I guess we'll serve some simple appetizers and munchies? Hot chocolate, decaf coffee and tea, and a warm grog?"

I nodded. "Works for me. Thanks for staying late to help out."

"If I may make a suggestion, Miss Holly, perhaps we should bring out some candles and candelabra, just in case we lose power as well." Mr. Huckle bestowed a gracious smile on me when I agreed.

On my way to the third-floor attic, where most of the off-season furniture was stashed, I spied Ella Mae on the second-floor landing. She quickly turned tail and ran back. Char, bundled up for the weather, emerged from their room. She picked up Ella Mae, wrapped her in a shawl, and carried the tiny dog in her arms.

"Ella Mae and I are going shopping!" She peered out the window on the landing. "Do you think the stores will be open?"

"Probably. Most of the owners live in easy walking distance of their shops."

Char barely listened. She was busy making cooing sounds to Ella Mae. "I fell in love with this little girl the second I saw her."

"Has your husband warmed up to her yet?"

"Geof! Honestly, he makes me so mad. He has chosen every dog we've ever had. They were all huge. The bigger they are, the more he likes them. I loved them all, of course, but this time, I'm making the choice, and he'll just have to go along with it. See you later!" She walked carefully down the stairs.

Trixie and I ventured up one more flight, where our apartment was on one end of the floor, and the storage attic was on the other. I unlocked the door, and Trixie zoomed inside as though she expected to find something fascinating. The open space was filled with out-of-season decorations and extra furniture. Oma, or maybe an employee, had been inconsistent about labeling boxes. It appeared that Oma kept everything. I guessed that was wise. One never knew what might be needed. I plowed through boxes until I found some full of candles and candleholders.

I made several trips downstairs on the elevator. Oma clearly had anticipated this kind of problem in the past. She had amassed a collection of battery-operated and regular candles. There was even a lantern for each room. Two hours later, with the assistance of Mr. Huckle, candles, lanterns, and matches waited everywhere, and I was beat. No wonder Oma needed a vacation!

Mr. Huckle, Shelley, and I warmed up leftover lasagna from the inn's lunch menu for a quick bite before everyone arrived for the initial mystery meeting. Zelda and the cook joined us, along with Twinkletoes, Gingersnap, and Trixie.

Twinkletoes feasted on something the cook called country chicken, which looked like chopped chicken and chicken livers to me. The dogs devoured the inn's roast turkey with gravy.

We ate by the fire in the dining area. Outside the huge windows, spotlights shone in the night, revealing snow that continued to float lazily down.

The Sugar Maple Inn did not serve dinner to guests. Oma felt breakfast, lunch, and afternoon tea were sufficient, plus she wanted people to go out into Wagtail to the restaurants. Some of them, like The Blue Boar, were only steps from the inn. Consequently, the inn always grew quiet around the dinner hour.

Val was the first to interrupt the tranquility. She stamped her feet outside on the porch, like an omen of what was to come, then burst through the front door, dragging a rolling cart behind her.

She spied us at our table, shed her boots, and walked toward us in pink, purple, and turquoise striped socks. Her dark brown hair flew with static when she whipped off a turquoise knit hat. "What miserable timing. The snow couldn't wait two days? Two lousy days?"

"How are the sidewalks?" asked Shelley.

Val nodded, unzipping her ski jacket. "Not bad. They scattered that paw-friendly stuff on them so the snow is melting pretty fast. I saw one of the golf carts depositing it on the streets, too."

"Want a bite to eat?" I asked. "We have plenty."

"No thanks, I'm good. I spent the afternoon cooking everything in the fridge so it wouldn't spoil. Didn't make much money today but I ate well. Lucky I have a gas grill."

Shelley offered to help Mr. Huckle clean up so Val, the cook, and I could focus on the mystery meeting.

There really wasn't much to do. I placed urns of hot coffee and tea on a long buffet table next to a crockpot of hot grog. The heady scent of oranges wafted from it. Insulated pitchers of hot chocolate were lined up next to whipped cream, marshmallows, Kahlúa, and peppermint schnapps, so guests could doctor their own drinks. Bottles of water and soda stood nearby. The cook had done a remarkable job of whipping up a few snacks to nosh on. I carried out beautifully arranged platters. Fresh fruit with a chocolate dip, artichoke and mushroom bruschetta, tangy cocktail meatballs, and a giant assortment of cheeses and other lovely items to nibble on, like olives, and veggies with a spinach dip. He hadn't forgotten the dogs and cats. A basket of round dog treats with a paw imprint sat next to a smaller basket of fishy-smelling treats in the shapes of little sardines, undoubtedly for cats.

Guests began to drift in along with residents of Wagtail. Mr. Huckle took their coats and hung them on a couple of racks he had discovered in the basement. I gathered they were delighted to find hot beverages waiting for them. They introduced themselves to one another and chatted excitedly.

Charlotte Tredwell still carried Ella Mae in her arms. The little dog now wore a pink dress with a bow just above a double ruffle on her rump. Geof carried two mugs of hot chocolate.

"How are things going?" I asked.

"Char hasn't set that poor dog down for more than two minutes, except to change her clothes. She's not a doll," Geoffrey sniped at her. "Let her play with the other dogs." He pointed at Trixie. "See the Jack Russell? She's not wearing a dress."

Trixie looked up at us and at Ella Mae as if she understood every word.

I had a feeling Geof might not be exaggerating. "Trixie loves to pal up with other dogs."

Confronted by the two of us, Char reluctantly set Ella Mae on the floor.

Both dogs wagged their tails and commenced with the proper protocol for introducing themselves.

"See? Now that's more like a dog," said Geof.

Char glared at him. "Your brother's here."

The second he looked away, she bent to pick up Ella Mae.

But it was too late. Trixie and Ella Mae had already scampered away to play.

Char's right hand flew to the base of her neck. She looked on, distraught.

I didn't really know what to say. I hoped that Char might loosen up a little bit over the weekend. "Don't worry about her. She seems to be having fun with the other dogs. Socialization is so important. Maybe this will be an opportunity for Geof to warm up to her."

"I think he's jealous of all the attention Ella Mae is getting." She glanced toward her husband, who had moseyed over to speak with a smaller man. "It's the story of Geof's life. Someone else always gets all the attention."

Geof's brother was short and slight, but they had the same nose and grayish-blue eyes, leaving little doubt that they were related. He unsnapped the leash on an elegant saluki, who didn't budge from his side. Long fur flowed over the saluki's ears. Her gentle eyes appeared wary of the other dogs. The gorgeous, slender cream-colored dog appeared to be shy.

Former supermodel Blanche Wimmer stood beside the saluki, drawing the attention of everyone in the room.

Blanche knew how to make the most of her figure, even though it was no longer model-slim. She wore tight leggings in a shiny bronze fabric. High-heeled ankle boots made her legs look even longer. But she had covered up her midsection and bottom with an oversized black sweater that slid off one bare shoulder. That little bit of flesh drew the eye upward. Her face had filled out and there was no way to hide the roundness under her chin, but Blanche was still startlingly beautiful.

Val called to me, and I excused myself, but as I turned away, Blanche strolled over to Charlotte, and I heard her ask, "Is he here?"

It struck me as odd but wasn't really any of my business. Still, a little part of me wondered who they were meeting.

Val enlisted my assistance to check in the participants. Not exactly rocket science. I simply ticked off the names on a list and handed each one a little Murder Most Howl tote bag that included the rules, the rhymes that led to clues, a deep dark secret about the person, a pen, a notebook, and a host of goodies from Wagtail merchants.

I recognized Max Hemmerich from the Tall Tails Bookstore. Snow glistened on his silvery hair and well-trimmed beard. He removed the ever-present reading glasses he wore around his neck on a cord and wiped them clean.

Lillian Elsner stood near him with her precious Yorkshire terrier, GloryB. Svelte and blonde, Lillian had been a guest at the inn. She liked Wagtail so much that she bought a house and opened a dog accessory store in town. After years as a politician's wife in Washington, DC, Lillian enjoyed the slower pace of life in the mountains.

While most of the other dogs mingled, GloryB watched Lillian carefully. She sat like a perfect angel, and held up one paw. Lillian laughed, reached for a dog cookie, and fed it to her.

The next blast through the door was my own Aunt Birdie. She allowed Mr. Huckle to take her coat as though she thought she were the queen of England. She made a show of parading over to me and kissing the air near both of my ears. "Who is the stunning man with that showy dog?" she whispered.

"Either Geof or Ian Tredwell, and they're both married."

"Mmm," she murmured. "Pity."

"What are you doing here?"

"Why, sugar—" she raised her voice "—I'm interested in everything my darling niece does. Besides, it's our family inn. I thought you might need some help."

What was she up to now? It might be a family inn but not on her side of my lineage. Birdie was my mother's older half sister, and as near as I could tell, that side of my family had fled Wagtail to get away from her.

Not having attracted the attention she evidently desired, Birdie floated off to the refreshment table, where she struck up a conversation with Max.

Norm Wilson wandered in and wasted no time introducing

himself and shaking hands with visitors. I observed him for a few seconds, impressed by his ability to talk with total strangers as if they were friends. He worked his way through the room like a politician.

I understood Val's irritation with him, though. I wouldn't like him, either, if I felt I had overpaid for something because of him. But at the moment, he seemed congenial and friendly. That was the only side of the man I had ever seen. I noticed that he had changed to duck shoes for the snow. Still no socks, though.

When everyone was seated and Val began to speak, one bag remained and one name was missing a checkmark: Robin Jarvis. I rose and stretched, noting that many of the local townspeople and merchants were in attendance.

After welcoming everyone, Val went over the basic rules. "Now don't forget to visit the stores. There's a list of participating merchants in your bags. In a small place like Wagtail, rumors fly around town, so don't be afraid to chat with them and ask questions. They might know the one thing that will help you put it all together. The first person or team to figure out who the killer is, his or her motive, and how he or she committed the murder wins. The first one to figure it out and tell me will be the winner. But don't worry, we have other prizes, too. To win, though, you must tell *me*."

While Val explained about the clues, I helped myself to a mug of hot cocoa. I cupped it in my hands, and took a sip, thinking things were going fairly well and that Zelda had been wrong, when a loud thunk was followed instantly by darkness.

The fireplaces still blazed in the dining area and the Dogwood Room, casting long shadows. Everyone seemed a little sinister in the dim rooms.

The sound alarmed several dogs, who jumped to their feet. Trixie took it calmly, but Gingersnap, usually the calm one, shot straight to me and jammed her head between my knees, her entire body trembling. I ran my hands over her shoulders, murmuring soft reassurances.

I couldn't help thinking of Mr. Huckle's sound advice. With Gingersnap glued to my side every step of the way, I grabbed a butane lighter from the kitchen and walked around calmly, carefully stepping over dogs, cats, and assorted bags and purses, lighting the candles I had set out earlier.

Most people took it in stride, and I heard a few jokes that questioned whether it was staged for their benefit. But when I passed Blanche, I noticed that she clutched her husband's hand as though she was frightened. Her saluki didn't seem to care.

Weegie's poodle had jumped into her lap. But little Ella Mae dodged around the room, sniffing everything as though nothing had happened.

Val handled it like a pro. So smoothly that I'd have thought the power outage was intentional if I hadn't known better. She positioned a large candle with three wicks so it lighted her face from below, giving her a frighteningly evil appearance. "Someone will be murdered tonight," she intoned. "Each one of you has known this person in some way. Your connection to him is in the packet you received tonight. Some of you were in love, some of you hated him, and some probably loved and hated our victim. Whether you share your secret connection to the victim is up to you."

I had to admit that the candles on the fireplace mantel and tables around the room added a certain ambience that wouldn't have existed with electric lights. It hadn't ruined the evening after all. On the contrary, it was charming and a little bit eerie. Perfect for a murder mystery event.

Val continued. "Three weapons are hidden in Wagtail. You have clues to help you find them. The weapons may be used to obtain information and clues from other players. If you are approached by a player with a weapon, you are obligated to share your clues and your connection to the victim. As you can see, the weapons are very powerful."

I lighted a candle on a side table next to an elderly man whom I hadn't noticed before and a horrified shriek escaped me.

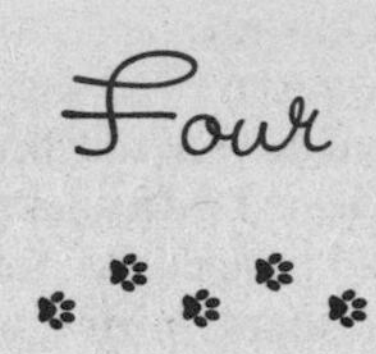

# Four

The old man slumped in his chair, one arm hanging limply over the side. His head sagged forward, his eyes closed. His white hair glowed in the candlelight. A bushy mustache covered his upper lip. He wore a black turtleneck sweater.

I felt completely foolish. My scream had drawn everyone's attention and agitated the dogs. Gingersnap, who had stuck close to me, barked once and sniffed him from a safe distance. Trixie raced to my aid, and I noticed Twinkletoes prowling close to the man's feet with great caution.

He had probably fallen asleep. I grabbed the candle next to him and held it near his chest for a closer look. The flame flickered, throwing distorted shadows on him.

I stretched my other hand toward his shoulder to give him a little shake.

A gust of air blew out the candle at the exact moment that he grabbed my wrist.

This time I screamed like the dead had come to life and jerked my hand away. All the dogs bounded toward me. One of them howled, long and mournful, probably the basset hound.

But the man didn't get up. He didn't even lift his head. I peered at him, reluctant to try to touch him again.

I nudged his shoe with my foot. No reaction. But in the dim light, I could see Gingersnap and Trixie wagging their tails.

Someone behind me chuckled. I turned to see Geof, who uttered dryly, "Mr. Boddy, I presume?"

I recognized his reference to the victim in the game Clue.

Participants sprang to their feet and clustered behind me. Still recovering from my fright, it took me a minute to get out of their way. I scooted to the side as they made note of his condition.

"He was poisoned," whispered Myrtle.

Mere inches from his hand, barely visible on the side table in the dark, the silver of the skull and crossbones on the green poison bottle glinted in the light of the fire.

I staggered away and collapsed in a chair.

Val slid into the chair next to me. "Wow! If I had known you were such a good actress, I would have asked you to play a role."

I kept my tone as level as possible. "I wish I had been acting."

"What?"

"He seized my wrist."

Val burst out laughing. "I'm sorry. Truly I am. He wasn't supposed to do anything like that. Your little shock aside, it played out much better than I could have hoped. The timing of the power outage was perfect."

"Yeah? You're not the one who has to keep the inn fireplaces stocked with wood."

"I thought you had a handyman for stuff like that."

"He quit this afternoon."

"What lousy timing. Okay, look. You came through for me when we had to move the meeting. I'll help you with the wood."

I couldn't see her very well in the dark, but I was touched by her offer. She had to be exhausted. I didn't want to gush too much, though. I had a feeling that Val was the type to brush off sentiment. "That's nice of you, thanks. I'll give you a call if it gets to be overwhelming."

"Good deal."

I watched people milling around in the dark. "So this is how it begins? With me screaming and making a fool of myself? I hope that's not how it ends! Who is that guy anyway?"

"The Baron von Rottweiler. He lives a very low key, under-the-radar life in Wagtail."

The flames from the fire lighted her face just enough for me to see her. "You know what I meant. Who is posing as the Baron von Rottweiler?"

"I almost missed the hot chocolate! Have you had any yet?" Val bounded from her seat and headed for the table with drinks.

A very evasive maneuver if you asked me. Had she conned Mr. Huckle into posing as the Baron von Rottweiler? I dismissed that idea. The legs were too long. Mr. Huckle was a small man.

Now Val had piqued my interest. In the glow of the fire, the people who milled around the Baron looked spooky. Several local people checked him out as well. I was glad to see their enthusiasm for the game.

"Excuse me. Perhaps you could help us?" Candlelight flickered on Blanche Wimmer Tredwell and her husband. He held out his hand. "Ian Tredwell." A receding hairline made Ian's broad forehead appear very large. He seemed pleasant but earnest, and at that moment, his brow creased into waves of wrinkles. "My brother mentioned that you have a back exit somewhere. I'm afraid we've lost him in the crowd. Would you be kind enough to show us the way?"

"Yes, of course." I picked up a lantern and led them and their saluki through the hallway. I didn't want to be nosy but I asked, "Is there a problem?"

"No!" said Blanche a little too quickly.

I glanced at the two of them as we walked.

Ian appeared to be calm. "We don't like to attract attention. You understand."

I guessed he meant his wife. No matter, it was easy enough to show them to the registration lobby. I unlatched the door and handed them the lantern. "You'll probably need this. Walk straight ahead for a few feet, then turn to the right. The walkway will bring you directly to The Blue Boar Restaurant and the main part of town. Can you find your way from there?"

They assured me that they could and strode off into the dark night. I locked the door, mentally kicking myself for not bringing two lanterns. When I turned around, a faint beam from outdoors shed some light on the room. I peeked out the window. The restaurants and stores were all well lighted! I smelled a rat.

I made my way back through the hallway to the main lobby.

The crowd had begun to thin. A few guests clustered near candles, looking over the clues and their secrets. Others took lanterns and made their way up to their rooms. Several people asked me for directions to a bar or a restaurant where they could chat over drinks.

Instead of cleaning up, I poured myself another cup of steaming hot chocolate, added a nice dollop of whipped cream, and handed Gingersnap and Trixie dog cookies.

I picked up a kitty treat and looked around for Twinkletoes. It was her habit to sit on the stairs at this time of night. I suspected she liked being petted by guests and told what a pretty kitty she was. But tonight, I didn't see her anywhere.

And suddenly, with a clunk as loud as the previous one, all the lights came back on. I turned my head immediately to see the Baron von Rottweiler more clearly, but the chair he had occupied was empty. Perfect timing for him to vanish before the lights came back on. I grew very suspicious. Why was Val keeping his identity secret?

The electricity was greeted with cheers, applause, and another visit from a trembling Gingersnap, who clearly didn't appreciate loud noises. I renewed my determination to find a handyman so I wouldn't have to worry about stocking the wood-burning fireplaces in case the inn really lost power.

Just to be on the safe side, I thought I'd better check the reception doors in case anyone else had left that way. Gingersnap and Trixie joined me on the walk back to the reception area.

Mr. Huckle stepped off the elevator as we passed by. I squinted at him. "You didn't come from the basement by any chance, did you?"

He smiled. "Why, Miss Holly! Are you accusing me of something?"

I was, actually. "That power outage was planned."

"Maybe a little bit."

"You stinker!" He was so darling, though, with that sweet old face and proper butler attire that I couldn't be angry with him. "Next time I'd better be in on the tricks."

"By all means." He suppressed a smile as he walked away, confirming my belief that he'd recommended putting out candles because he knew he would be shutting down the power temporarily. What a scamp.

I was a little bit miffed that he and Val hadn't let me in on their plans, but maybe it had worked out better that way. If I had known there would be a dead man, I would have pretended to scream, and it wouldn't have sounded as authentic.

I straightened up and made sure everything was in order in the registration lobby. Our little gift shop was locked, as was the door to the basement. Trixie raced ahead of me when we returned to the main lobby but I noted that Gingersnap stayed close by, no doubt fearful of yet another big bang. I double-checked the doors to the back terrace that overlooked the lake and the mountains to be sure they were securely locked.

The snow was really coming down. I paused for a few minutes to watch it in the beams of the outdoor lights. There was just something magical about snow. Everything seemed so peaceful.

I tore myself away from the windows to clean up the leftovers—not that there were many. I loaded platters in my arms and carried them to the commercial kitchen. On my final trip, I told Trixie to behave. "Gingersnap, you're in charge of her. I'll be back very soon."

The commercial kitchen was the only place in the inn where dogs and cats couldn't go. Although the town had asked for official waivers from the laws regarding animals on the premises where food was served, everything was still pending. They skirted the law by keeping animals out of the food preparation areas.

I arranged the few leftovers in glass storage containers, then rinsed off the platters and popped them into the dishwasher so they would be clean when the cook arrived in the morning. With the dishwasher running, I picked up the leftovers and returned to the lobby. Gingersnap and Trixie waited for me just outside the door. I praised them for being good dogs and crossed to the other kitchen in the Sugar Maple Inn.

Oma had reserved one large room for family use. I had spent many happy hours there as a child. It was an open plan kitchen with enough space for a farmhouse-style dining table, a blue island that verged on turquoise, and a comfy seating area in front of a stone fireplace that was original to the building. The back door led to Oma's little herb garden.

The dogs could have gone through the pet door but they waited for me. My hands full, I backed into the door to push it open.

Behind me, I heard a little snap. Trixie's claws scrambled against the hardwood floors. Yelping, she raced through another pet door, located at the bottom of a built-in bookcase.

Gingersnap was on her tail and through the pet door in an instant.

Eyeing the door, I set the food on the island. I had recognized that snap. It was the sound of the bookcase closing. Oma had hidden two secret stairwells in the inn when she renovated. No doubt the result of reading too many mysteries.

This one led up to a second-floor exit and to my apartment on the third floor, opening in my dining room.

Taking a couple of deep breaths, I considered my options. If this were a movie, and I dared to open the door, I would surely find a one-eyed monster with pointy claws for fingers. I listened. Neither Trixie nor Gingersnap was barking. Did they know the person who had concealed himself there as we entered the kitchen?

Most of the employees probably knew about the hidden stairs. Was this a continuation of tricking me for purposes of Murder Most Howl? Would I find a second body or scream loud enough to bring guests running? It would be amusing for them because they would hear the scream but not be able to find me in the secret staircase.

I exhaled noisily. The sensible thing to do would be to fetch assistance. Casey Collins would be here soon for the night shift. But then it would be a big joke, and when Oma returned, everyone would tell her the story about the time I was so scared that I waited for Casey to look behind the bookcase. Oma had run this inn for decades by herself. She would never have waited this long, pondering the situation. She would have opened the bookcase and demanded that the person show himself.

I squared my shoulders, picked up a wine bottle to bash over a head if need be, and opened the bookcase door.

Was that purring I heard? "All right," I said. "Who's in here?"

"The living dead." The Baron von Rottweiler loped down the stairs holding Twinkletoes and his wig in his arms. The two dogs followed him, gazing at him with adoration. They had known who he was all along. I felt pretty silly now that I knew who he really was.

He stopped and whispered, "Any guests with you? Wouldn't want to spoil the game."

"Holmes Richardson, why do you always scare me half to death? There's no one here but us."

I backed up and set the wine where it belonged.

He ambled through the doorway, grinning. Tall and sandy-haired, Holmes had vivid blue eyes that always made me melt.

After my parents moved away from Wagtail, they sent me back to spend my summers on the mountain with Oma. My cousin Josh came too, and Holmes, the grandson of Oma's best friend, Rose, rounded out our little trio. Oma set us to work, rarely differentiating between genders. We all made beds, cooked and washed dishes, carried luggage, checked guests in and out, and learned the business from the ground up. Josh, who now traveled the world, had been Holmes's best friend. And I had never forgotten the first boy who ever kissed me.

Turned out he didn't look half bad in a big white mustache. Holmes worked as an architect in Chicago and, alas, was engaged to be married. "I can't believe I didn't recognize you! What are you doing here?"

Holmes set Twinkletoes on the floor. She wound around his ankles. "Grandma Rose told me about Murder Most Howl when I was here for Christmas. I had no shame—I begged for a part." He peeled off the mustache. "I missed seeing you over the holidays. Where were you?"

"Hungry?" I asked, showing him the food I was about to stash in the fridge. "I had hopes for an old-fashioned Christmas here at the inn but my parents made such a stink that I wound up driving to Florida to see my dad. Four days in the car—two days there, two days driving back. Hardly worth the trip."

"Bummer. I spent Christmas Eve with my fiancée and her family, then flew here to be with my family. It was all a big rush."

"Did she come with you?" I had never met the woman who had captured his heart.

He sucked in air. "No."

Men. Maybe I was reading something into his response, but it sounded like I had hit a sore spot. I itched to know more but he appeared to be concentrating on red peppers and dip. "I can't believe you came back to Wagtail just to play the Baron von Rottweiler. Essentially your part is over now, right?"

"I guess it is. But I don't want to miss out on all the fun. My life in Chicago is pretty mundane."

"Chicago mundane?" I snorted. "It has everything in the world that anyone could ask for."

"You lived in Washington, DC. You must know how it is. It's invigorating in the beginning, but after a few years, you go to work and come home." Holmes shrugged. "Wagtail is like a vacation for me." He tossed pieces of broccoli to Trixie and Gingersnap, who caught them in their mouths. "You okay? I was a little hesitant about grabbing you, but your first scream was more like a loud mouse squeak."

"I'm fine. Just a little miffed about not being in on the plan. Is the power really out at Hair of the Dog?"

"That part was true. Half of Wagtail is out. Luckily it's the other end of town. I promised Val I'd pitch in tomorrow. She thinks the participants will have questions as they get going."

"Won't they wonder why the Baron von Rottweiler is suddenly alive again?"

Holmes laughed. "The old guy's dead. I'll be there as myself."

"So what's the story with the poor deceased baron?"

"Haven't you read the information Val gave you?" He tsked at me.

"Hey, I've been a little busy."

"Don't get testy. The old baron ran a guard dog–training business. He kept a low profile but was quite the ladies' man with three wives, a bunch of mistresses, and a few illegitimate children, all of whom have descended upon Wagtail. Not to mention his shady business practices, which aggravated locals and visitors alike."

"Okay, I get it. He was a crumb."

"Val had to exaggerate to give each of the participants a role in the baron's life, but the more I thought about it, the more I realized that she wasn't too far off from the truth about some people."

"Not you, I hope."

Holmes wiggled his eyebrows like Groucho Marx. "Thanks for the snack. See you in the morning." He loped out the door.

Trixie looked up at me, Gingersnap whined, and Twinkletoes stared forlornly at the door as it shut. "He's engaged," I reminded them.

I stashed the food in the fridge and returned to the lobby.

Casey had just arrived. He deposited a laptop and two

immense books on the desk. Twinkletoes jumped up immediately to inspect them.

"I'm so glad you have power," he said. "My mom's house is in the dark." Casey's round metal-framed glasses were fogged up, making him look like an eyeless cartoon character. A shock of dark coffee-colored hair hung in his forehead, as usual. It always made me think of young Harry Potter. In addition to working at the inn, Casey was studying at the community college over on Snowball Mountain.

He peeled off his glasses and jacket, rubbed his eyes, and said, "Big history test tomorrow. I'm hoping classes will be canceled because of the snow but my mom says I can't count on that."

"Sounds like good advice to me."

He bent to pat Trixie and Gingersnap. "A guy can hope. It better be quiet here tonight so I can get some serious studying time in."

"I think you're in luck. We have a full house but it should be fairly calm. I don't think we have any rabble-rousers among them."

He seemed relieved and settled in at the desk.

I started my nightly rounds by walking through the library and into the cat wing. I climbed the stairs to the second floor and strode through the hallway past the guest rooms.

Everything was quiet. We headed outside to the puppy potty for Trixie and Gingersnap. The snow had stopped. The cozy scent of smoke from the fireplaces drifted to me. Warm lights shone in some of the inn windows. I imagined guests were sitting by the fireplaces in their rooms going over their rhymes and clues.

A golf cart, better known as a Wagtail taxi thanks to the strict rules against cars, pulled up at the door. A woman stepped off it and rubbed her upper arms.

"Good evening. You must be Robin Jarvis." I took her bag and led the way inside.

"How did you know?" she asked.

"You're the only one who did not pick up your information for Murder Most Howl."

"I hope it's not too late!"

She sounded panicked.

"Of course not. I'll bring it up to your room as soon as we get you settled."

"Brr. I had no idea it would be so cold here." Robin brushed snow off a fashionable jacket that wouldn't keep anyone warm.

I guessed Robin to be in her forties. Pleasantly plump, she wore her chestnut brown hair short. Just long enough to tuck behind her ears. While I checked her in, she made a big fuss over Trixie and Gingersnap, who wagged their tails and vied for her attention.

She cooed at them before turning to me. "I had hoped to get some hiking in. Do you think the trails will be open with all the snow?"

"I guess it depends on how much we get tonight. You can probably hike on some of the lower trails." I eyed the woman, who obviously loved dogs but didn't bring one with her. "You know, they always need dog walkers at the shelter. If you do hike, maybe you could take a dog with you?"

She looked at me as though I had given her a gift. "I would love that!"

It was almost midnight when we left Robin by the fire in her room clutching her Murder Most Howl bag. We returned to our quarters on the third floor, ready to pack it in for the night. In the latest renovation, Oma had carved out a beautiful apartment with me in mind. It ran from the front of the inn to the back. On the north side, a bedroom balcony overlooked Wagtail. To the south, a terrace off the family room offered a view of the lake and the mountains. Oma had thoughtfully provided a second bedroom for company. A darling dining room doubled as a little library where one of the bookcases pushed open to the stairwell where Holmes had hidden. The pet door on the bottom shelf allowed Trixie and Twinkletoes to roam the inn. I knelt and closed it for the night, so they wouldn't accidentally sneak out, as they had on occasion.

My TV had once again magically turned itself on. After my move to Wagtail, the remote control had been lost among all the moving boxes. Trixie and Twinkletoes knew where it was and kept turning the TV on by themselves. I had since located it but the little rascals continued to turn on the TV when they felt like it.

I clicked on the gas fireplace. Flames ran along the little starter and flickered into a blaze. Instead of changing into jammies, I kicked off my shoes and hit the kitchen for a snack. After feeding Twinkletoes shrimp and herring aspic concocted at the inn, I made myself a mug of steaming hot hibiscus tea, grabbed two Sugar Maple Inn dog-safe raisin-free oatmeal cookies, and settled in one of the cushy chairs in front of the fireplace. Trixie bounded onto the matching ottoman and crept closer, her tail wagging nervously in anticipation. Gingersnap sat down and politely offered her paw to shake.

I broke off pieces of one cookie and shared it with them. When I awoke an hour later, the remaining cookie was gone, Trixie was next to me on the chair, upside down, all four feet in the air, Twinkletoes sprawled across my lap, keeping me warm, and Gingersnap had curled up on the ottoman with her head on my feet. With great reluctance, I roused them so we could stumble off to bed.

I woke to wild yelping. It was still dark outside. Trixie ran to the door and back to me. Ugh. That could only mean one thing.

At times like these, I wished I still lived in a small townhouse with a tiny fenced-in backyard where no one would see me letting the dog out. I pulled on warm woolly pants and tucked my nightie into them. I stuffed my feet into boots, and slid my big puffy jacket on. I tried not to clomp down the stairs so I wouldn't wake the guests. Gingersnap stuck by me, but Trixie sped ahead and waited for us by the door. Someone must have entered during the night because puddles of melting snow lay on the floor. Casey wasn't at the desk. Maybe he had gone for a mop.

Trixie flew outside when I opened the door. Wildly whirling snow was so dense that I couldn't see more than a few feet. In less than two seconds, Trixie, whose fur was mostly white, disappeared from view. Gingersnap bounded after her. Fortunately, her reddish fur made her more visible.

Trixie ought to be headed for one of the doggy potty areas. I pulled up my hood and stepped off the porch into the wind. Snow blew everywhere. "Trixie?" I called. Hopefully she would find her way back to me with her powerful dog nose.

I ventured forward a few steps, trying to see Gingersnap. Over the howl of the wind, I thought I heard Trixie bark. I stopped to listen. Bent over against the driving snow, I forged ahead. Even the streetlights of Wagtail fought a losing battle with the heavy snow.

"Trixie!" I yelled.

This time, I heard frantic barking. I rushed forward blindly. Why didn't I have a black dog who would be easy to see in the snow? "Trixie!"

The barking continued. I thought I was headed in the right direction but even Gingersnap had vanished in the heavy snow. I hurried along the salted sidewalk. Snow had collected in spite of the treatment, and now blew across it, but at least I wasn't knee deep, trying to trudge through the stuff.

Trixie's incessant barking grew louder. I began to fear that she had fallen into something or was trapped.

Stinging snow hit my face, eliminating the last vestiges of sleepiness. "Trixie!"

She darted in front of me, nearly tripping me. I bent to pick her up but she barked and backed up. "Trixie," I growled. "It's the middle of the night in a blizzard. This is no time to play keep away."

She backed up more, just out of arm's reach. I was getting frustrated with her. "Why are you doing this to me? Did you forget that we have a nice warm bed back at the inn?"

And then she sat down. Right next to the leg of a man on a bench.

For the third time in less than twelve hours, I screamed.

# Six

The moaning wind drowned my scream but not my horror. I stepped closer. Was he real or a prop?

The streetlamp next to the bench offered precious little light in the swirling snow. But the brightly lit storefront window display of Tall Tails, the local bookstore, helped somewhat. Icy snow covered his knit beanie-style hat and clung to his eyebrows and lashes. His eyes were half open as if he was drowsy. He wore a navy blue jacket. The swirling wind that made it difficult for me to stand didn't appear to have an impact on him.

Gingersnap inched her nose closer to his body as though she wasn't quite sure what to make of the snowman.

My breath caught in my throat when I realized a bottle lay in his lap, covered with snow. Had he been too drunk to get up and save himself?

Surely not. I dared to reach forward and dust the surface of the bottle. It was the faux bottle of poison that had allegedly killed the Baron von Rottweiler! One of the weapons for Murder Most Howl. So the guy was a fake. Val must have been up half the night setting it up.

I looked down at Trixie. "He's not real, sweetie. Though I agree that he sure looks human."

No sooner were the words out of my mouth than it occurred to me that dogs used their noses more than their eyes. Even in this blizzard, Trixie should have realized far sooner than me that the man was a plastic prop.

Gingersnap delicately pawed his knee.

I peered at the frozen man's face again. All the ice crystals on it had to mean he wasn't a real person. No one could sit there covered in ice and snow like that. He'd freeze to death.

Wait a minute. What a coincidence that he was sitting where tourists would find him. Had Val counted on someone making a fuss and thinking the guy was real?

The face seemed odd, almost like a mask, yet vaguely familiar. I had to call Val to find out for sure. If he was a fake, I would be the butt of a joke that no one would ever let me forget. But I hadn't bothered to bring my cell phone.

This time, Trixie allowed me to pick her up. Gingersnap and I walked back to the inn. No one sat at the front desk, and the melted snow hadn't been cleaned. I wondered where Casey was. Maybe he was getting a snack in Oma's kitchen.

I set Trixie down and used the phone on the desk to call Val. She answered with a sleep-fogged voice. While I felt a little bit bad about waking her, she deserved it if she had left that fake body out there without telling me.

"Val, did you arrange for a second body to be found with the poison bottle?"

"Huh? Who is this?"

"It's Holly. Is the guy on the bench one of your props?"

"What are you talking about?"

A shiver ran through me. "Are you kidding?"

I heard her moan. "I don't joke at five thirty in the morning."

Was it that late? Guests would be rising soon! "I'm going to call Dave. He won't be happy if you're lying about this."

Her words were measured. "Holly, I do not know what you're talking about. Where is this guy?"

"On a bench near Tall Tails."

I said good-bye and phoned Dave Quinlan. Officer Dave, as he was fondly known around Wagtail. He sounded almost as groggy as Val. But his voice cleared up as soon as I told him I thought we had a problem and described the man on the bench. "You're sure he's dead?"

"I'm not even sure he's real, but Val insists that he's not part of the mystery weekend."

Soft giggling caused me to turn around. Myrtle and Weegie were watching something in the Dogwood Room. Oh boy. Guests were up and about but I didn't smell coffee yet. "Dave," I said into the phone, "meet me in front of Tall Tails in ten minutes."

"Okay." He hung up.

Trixie and Gingersnap had joined the group in the Dogwood Room. I walked over to see what was going on, dismayed to find that Puddin', Weegie's poodle, was licking Casey's hand. He was splayed on the sofa, dead asleep, not unlike the first time I had met him. One arm hung off the edge, and his stockinged feet relaxed on the armrest.

Trixie joined Puddin' in licking his hand, and Gingersnap kissed his face.

Suddenly, Casey shouted, "Seventeen seventy-five!" and jerked up to a sitting position. He blinked at us. "Did I fall asleep? Nooo," he wailed. "I have an exam this morning."

The front door opened. Shelley and the cook came in with a blast of frigid air.

Casey pushed his glasses on his face, grabbed the books that lay about him, and hurried to the front desk.

"Isn't he adorable?" whispered Weegie to Myrtle. "Reminds me of that boy who played Harry Potter. We could help him study."

"And let someone else be the first to find the clues? No, ma'am. We got up early to win, not to tutor some kid who—"

she raised her voice so he would hear "—should have been studying all along and then he wouldn't be in this fix."

"All right," conceded Weegie. "I do have to let Puddin' out anyway."

But I noticed that when Myrtle wasn't looking, Weegie whispered something to Casey about helping him when they came back for breakfast.

The scent of coffee brewing finally filled the air, making me reluctant to head back out into the predawn darkness and cold. But Dave would be there any minute.

I headed for the stairs in a rush but Shelley nabbed me. "Holly!" She lowered her voice to a whisper. "I have a little problem and could use your help."

Uh-oh. This day wasn't starting well. "Is it an urgent crisis or can it wait an hour?"

"It can wait. What's going on?"

"There's either a dead man or a prop on a bench outside but I'm not sure which it is."

"Good heavens!" Shelley waved her hands horizontally. "No problem. This can definitely wait. Did you call Val?"

I nodded. "She says it's not a prop." I sprang up the stairs to my apartment as fast as I could, swapped my nightgown for a turtleneck, opened the dog door so Twinkletoes could come and go as she pleased, grabbed a warm coat for Trixie, and hurried back downstairs. Trixie was agreeable about putting the coat on and dashed out the door with Puddin' at the first opportunity. Gingersnap parked herself just inside the door, her eyes trained on the stairs as if she expected more guests to wake soon and didn't want to miss them.

The blizzard had died down but snow fell so heavily that it still obscured vision. I stepped out on the porch, where Myrtle and Weegie had paused to pull on gloves.

"My goodness, Myrtle," said Weegie. "Maybe we should have a cup of coffee first. I can't see my own hand."

"If we wait, someone else will snap up all the clues."

"I doubt anyone else is crazy enough to be out in this

weather." Weegie looked over at me. "What are you doing out here?"

I paused a beat too long. What could I say? There might be a man frozen to a bench? "I have to meet someone." That was true!

But my moment of hesitation caught Myrtle's interest. She knocked her elbow against Weegie's, then pulled her hat down on her head more firmly. "She's putting out clues!"

I had to hurry but I took the time to deny it. "They were all out yesterday." I said good-bye, suspecting they would follow me anyway. They did. Puddin' ran ahead with Trixie, who raced along the sidewalk in the direction of the bench.

I was pleased to see that the streetlight shed more light on the man now that the wind had died down.

Dave was already there and leaning over to examine the man more closely. Formerly a naval sailor, Dave lived in Wagtail and kept an eye on it, even though the sheriff's headquarters were on Snowball Mountain. Early to mid-thirties like Val and me, Dave had grown up in Wagtail. Sometimes he had a hard time convincing the older folks who had known him as a little boy that he was an adult now and in charge.

He straightened up and asked, "You're sure this isn't some kind of stunt for Murder Most Howl?"

Myrtle lunged forward. "Of course it is! There's the poison bottle that disappeared last night." She grabbed the bottle and waved it in the air, doing a little dance. "I told you the early bird gets the worm. Or in this case the poison!"

Dave looked on in horror. "Ma'am, I'm afraid I have to take that. It's evidence." He held out his gloved hand for it.

Myrtle clutched it to her and looked at me. "Isn't this one of the weapons?"

I was pretty sure that it was the same bottle Val had used the previous night. I glanced at Dave. "I think it *is* one of the pretend weapons for the game."

Dave frowned. "So this guy could be a fake after all? May I please see the bottle?"

Myrtle stood her ground. "No! We found it fair and square."

"Ma'am, I am the local law enforcement officer. Now hand me that bottle."

Weegie nudged her friend. "Better do it, Myrtle."

The second Dave took it into his hand, he threw a dirty glance at me. "You knew this was a prop, and you called me out here anyway?"

"Just because the bottle is fake doesn't mean the man couldn't be real," I protested.

Val arrived at that moment and overheard me.

I looked at her, hoping with all my might that the guy really was a prop. She might pull *my* leg, but she'd have to be honest with Dave.

A screech shuddered out of her mouth. "Good heavens. He's not part of the game!"

Behind me, Weegie exclaimed, "You mean that's a real person? Someone sat down right here and died?"

No one answered her.

Dave touched one of the man's frosty eyebrows. Apparently unconvinced, he tried to lift the edge of the knit cap. "It's frozen to his head." He stepped back. "Looks like Norm, doesn't he?"

That was why he looked familiar!

Dave focused on Val. "You sure you're not pulling a fast one?"

"Honest! The participants only have today and a few hours tomorrow to solve the death of the Baron von Rottweiler. I decided a second murder would be too much for them to handle."

Dave's mouth puckered. "So help me, if I call the rescue squad and this turns out to be part of your murder mystery—"

"It's not!" Val protested. "I don't know if he's real or not—gosh, I hope not—but I had nothing to do with it."

Dave pulled out his radio and called for an ambulance.

When he was through, he leaned forward and unsnapped the top of the man's navy blue jacket. He tugged at the zipper but it didn't budge. He slid his fingers along the side of the neck and wedged them under the man's turtleneck.

I saw Dave's shoulders jerk. He backed up. "I think we have a corpse."

"Don't they freeze people on purpose sometimes?" asked Val. "Maybe they can revive him in the hospital."

"That's right." A glimmer of hope crept into me. "They lower their temperatures so their hearts hardly beat."

"Yeah? Well, if his heart is beating at all, I'd be surprised." Dave scanned the area.

"What are you looking for?" I asked.

"Footprints. It came down so hard and fast that the snow melt stuff couldn't keep up but the snow also did a great job filling any tracks."

Val cocked her head. "You mean the footprints from this guy?"

"Or someone else."

"Duh. If someone was with him, wouldn't they have called for help?" asked Myrtle.

Dave simply lifted an eyebrow.

"Surely you don't think this was a murder!" I blurted.

"I have to treat it as a crime scene until we know otherwise."

A beaming couple with pleased smiles hurried toward us. "Is this the next victim?" asked the man.

Dave stared at them, clearly appalled.

Thankfully Val had her wits about her. "No. I'm so sorry. This isn't part of the mystery weekend."

Although snowflakes continued to fall, the sky was growing lighter. More people were gathering around to see what was happening.

"Folks," said Dave, "I need you to step back, please. Sir! Please stay on the sidewalk!"

How could we get people to stop tromping on the snow in what I now feared might be the scene of someone's death? There was only one solution. I pointed toward the inn. "Free coffee for everyone at the Sugar Maple Inn this morning. And in just a short while, we'll be giving away a secret about the location of a weapon."

Val glared at me, her eyes wide. "You're giving away secrets?"

"I had to do something to get them away from here."

"How do you know the weapons haven't already been found?"

I hadn't thought that part through. "Surely not all of them have been discovered yet. Besides, I can peek to see if the candlestick is where I left it." I hoped it was still there.

Surprisingly, almost everyone except Myrtle and Weegie hurried toward the inn. Either they were desperate for that weapon or they were as cold as I was. I looked down at poor Trixie. Her little paws must be chilled to the bone.

Myrtle coughed politely. "Um, could I have the bottle back now?"

"Myrtle! For heaven's sake. Someone died," hissed Weegie.

"Don't you get it? It's an act. If this guy is real, then why did he have a game piece in his lap? They're putting us on."

"I can see why you would think that," said Val, "but I'm in charge of Murder Most Howl, and I can assure you that this is not part of the game."

Honestly, Myrtle looked at us so innocently that I wondered if she understood what was happening. Val turned to Dave with her palms up as if she was pleading with him, but I knew he wouldn't give up the bottle.

"How about this?" I offered. "You can't have that weapon but Val and I will come up with a replacement for it. That way you won't lose out on the power of having a weapon. Give us an hour or two?"

Myrtle scowled at me but Weegie said, "That sounds fair. I'm freezing anyway. And look at poor Puddin', she's shaking, even in her wool coat! C'mon, Myrtle. Let's have breakfast. You got what you wanted."

I was relieved to see emergency medical technicians calmly striding toward us. I unzipped my jacket, picked up Trixie, held her close, and wrapped the jacket around her. Val and I backed away to give the EMTs room. There was no mistaking their astonishment.

The tallest one scratched the back of his neck. "In all my years I've never seen anything like this."

Another one worked at unzipping the navy blue jacket. He slid his hand inside the man's clothing but shook his head.

The tall one pulled out a phone, walked away a few steps, and made a call.

"They'll take him to the hospital," said Dave. "I think he's beyond help but I'm no doctor."

The EMTs had trouble moving him to the gurney. After a few awkward attempts, they lifted him in a sitting position. Dave stopped them briefly and felt the man's pockets. He managed to withdraw a wallet and motioned for them to continue.

Dave flipped the leather wallet open and found identification. "Just as I feared. It's Norm Wilson."

# Seven

The EMTs rolled Norm away on his back, his feet jutting into the air reminiscent of a dead bug. I turned away.

I barely knew the man but the heavy gloom of death hung over me. It was so sudden and unexpected. And now I felt guilty for excluding him from planning Murder Most Howl. It had been Val's decision, not mine, but he'd seemed so eager to help. It wasn't important, just unkind of us. We really ought to treat everyone with more kindness. We never knew what might happen.

"Looks like I'll be paying a visit to Norm's wife, Savannah." Dave gestured with a halfhearted wave. "The worst part of my job. See you guys later."

By the time Val and I returned to the inn, the sun was valiantly trying to peek through gray clouds and the snow had tapered off considerably. Stepping inside the inn was a bit of a shock. The dining area was packed. Cheerful chatter filled the air. At two tables, diners exchanged good-natured banter about the murder of the Baron von Rottweiler.

A cry went up. "Clue! Clue! Give us the clue!" They rapped on the tables like a rowdy crowd in a bar.

"Better go see if the candlestick is still there," whispered Val. "I'll try to hold them in check."

How was I going to pull this off? Surely someone would notice if I kneeled on the floor and moved the books. If that happened, I would simply have to hide the candlestick again. Assuming they didn't overpower me first in their zeal to nab it.

I sidled into the library and, from a distance, peered at the bottom shelf where I'd left the candlestick. Someone had found it all right. In his or her excitement, that person hadn't even bothered to clean up. Books lay on the floor in little heaps. I knelt to put them back. Now what? I had promised a clue!

"*Psst.* Holly!"

I looked over my shoulder.

Shelley twisted a dishtowel in her hands. She motioned me over to the window seat. "Do you have a minute now? I need to do something about this before Val finds out."

I shoved the last book into place and sat down on the window seat next to her. Snow blew past us outside with a ferocious howl.

Val handed me a piece of paper.

*Chop chop choppity chop*
*Cut off the bottoms*
*Cut off the top*
*What's left over we'll put in the pot*
*Chop chop choppity chop*

*—Australian Children's Rhyme*

"What is this?"

Shelley's face flushed. "The clue for the weapon I'm supposed to hide!"

"For the cleaver? That's cute. I've never heard that rhyme before."

"Cute?" Shelley hissed. "It's the worst clue ever! Where am I supposed to hide it? In a pot? No one would ever find it."

"You haven't hidden it yet?"

"No! I didn't know what to do with it. Val's going to be furious if she finds out."

"Perfect. Where do you want to hide it? We can make up a clue, and I'll announce it."

Shelley looked out the window at the snowy vista. "Can it be somewhere close by?"

"How about the dock? I'll tell them, *Hickory dickory dock, the mouse went up the clock*."

"You're as crazy as Val. They'll be looking for clocks!"

"Do you have a better idea?"

"No. But I don't want to go out in that awful weather." Shelley looked miserable at the mere thought.

"I'll do it. You might need to distract them, though. The dock is visible from the windows."

"Would you?" Shelley brightened up considerably.

"Sure, where's the cleaver? I'll do it right now."

"In the kitchen."

I followed Shelley and slipped the weapon inside my jacket.

Val poked her head into the kitchen. "I've been pouring coffee and ran out. Where's the coffeemaker? What are the two of you hatching in here?"

I whipped past her, leaving Shelley to come up with answers.

Trixie followed me to the office. I grabbed some floral wire to tie the cleaver to a post, and we stepped out into the snow. Even though it had slowed, I couldn't see the lake. If Trixie hadn't had black ears and a black spot on her rump, I would have lost sight of her. It was deep enough for her to have to jump like a bunny to cross the pristine lawn. Negotiating the walk down to the lake was tricky. I fell and slid, which Trixie thought great fun and reason to leap over me. She yapped with delight at our new game.

"You're not helping." I reached out to nab her but she darted out of reach, her little tail wagging nonstop.

I made it to the dock and had second thoughts. We really didn't want people having to slip and slide down the hill to get to the dock, did we? Huffing more than I'd have liked, I called Trixie and made my way back up to the inn. A different nursery rhyme ran through my head. Stomping to shed snow, I returned to the office, peered into what Oma called the emergency closet, and found just what I needed. I seized the broom and tied the mock cleaver onto it with the florist wire. Now where to hide it?

It only seemed fair for one of the other merchants to benefit from it. After all, the candlestick had been found by someone in the inn. I looked down at Trixie. "Ready for another trek out in the snow?"

She gazed up at me and perked her ears. I took that as a yes.

Armed with my broom, I felt a bit like a Halloween witch as we walked out into the white world. The Blue Boar wasn't open yet, but a young guy was cleaning snow off the restaurant's deck. He looked to be in his mid-twenties. Most of his hair was hidden under a knit ski hat but I caught a glimpse of friendly brown eyes when he flashed me a smile.

"Hey," he said.

A common Southern greeting. He was local or from the South. I responded with "Good Morning," thinking that the owner of The Blue Boar was a savvy guy around Oma's age. He wouldn't hire a louse, even to shovel snow.

"Do you work for The Blue Boar?" I asked.

He stopped shoveling and stepped toward me. "Just do odd jobs when they need me. Are you Mrs. Miller's granddaughter?"

"How did you guess?"

He looked down at Trixie. "Not to slight you any, ma'am, but your dog's getting a reputation around town."

Trixie didn't seem upset by that. She edged closer to

smell his boots. Trixie *had* found a few bodies. I could imagine what local people thought. They probably ran when they saw her coming.

I offered my mittened hand. "Holly Miller."

He laughed when our gloves were too bulky for a handshake. We tried a mock high five. "Shadow Hobbs. My mom owns The Cat's Meow."

"I was just headed to her store. What else do you do for The Blue Boar?"

"Whatever they need. I bring them firewood, and fix dishwashers, and—"

That sparked my interest. "You can fix appliances? Do you mow and do yard work?"

"Sure, but usually not when there's a foot of snow on the ground." He grinned at me.

"We could use some help around the inn. Would you be interested in doing some work for us?" I could try him out to see how he did.

"Yeah, I'd like that. I'll be over when I finish up here."

I waved at him and hurried toward his mom's store. The front window of The Cat's Meow featured an artfully displayed collection of items for cats and the people they owned. One of the resident cats, a long-haired tortoiseshell kitty named Mimi, sat in the middle of an assortment of stuffed toy cats and kittens, watching the snow fall. To her right, I recognized Zelda's cat, Leo, draped over the perch of a fancy cat tree. Leo certainly got around.

The store wasn't open yet but I could see Delta Hobbs working inside. I rapped on the window. The bell on the door rang when she opened it. Trixie ran inside, eagerly sniffing everything she could reach. I had been in Delta's store before but only knew her in a shallow sort of way.

Delta smiled at me, pushing thick dark hair off her shoulder. "You're an early bird today."

"I just wanted to leave this broom here. There's a clue attached for Murder Most Howl."

"Oh my word!" Delta took the broom and spun it in her hands. "Thank you so much, sweetheart. I was hoping I'd get some clues that would bring them in here." She paused for a moment, and one eye squinted. "I'll put it in the store window. What do you bet half of them will walk right by it?"

I thanked her in a bit of a hurry, knowing that they were probably getting anxious about the clue back at the inn. Trixie and I shot out the door.

To my left, I spied Dave draping the area around the bench with crime scene tape.

I hurried over to him. "Does this mean Norm was murdered?"

Dave shook his head. "Nope. He's dead, though. We're waiting for autopsy results."

"Then why the tape?"

Dave shot me a deadpan look. "I don't know how he died."

I guessed that made sense from a law enforcement perspective. "Come by the inn for some breakfast when you're done?"

"Thanks, I'd like that."

When I walked past the window of The Cat's Meow, Delta was arranging the broom among the other items on display.

We were halfway back to the inn when a wind blew in, lifting the snow and obscuring everything. I knew where I was but the snow swirled around me so thick and fast that I could have easily lost my way. I called Trixie and bent down to grab her. Clutching her in my arms, I forged ahead, bent over against the stinging ice crystals that flew through the air. Trixie didn't even squirm. I thought she probably wanted us to reach the inn soon, too.

I breathed with relief when I could make out the front steps. Still carrying Trixie, I staggered up the stairs and into the warmth of the inn.

Mr. Huckle swooped down on me and took Trixie. "Miss Holly! We were worried about you." He unfastened Trixie's coat and removed it.

"We're fine, but it's a blizzard out there." I shed my jacket and boots, and hurried to the center of the dining tables.

"I would like to apologize to everyone for taking so long. Trust me when I say you really don't want to be outside right now anyway. Let's hope this snow dies down. Here's the clue you've all been waiting for." I hoped I remember the words of the children's rhyme correctly.

*'Twas a stormy night*
*When two little kittens began to fight.*
*The old woman seized her sweeping broom,*
*And swept the kittens right out of the room.*

*—Anonymous (circa 1880)*

Participants scribbled the words. A few called out for me to repeat it. I was happy to oblige.

The scent of hearty blueberry buckwheat pancakes and hot sausages laced with sage wafted to me, reminding me that I hadn't eaten yet. Now that everything was getting under control, I thought I could pause for a moment to eat and savor some much-needed coffee.

But first, I made sure Shelley knew that coffee was on the house for everyone this morning. Oma might not like that much but she probably would have done something similar had she been in my shoes. A number of the tables opened up rather quickly as people donned their coats and jackets and headed outside discussing clues.

"Mr. Huckle, have you eaten breakfast?" I asked.

"It's been rather busy, Miss Holly."

I invited him to join me and sat down at an empty table. Mr. Huckle hustled over eagerly, took a seat, and leaned toward me. "Is it true that someone was found frozen?" he whispered.

"News gets around fast."

"Half the out-of-towners were chattering about it this morning. Anyone we know?"

"I'm afraid it was Norm Wilson."

"Norm! Well! I'm very sorry to hear that. *Hmmpf*," he snorted quietly.

"Do you know something about this?"

"Oh my, no! I was just thinking that's what comes of not wearing socks in the cold of winter."

I seriously doubted that Norm had succumbed to the frigid temps because of his bare ankles. Socks probably wouldn't have made much of a difference unless they were extremely thick and warm. "I imagine he had a heart attack, don't you?"

"He *was* on the portly side. How very odd. I suppose he didn't have the strength to stand and walk."

"Dave said they'll be sending him for an autopsy."

Mr. Huckle frowned. "He was here last night. He didn't seem ill to me. I've heard of people falling and freezing to death, but I can't say that I have ever known anyone to sit down on a bench and freeze. Seems a bit peculiar."

I was about to agree with him when we heard thumping noises on the front porch. But no one entered.

# Eight

Mr. Huckle and I exchanged a glance and hurried to the door. We found Shadow Hobbs cleaning snow that had blown onto the porch.

"Come on in and have a cup of hot coffee. You've been out in the snow for hours," I said.

"Thanks, but I don't want to track snow inside. I shoveled the walk between the inn and The Blue Boar, and sprinkled nontoxic ice melt on it. I hope that's okay. I also cleaned up the doggy potty area. It looked like it needed it. You know, it shows more in snow than in the grass. And the snow had gotten too high for little dogs."

He was a gem! I looked at those sweet brown eyes and felt as though I'd discovered a gold mine. He hadn't been told to do those things. He simply took it upon himself because they needed to be done. I had stumbled upon the perfect handyman! He was clearly a self-starter who didn't need to be told every little thing. Oma would be thrilled that I had hired him.

Brown curls peeked out from under his knit hat. He wasn't as tall as I'd thought. Probably five inches short of six feet.

His face was adorably earnest but someone really ought to tell him that the fuzzy triangle of beard just under his lower lip was not that attractive.

"This is wonderful!" I exclaimed.

A smile lit his face. "Yeah? I, uh, need to take a quick break. Something, um, came up, but if you've got anything else for me to do, I can come back in an hour or so."

"That would be terrific. We need someone to bring firewood in from the woodpile in back."

"Sure. I can do that. I can even split it for you if you want."

I loved him more every time he opened his mouth. "We'll see you later then?"

He nodded. "You bet."

I closed the door and said to Mr. Huckle, "I think I've found our new handyman."

Mr. Huckle raised his eyebrows. "Perhaps you shouldn't be hasty about this."

My breath caught in my throat. "Is there something wrong with Shadow?"

Mr. Huckle paused. "I believe hiring a new employee is something your grandmother would rather do herself."

I was a little put out with Mr. Huckle. Maybe that was true, but Oma wasn't here, and I *was* co-owner of the inn.

Breakfast on my mind, I returned to the dining area but Myrtle rushed at me like a tank. I could tell from the determined look on her face that I wouldn't get a bite of breakfast anytime soon.

"No one believes that we have a weapon. We're losing precious time here. Where's the substitute poison bottle?"

Oy. I had forgotten all about it. "I'll work on that right now!"

I whipped into the kitchen to swipe anything I could. The muffins looked good. "Hey, Shelley, I need an empty bottle as a replacement weapon. Do you know where Oma might keep something like that?"

Shelley loaded a tray with dishes full of French toast. The scent made me want to stay put and eat. "Have you checked your grandmother's stash in the attic? She saves all kinds of things. This isn't the first murder mystery weekend. I bet she has some props up there somewhere."

"Why didn't I think of that? Of course!" I dashed out of the kitchen and across the dining area. Trixie and Gingersnap ran with me, their noses turned up in the direction of the muffins I had grabbed.

As soon as we were in the private kitchen, out of Myrtle's sight, I paused and shared a muffin with the dogs. "Here's the deal," I told them. "We're looking for a bottle. The sooner we find one, the sooner we can stop and eat a real breakfast." They listened intently, their bright eyes focused on me—or the other muffin.

"If we don't find one, we may not eat more until lunchtime."

They snarfed their share of the second muffin, and as if they had understood every word, they shot through the doggy door and started up the hidden staircase, leaving me behind.

I dashed after them. We climbed the stairs to our apartment, walked through it, and stopped at the door to the storage attic. Twinkletoes magically appeared as if she had a notion something exciting would happen there. I unlocked the door, and the three of them launched into the attic with enthusiasm.

While they sniffed around, I scanned the large attic room hoping to see a stash of old bottles or boxes labeled *Mystery Weekend* or something along those lines.

Across the room, a box crashed. Trixie and Gingersnap ran to their safety zone—me. Twinkletoes stalked away with her head and tail held high, pretending she had nothing to do with the loud noise.

The box that had tumbled was labeled with my father's name. Curious, I opened it. The dogs, feeling safer now, sniffed it eagerly. Twinkletoes jumped inside, purring. She investigated each corner and pawed at some old books. Apparently deciding it wasn't worth her interest after all, she vaulted out of the box, leaped onto a table, and washed her fur.

The contents were a fascinating look at my dad's childhood. He read Tom Swift, the Hardy Boys, and *Treasure Island*. Nestled beside the books were a well-worn stuffed bunny, old 45 records, a stack of his report cards tied with a ribbon, and a host of other things. All interesting and worth a look at another time, but right now, I needed a bottle. I jammed everything back into the box and was stashing it near the wall when I hit pay dirt.

An ornate display cabinet with gilding along the curving lines was almost hidden behind taller furniture. Through the glass doors I could see a collection of knickknacks and what appeared to be an old tea service. I wedged between a bookcase and an armoire to reach it. In a back corner was an old green bottle. Not too big, it looked like something that might have contained medicine at one time. Perfect.

I called Trixie, Gingersnap, and Twinkletoes, locked the door, and pressed the button for the elevator. The second I did that, Trixie backed away in fear and shot toward the stairs. I was beginning to think she might never get over her fear of confined spaces. Gingersnap, older and wiser, stepped into the elevator as though it was perfectly normal. Even Twinkletoes pranced into the elevator without hesitation.

Trixie was faster than the elevator, and the smart little girl was waiting for us when we stepped off. How could she have known on which floor we would exit?

Gingersnap and Twinkletoes turned right toward the murmuring voices of diners. Trixie and I hustled in the other direction, to the office.

Luck was with me. In less than a minute I found printable skull and crossbones poison labels on the Internet. I was even able to add the words *Official Murder Most Howl Poison Bottle* to the image. I printed it on a large address label and stuck it on the bottle. Voilà! "Trixie," I said, "prepare to finally eat breakfast." Coffee, I needed coffee in the worst way. I sped back to the dining tables, knowing I would finally be able to sit down and catch my breath.

Myrtle, Weegie, and Sylvie sat at a large table with the rest of their book club.

Trixie had the audacity to lick Puddin's breakfast bowl in case she had left a morsel.

I proudly announced, "Myrtle, this is the official replacement bottle. I apologize for the delay."

Sylvie reached for it.

Myrtle clutched the green bottle to her chest. "Oh no you don't. I see that I shall have to guard this with my life."

I hoped not!

Sylvie scoffed at her. "Do you really think I'm going to run off with it?"

"Yes," said Myrtle. "That's exactly what I think you're going to do. If you had gotten up early like Weegie and me, instead of lounging until daylight, you might be entitled to the benefits. Now then, perhaps you could disclose your relationship with the Baron von Rottweiler?"

"I just wanted to have a closer look at it."

Holding it firmly between her hands, Myrtle raised it in the air slightly. "You may admire it from afar. And now I'd like to know your connection to the baron, please."

The corners of Sylvie's mouth turned down. "Very well. I'm not ashamed. I was his first wife. Apparently, he left me for some much younger trollop."

Weegie scribbled furiously in a notebook. "Well! I call that motivation for murder."

Myrtle eyed her friend. "I don't believe you've told me your connection to the baron, Weegie."

Weegie pulled a tissue from her purse and dabbed at her eyes. "I'm his third and current wife."

"Reaaaly," drawled Myrtle.

"You can't think I killed him. I loved him!"

She put on a good act, making me grin.

Sylvie laughed. "We have a lot in common, apparently."

But Myrtle didn't appear to be amused. Her eyes narrowed. "Have you obtained any other clues?"

"You're a pest, Myrtle." She pulled a clue from her pocket. "I don't think it means much."

*The Baron von Rottweiler's third wife has a brother, who recently made dinner for his mother and sister at their mother's house.*

"There was another clue about his third wife," said Myrtle. "I'll have to check my notes."

It was an innocent comment, but Myrtle said it as though she thought Weegie might have really killed someone.

Myrtle scanned the rest of the members of her group. They jumped up simultaneously, scrambling to depart.

"Not so fast," said Myrtle. "You don't get to run away. I would like to know your secrets, please."

Some of them looked defeated but I noticed that a couple of them seemed pleased. Were they planning to lie to her?

I spotted Mr. Huckle finishing his breakfast at a table near the window. I strolled over to join him, ready for my much-deserved coffee. "I think we have everything under control now."

"I hope so, Miss Holly," he said.

Across the room, Charlotte Tredwell watched Puddin' and Trixie play with Ella Mae. Puddin' and Trixie each outweighed little Ella Mae but there was no question that the tiny ten-pound dog thought she was bigger than either of them.

Charlotte's husband, Geof, chowed down on French toast, pausing only when Robin Jarvis made an appearance. Geof jumped up and pulled out a chair for her. Charlotte looked on, evidently used to such gentlemanly behavior.

Robin and Charlotte launched into a conversation, leading me to believe they knew each other. Robin's pale complexion contrasted with her dark hair. Bags under her eyes made her look tired and as if she had just rolled out of bed. But she had taken the time to accentuate her almond-shaped eyes with eyeliner, and despite her exhaustion, she drew admiring glances from a couple of men in the room.

I took a deep breath and gazed around. People were laughing and lingering over coffee. I could hear them accusing one another of murdering the baron.

Finally, everything was going fine. Myrtle had her faux bottle of poison, the Sugar Maple Inn had electricity, and it appeared that Shadow would make a pretty good handyman for the inn. At that moment, the sun even made an appearance in a chunk of clear blue sky. The air might be chilly and the ground might be covered with snow, but it was going to be a beautiful day.

And then Dave walked in the front door with Holmes on his heels. They shed their coats and boots and headed toward us.

Dave wore colorful woolly socks that couldn't possibly have been part of his uniform. They showed a fun side of him that I rarely saw.

The two of them greeted Mr. Huckle, and Dave asked, "Could we speak privately? In your grandmother's kitchen, maybe?"

Uh-oh. That couldn't be good. "Sure."

Shelley arrived with a pot of steaming coffee and a basket of breakfast breads.

"We're moving to Oma's kitchen," I muttered, picking up my mug and taking the basket of rolls from her. "I'll help you serve."

Shelley didn't miss a beat. She snatched up two mugs and followed us. She leaned toward me and whispered, "Don't you dare help me serve. I need an excuse to come to the kitchen and hear what's going on!"

Holmes grabbed cutlery on his way. When we were in the private kitchen, Holmes asked Shelley, "Any chance you've got some grits cooking in the back?"

Shelley was circling the table, pouring coffee for everyone. "How about cheddar cheese grits with eggs and smoked sausages?"

"Be still, my heart. Bring it on, Shelley. I never get grits in Chicago." Holmes struck a match and poked the fire into a warm, comforting blaze.

If Dave hadn't insinuated that something was awry, I'd have gladly spent the entire day lounging by the fire in my Oma's cozy kitchen.

Dave ordered the same thing as Holmes but I asked for French toast. "How about grits, eggs, and dog sausage for Trixie and Gingersnap, please?" After the time I spent outdoors in the chilly morning before dawn, I figured I deserved French toast with butter and maple syrup. But the dogs should probably have a more fortifying meal.

Dave seemed distracted. He sat at the farmhouse table, stared at his coffee, and appeared to be deep in thought.

"What's wrong?" I asked.

Dave looked around the table at us. Taking a deep breath, he spoke in a soft tone. "Norm was murdered."

# Nine

Holmes, Mr. Huckle, and I jerked back in shock.

"How could they have done an autopsy so fast?" I asked.

A worry crease edged between Dave's eyes. "Norm couldn't be revived but the emergency room doctor managed to get some fluids to test. He thinks Norm died of hypoglycemia."

"Isn't that low blood sugar? Was Norm diabetic? Maybe it wasn't murder but a terrible accident." I held my breath waiting for his response.

"His wife, Savannah, says he wasn't."

My last ray of hope fizzled.

"Is taking insulin the only way to get hypoglycemia?" asked Holmes.

Dave held up a hand to stop him. "Apparently not, but there's more. Norm had what appears to be an injection site reaction. The doctor described it as a red inflammation around a spot where a substance was injected. Given the low blood sugar, that substance was very likely insulin."

Shelley delivered our meals, and we fell into silence while

Trixie danced in circles, yelping for her food. As Shelley set my plate in front of me, she whispered, "What's going on?"

"Norm was murdered."

Shelley gasped. She set breakfast bowls on the floor for Gingersnap and Trixie, then sat down with us.

Holmes quickly filled her in about Norm.

"Injection site?" murmured Shelley. "We don't have much of a drug problem here in Wagtail. You think Norm was into drugs?"

"It doesn't appear to have been self-inflicted," said Dave rather dryly. He left it at that, but I wondered how they could know Norm didn't give himself the shot.

Mr. Huckle had been listening quietly. "I believe insulin is only available by prescription. That should make it easy to narrow down the field of potential culprits. Officer Dave, I presume your position entitles you to demand a list of those persons who have bought insulin at the local pharmacy?"

"Good idea." Holmes relaxed. "There were a lot of people in Wagtail who didn't care for Norm. But finding out who buys insulin will narrow down the list. I bet you end up with just a few potential suspects." He dug into his food. "Mmm, mmm. My best to the cook, Shelley!"

"I'm headed to the pharmacy after I eat." Dave swiped a fork through his grits. He still seemed worried.

"You haven't told us something," I said gently.

Trixie placed her front paws on the edge of my chair and cocked her head adorably. Not to be outdone, Gingersnap, who normally had much better table manners than Trixie, tried to lay her head in my lap.

"I haven't had one bite yet," I hissed at them. "Don't I get to eat?" They didn't appear to think so.

Dave looked me straight in the eyes. "You found him. You were there."

I wasn't following his train of thought. "That doesn't mean I killed him."

"That's not what I'm saying. The killer left us a message. A clue, to be more precise."

Now he had my attention. "Of course! The bottle of poison."

"Norm had a bottle of poison with him when you found him?" asked Mr. Huckle.

"The pretend poison bottle for Murder Most Howl was on his lap."

"The one I carved?" asked Holmes.

"You made it?"

"I carved all four of the weapons."

"They're amazing!" I stared at Holmes in awe for a moment. I thought I knew him so well, but he continued to surprise me. What other hidden talents did he have?

I struggled to shift my thoughts away from Holmes and turned to Dave. "You can't possibly think the presence of the poison bottle had any significance."

"It means something all right. I just don't know what."

Holmes swallowed the last bite of his treasured grits. "You think someone who is playing the game left the bottle there to taunt you?" He shuddered. "That would be sick."

Dave nodded. "I hope that's not the case but I can't ignore the possibility. Or someone from Wagtail might have had a beef with Norm and left the bottle there to throw us off track and make us think an out-of-towner did him in."

"Other than killing the poor old Baron von Rottweiler, does the bottle have any symbolic meaning in the game?" asked Holmes.

I finally cut into my French toast. Fresh blueberries on top had been dusted with powdered sugar but that didn't stop me from drizzling maple syrup over it, too. "Not that I know of. It was just a tool that gave a player the power to demand information from other players."

Mr. Huckle touched the fingertips of his hands together. "I suppose Norm might have found the bottle and just happened to have it with him. Perhaps it's not related to his death at all."

"I'll say one thing. There was no shortage of folks who loathed Norm." Shelley's eyes met mine and widened. She jumped up. "Goodness! I have to get back to work before my boss yells at me." She patted my shoulder on her way out.

"I don't see how his death could have anything to do with the game," I said. "The bottle in his lap must have been a coincidence."

"No matter how you look at it—whether he found it and had it with him when he died or someone left it there on purpose—that poison bottle is going to lead me to information about his death." Dave seemed to feel relieved to have told us the bad news. He finally ate his breakfast with gusto.

"Anything we can do to help?" asked Holmes.

"Keep your ears to the ground. Let me know if you hear anything, no matter how insignificant it might seem."

"Did his wife call you last night when he didn't come home?" I asked.

Dave took a long swig of his coffee. "Nope. She went to bed at ten and didn't realize that he never came home until I called her this morning."

"So no alibi," mused Mr. Huckle. "Not that Savannah would need one," he hastened to add. "She's very sweet."

"Norm was here for the Murder Most Howl introduction last night," I said. "I didn't notice anything strange about him. He wasn't arguing with anyone."

"Did you see him leave?" asked Dave.

"I didn't. Mr. Huckle, how about you?" I asked.

"As a matter of fact, I did see him take his leave. No socks, as usual, but I helped him with a navy blue jacket. He departed alone. I'm afraid I did not note the exact time. Probably around nine thirty or so."

The door banged open and Val barged in. "There you are! Shelley told me what happened to Norm." She slid into a chair as though she was exhausted. "Can't say I'm surprised."

"You didn't like him, did you?" asked Holmes.

Val ran a hand through her hair and took a deep breath. "I

haven't made a secret of that." Her shoulders sagged as she exhaled. "Norm was a no-good, miserable worm. Maybe even worse than that. Nevertheless, I'd like to think I'm a big enough person not to find joy in anyone's demise, especially if it involved murder. But you won't see me shedding any tears for that vile man. Is that the French toast? Shelley's bringing me some. Looks good."

I glanced over at Dave, who, as I expected, watched Val carefully. Couldn't she have just said it was a tragedy and left it at that? Eager to change the subject, I asked, "Where did you go?"

"The shock of seeing Norm frozen this morning made me forget that I still had to put out the dog and cat clues. The dog clues are cookies and the cat clues are filled with catnip, so I thought it best to wait until morning to hide them."

"How is a dog cookie a clue?" asked Holmes.

"Sweet Dog Barkery baked them in special shapes, like a dinner plate, wedding bells, and a book. Of course, if a hungry dog like Trixie should find one and take a bite out of it before a person knew what the shape was, he'd be out of luck."

Holmes roared. "So all over town dogs and cats are leading their people to clues but the people might not even realize they're clues until it's too late?"

We all chuckled but in such a pathetic, joyless way that I knew everyone was upset about Norm's demise.

Shelley arrived with Val's breakfast and joined us with a plate of French toast for herself. "The breakfast rush started early this morning. And then Myrtle went and scared half the people away by demanding their secrets. There's a surefire way to clear out a room."

Mr. Huckle rose from his seat. "I shall keep an eye on the remaining diners while you eat, Miss Shelley." He left the room, and I could hear him greeting someone before the door even closed.

Val winced. "I hadn't thought of it that way. Well, live and learn. Myrtle can't be everywhere. Has anyone else found a weapon?"

"Someone must have the candlestick because it's not where I hid it." Gingersnap bumped my elbow with her nose. "What's with you today? You're usually so well behaved." She gazed at me with sweet brown eyes. She probably missed Oma. I relented and shared a bit of my breakfast with her and Trixie.

"So, Val," said Dave. "Did Norm come by your pub a lot?"

I held my breath. Even though Dave was trying to make it sound like casual conversation, I suspected he was interrogating her.

Val didn't blink. She didn't even look up from her French toast. "Nope."

I tried to hide my smile. Val was no dummy. She moved to Wagtail just before I did but she had probably met a lot more people at her pub.

"Never?" asked Dave.

Val shrugged. "Everyone comes in now and then."

I could see Dave's jaw tensing. She was being a little bit too cavalier.

Holmes's eyes met mine. "I hang out there," he said. "And she hasn't knocked me off yet."

Val shot him a grateful smile but the look on Dave's face told me he wasn't finished with her.

"Thanks for breakfast, Holly." Dave rose. "I'm off to the pharmacy."

I couldn't help noticing that he took one last long glance at Val before he left.

She must have noticed it, too. She closed her eyes for just a couple of seconds, and her body relaxed. "Did either of you see who took the original faux poison bottle last night? It was on the table beside you, Holmes. Did you see who took it?"

Holmes set his mug on the table. "Not me. Are you kidding? People crowded around me like dogs after a piece of bacon. I had to play dead, remember?"

Val shifted her gaze to me.

"The Tredwells asked me to show them out the side door in the dark. I wasn't even in the room part of the time."

Holmes sat back in his chair. "It could have been anyone. In the dark, it would have been easy to pick it up. Besides, it was small and easy to hide in a pocket or a purse."

After breakfast, I stopped by my apartment to change into something a little more coordinated than the clothes I'd thrown on that morning. Twinkletoes followed me, rubbing my legs and meowing.

With a gasp, I realized she hadn't been fed! I swung her up into my arms. "I'm so sorry, sweetie pie. What would you prefer? Liver? Beef? Salmon?"

She purred nonstop. I eyed the bowls of dry food. They weren't empty. It made me feel a little bit better about not feeding her. "I'm so sorry, schnookums. Our routine was interrupted." That wasn't a good excuse, but it was all I had. I spooned beef au jus into her bowl and set her down. She curled her black tail around her body and ate daintily.

I retreated to my bedroom, where I changed into a navy and white striped sweater, jeans, and short boots. Pulling my hair back, I pinned it up in a practical makeshift twist, added dangling red earrings, a red scarf, and a white vest. That ought to keep me warm for a bit if I had to go outside again.

I trotted back downstairs and found that Gingersnap had ventured out to her favorite spot on the porch. She didn't seem to mind the chilly weather. In fact, she appeared to like it.

Twinkletoes already lounged in her favorite sunbeam in the Dogwood Room. Through the windows, I could see Shadow carrying wood from the covered pile.

I walked to the reception area and discovered a stash of wood just inside the door.

The doors slid open and Shadow deposited more firewood. "Hope this is okay," he said. "I didn't want to track snow through the inn. When I've got enough, I'll change into indoor shoes and take wood wherever it's needed."

I was so surprised by his thoughtfulness that I hardly knew what to say. "That would be great! Thank you for being so considerate." I was going to hire him full time if he would have us.

Before returning to the office, I found Marisol, the housekeeper, and told her Shadow would be bringing firewood up to the rooms.

When I settled in the office, Twinkletoes snoozed on one end of the sofa and Trixie slept on the other end with all four paws in the air. I took care of some paperwork and made phone calls. After the busy morning, I ate a turkey sandwich at my desk for lunch. I shared it with Trixie and Twinkletoes, who had what I thought was an odd affinity for a cat—a love of bread!

Pleased with my progress, I pulled a couple of employee files to see what Oma did when hiring someone new. It didn't seem too difficult. I was flipping through them when I heard the sliding glass door whoosh open and angry voices.

Zelda backed into the doorway to the office. Without turning to look at me, she said, "I think we've got trouble."

# Ten

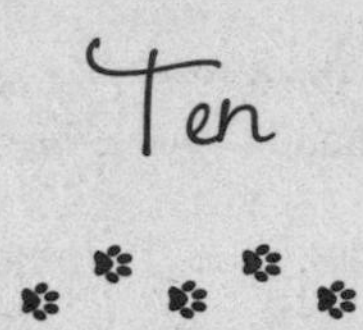

The very first face I saw belonged to my own Aunt Birdie. The scowling expression of my mother's older half sister was the norm for her. Aunt Birdie complained about everything. As usual, she had dressed stylishly in a black faux fur coat with a fluffy white collar that did nothing to soften the gaunt lines of skin stretched thin over high cheekbones or the angry blaze in her eyes.

Peaches Clodfelter followed her. The pompous woman had once been married to the richest man in Wagtail. She had fallen on hard times but she still managed to have her brassy orange hair swept up in a lacquered coif that must have been done by a hairdresser. Lean and angular like Aunt Birdie, her nostrils flared, and she jabbed a stick-thin finger at me. "How dare you?"

"Have you no shame?" asked a man whom I didn't know. Sparse black and gray hair stuck out from his very round head. His lips were so thin they were little more than edges for his mouth. He wore his shirt unbuttoned at the neck, making room for a substantial double chin. In spite of the cold weather, he wiped sweat off his forehead.

Each of them clutched a small folded sheet of paper.

I forced a little smile. "What's going on?"

"That's what we'd like to know!" said Aunt Birdie. "The gall. The unmitigated gall! How could you do this to your own aunt?"

Zelda and I exchanged a look.

"I have no idea what you're talking about."

The three of them glanced at one another.

"You first," said Birdie.

"No, no. You're family. You go first," protested Peaches.

I reached across the reception desk and each of them sheepishly handed over their slips of paper. With Zelda looking over my shoulder, I unfolded them one at a time. Evidently they hadn't seen one another's papers because they all leaned over to read them upside down.

The first one said:

*Peaches Clodfelter's daughter is in prison.*

The second one was worse.

*Larry Pierce, chef at Café Chat, is having an affair with Peaches Clodfelter.*

I looked up at the chubby man. "I presume you're Larry Pierce?"

"What if my wife hears about this?"

I could see panic in his eyes. I unfolded the third one.

*Birdie Dupuy stalks Max Hemmerich.*

I bit my lip so I wouldn't laugh. I couldn't imagine Max, a sophisticated bookaholic, being interested in staid Aunt Birdie.

She had turned the color of cooked beets. "That's just not true! I've never been so embarrassed in my life."

Peaches guffawed. "Not true? It's hysterically funny! You follow that man everywhere."

"I do not. But I bet your daughter Prissy looks awful in those orange prison jumpsuits."

Peaches gasped. "How can you be so cruel? You know that's the worst thing that ever happened to me."

Could they all be true? I read them again. The only one I knew for sure was that Peaches Clodfelter's daughter was in prison. I eyed Larry and Peaches. An unlikely couple, but didn't they say opposites attract? And hadn't Aunt Birdie arrived at the meeting last night on Max's heels? "I'm sorry about this, but I don't know why you came here. I didn't have anything to do with these," I said.

"You're the mayor," spat Peaches. "You have to do something!"

"I am not the mayor. Oma is the mayor, and she's away. There must be some kind of vice mayor or someone filling in for her." No sooner were the words out of my mouth than I realized that old Mr. Wiggins was the vice mayor. No wonder Peaches didn't want to go to him. He was the ex-husband whose money she ran through.

Birdie gasped. "In the first place, we can't go to him because he's a horrid gossip. It will be all over Wagtail! And in the second place, this is your fault. You're totally responsible. These are clues for Murder Most Howl."

I flipped them over and studied them. Plain paper, probably printed by a computer. "They're not clues. I hid some myself, and I can assure you they came in cute little red envelopes."

As though they had practiced it, all three of them raised little red envelopes simultaneously.

I took a deep breath. *Val!* But why would she do something like this? If the notes were true, and I had a sinking feeling they might be, given the rather desperate reaction of

Birdie, Peaches, and Larry, they were unkind if not downright malicious. And even more important, they had nothing to do with the game. There wasn't any mention of the Baron von Rottweiler, unless one was to presume that the baron knew these things and that's why someone killed him.

"I'll take these straight to Val, and I'll let you know what she says."

"Val?" screeched Peaches. "I should have known she was behind this. She hears gossip all day long at that scuzzy bar of hers. I heard she was run out of town at the last place she lived."

I glared at her. That was as unkind as the clues they brought to me. It was absurd, too, like something out of an old movie. People weren't ejected from towns anymore. Were they?

"What if there are more?" asked Larry, breathing heavily. He wiped his forehead with his palm. "What if they're all over town?"

"Where did you find these?" I asked.

Birdie mashed her lips together. "A total stranger marched up to me in the middle of Sweet Dog Barkery and asked if I was Birdie Dupuy. I thought he had probably read some of my articles on antiques, but then he asked me if I murdered the Baron von Rottweiler and shoved this clue at me. Can you even imagine my embarrassment? I was so humiliated that I like to have died right then and there." She raised her chin defiantly.

Larry leaned toward me. "One of my waiters brought me this. A customer asked him about it! Every single one of my employees has probably heard about it by now."

Peaches slapped a hand just below her throat and moaned. "It will be all over town. I can never show my face in this town again!" I assumed she meant her affair with Larry since Prissy's incarceration wasn't a secret.

"I'll talk to Val right away and find out how many more there are." I still couldn't believe she would have done such a thing. I slid on my jacket and dressed Trixie. Bypassing Peaches, Birdie, and Larry, who murmured in a little huddle, we headed for the front door. Gingersnap lounged by the fire in the Dogwood Room. I whistled for her. "Gingersnap? Walkies!"

She scrambled to her feet, walked to the door, and waited for me to open it. I paused for a moment, wondering if Gingersnap wore a coat in the winter. She had typical long golden retriever fur. Probably not.

Gingersnap and Trixie raced outside and down the porch stairs to sniff other dogs being walked. I stayed on the sidewalk, admiring the heavy snow dressing up branches. Even the gazebo looked more glamorous with a pristine snowcap.

I paused briefly at the sight of Geof and Robin chatting on a walking trail near the inn. No sign of Char or Ella Mae. That didn't mean a thing, I told myself.

Hair of the Dog was on the other end of town, but strolling through a light sprinkling of snowflakes was magical. The dogs romped with joyous abandon, sniffing every tree, and tracking scents.

We turned right and walked to the end of the street, where Hair of the Dog occupied a Tudor-style house. Someone had built a snow couple drinking something with snow whipped cream on top. An unmistakable snow poodle sat with them.

I opened the door, setting off a bell, and both dogs shot inside.

"Sorry!" called Val from the back. "We won't be open until this afternoon around five."

She didn't have much time to get everything ready. "It's Holly." I raised my voice so she would hear me.

"I'm glad it's just you." Val emerged from the back, wiping her hands on a towel. "We have some locals who might be a little bit too addicted to coming here. Not that I mind. I love the business but they're very cranky that they can't lounge around the pub this afternoon."

I removed Trixie's coat and my vest before pulling the clues from my pocket. I didn't really know what to say. I didn't want to accuse her of anything, so I just handed them to her.

Val read them silently. "Whoa. This is some powerful stuff. Where'd you get these?"

I exhaled with relief, thanking my lucky stars that she wasn't the one who wrote the scandalous clues. "Aunt Birdie, Peaches, and Larry brought them to me. Some of the Murder Most Howl participants found them in red envelopes."

Val blinked a few times, a crease forming between her eyes. "Do you think they're true?"

"I know for a fact that Peaches's daughter is in the slammer. I don't know about the others but Larry was pretty worried about his wife hearing about his alleged affair with Peaches."

Val stared at the slips for a moment. "I know Birdie is your aunt, but I fear she might stalk Max. She never comes in here. It's not her kind of place. I get that. But every time Max walks through the door, I can guarantee that Birdie will follow a few minutes later."

That was all I needed—my crazy aunt stalking someone. "I think I'd better have a chat with her about that."

Val flapped the clues against her hand nervously. "Why would anyone do this? It's as though someone in town took advantage of Murder Most Howl to expose some very personal secrets."

"Not to mention messing up the game. The players won't know which clues pertain to the game."

Val's eyes opened wide. "This is a nightmare! Wagtail will get a terrible reputation. I almost invited a reporter to come for the weekend. I'm glad I didn't do that! But with social media, complaints will be all over the place in no time."

I paced the room. We had to correct this mess. But how? "What if we make it fun for them?"

"Oh, right." Val's voice dripped with sarcasm. "What are

we going to do? Tell them the game wasn't complicated enough so we threw in red herrings that have nothing to do with it?"

"I have an idea. I think we can deal with the guests. The locals whose secrets are being exposed are going to be the big problem."

"They'll all blame me." Val clutched the top of her head. "They'll hate me!"

"Do you have a list of the clues?" I asked.

"Of course. What good will that do?"

"I don't know if this will work but it's worth a try. We set up a clue inspection center at the inn. You, Shelley, Zelda, and I can take turns manning it. Players bring their clues, and we check them against the master list. We keep any that don't belong. We'll—" I thought fast as I talked "—set up a bowl with little slips of paper awarding them prizes like a free drink here, or free afternoon tea at the inn, or a free dog cookie or cat treat. The person who presents the most slips for inspection gets a free dinner for two here at Hair of the Dog."

Val stared at me for a long moment. "That could work. Everyone wins something just for showing us the slips. At least we could take the malicious ones out of circulation." She bowed her head. "But it only takes care of half the problem. I don't believe this is happening. What kind of sick person would leave ugly notes like these about the people of Wagtail?"

"It has to be someone local. The people visiting wouldn't know all those scandalous details. Oh boy. If there are more and these are typical, we're going to have a huge ruckus."

"Yeah, well, I am *not* taking the blame. Some twisted creep did this, and believe me, Holly, I will not rest until I find out who it was." She checked the time. "I can run off little prize certificates but I won't have time to man the desk. I'll see if I can find someone to pitch in."

Gingersnap and Trixie shot out the door when I opened it. Although the walk had been cleared, they romped through the snow, with Trixie jumping through it more like a rabbit than a dog.

I wished I felt their glee. It seemed like problems had piled up since Oma's departure. I gave myself a little pep talk. It wasn't so bad. I would hire Shadow as soon as I saw him. We would collect the scandalous clues and get them out of circulation. Guests would be happy with little prizes. That should save the mystery weekend. All we had to do was find the real killer who had done in Norm, and the mean-spirited person who left the outrageous notes clearly intended to cause hostility among the peaceful residents of Wagtail.

Back at the Sugar Maple Inn, fires blazed in the dining area and the Dogwood Room. Gingersnap made a beeline to guests, wagging her tail and expecting their adoration. Trixie found Ella Mae and the two of them frolicked through the lobby. I deposited our coats in the private kitchen and poked around for a bowl. An adorable blue ceramic bowl with white snowflakes painted around the rim was reminiscent of Christmas, but given the weather, I thought it appropriate. Trixie followed me to the desk near the front door. I placed the bowl on it for the prize slips.

Shadow ambled toward me in stocking feet and no shoes. "I think I'm done here unless you need anything else."

I asked him to accompany me to the office. On the way there, I asked if he knew anything about plumbing.

"Sure. My mom says there's not much I can't do with my hands. I built a new bathroom on her house."

That was all I needed to hear. If he could build a bathroom, he could surely fix a leak! "How would you like to work here as the handyman?"

"For real?" he asked. "You mean like all the time?"

I nodded as we walked into the office. "You would help the housekeeper with things like leaks and replacing lightbulbs that are high. Keep the grounds orderly and clean outdoors. Mow, prune trees, shovel snow, clean up the doggy toilet areas. Haul wood inside like you did today."

"Yes!" he shouted. Looking a bit abashed by his own enthusiasm, he added, "I'm not much for sitting around in an office and pushing papers. It sounds about perfect."

I asked him to have a seat and handed him forms to fill out. Meanwhile, I wrote a check for the hours he had worked that day.

Shadow seemed surprised when I handed it to him. "Thanks, Holly. I . . . I don't know what to say except I really appreciate this. It means a lot to me."

I wasn't sure which one of us was more pleased. It was a load off my mind to have someone around who could fix the little things that went haywire. Not to mention keep the grounds clean and safe.

As I walked him out, Zelda's tabby, Leo, followed the book club guests inside.

Zelda frowned at her cat. "What are you doing here again, big boy?"

Weegie laughed. "He followed us all the way back to the inn. It was just the cutest thing. I thought Puddin' would bark at him but they acted as though they were old friends. I don't understand. At home Puddin' would have barked her fool head off if a cat came near."

Leo made a beeline for Shadow and wound around his ankles, rubbing his head against Shadow's legs. Shadow bent over and scratched behind Leo's ears.

Zelda nodded at Weegie. "It's the attitude in Wagtail. Visiting animals know it's not their home, so they don't feel they have to defend their territory. And the people in Wagtail send out vibes of acceptance. We love dogs and cats. They sense that. It lets them know they can be friends with other animals."

"You're the pet psychic, right?" asked Myrtle.

"Yes. Would you like me to tell you what Puddin' and Leo are thinking right now?"

The group gathered around her, murmuring their agreement.

Zelda took a deep breath and rotated her hand just below her chin. "Leo is happy to see Shadow. They're old buddies. Puddin' thinks Leo is a very cool cat and would like to eat one of the treats that Weegie bought in town."

Sylvie and Myrtle appeared skeptical but Weegie gasped. "There's no way you could have known about that. I have a peanut butter dog cookie in my bag." She spoke to Puddin' in a high voice. "Puddies can has da' cookie as soon as we go up to our woom."

Puddin' wagged her tail as though she understood.

Myrtle laughed. "What a cute parlor trick. I have to remember that for parties at home."

Shadow glanced at me with big eyes. "This is gonna get ugly. I'll see you tomorrow?"

I thanked him again, and he hustled out the door as though he feared the group of ladies were about to start a war.

"It's not a trick," said Zelda. "I realize some people have difficulty imagining that I know what animals are thinking but—" she shrugged "—I do!"

Sylvie inhaled sharply. "Can you read our minds, too?"

Myrtle scoffed and addressed Zelda. "Not to offend you, dear, but that's nonsense." She turned to Sylvie and whispered, loud enough for us to hear, "It's impossible, Sylvie."

To her credit, Zelda smiled and spoke in a calm voice. "I can probably guess what most of you are thinking right now, but I can't read the minds of people."

Weegie tilted her head thoughtfully. "Wouldn't it be awful if someone knew what everyone was thinking? Talk about no privacy! We'd all have to hide in our homes."

Sylvie shook her fingers through her hair, loosening it from hat head. "I'm glad you're here, Holly. We found some very odd clues today. Maybe you can help us make sense of them?"

"I'm so glad you asked. We've instituted a new policy, and you can win prizes for some of those clues." My words were magic—every single member of the book club started searching pockets and handbags for clues.

Sylvie handed me her two clues first.

*The Baron von Rottweiler poisoned his second wife.*

I unfolded the next one.

*Shadow Hobbs has a criminal record.*

# Eleven

A chill rattled through me right down to my bones. Why hadn't I checked around? Why hadn't I asked people about Shadow? He had been so helpful. Maybe it wasn't true. Maybe the vicious person who had written these clues had mixed the truth with lies.

Or maybe not.

Gathering myself, I spoke as cheerfully as I could. "One of these is a fake clue. You win a prize! Everyone follow me, and we'll go through all your clues."

We trooped to the main lobby where Val was just coming through the door.

"Our first customers, Val," I said with fake glee, hoping no one would notice my distress.

She dumped the prize slips into the bowl. I mixed them up and held the bowl out to Sylvie while Val made a notation that Sylvie had turned in a clue.

"Good luck!" I said.

"A drink! I get a free drink at Hair of the Dog tonight!"

Her enthusiasm attracted more people, and before I knew

it, Val and I were checking clues, making a list of who had turned them in, and telling everyone to spread the word.

*Mr. Huckle was fired from his last job.*

I knew all about that. It wasn't because of anything he did. How dare someone malign that sweet old man when it was all the fault of that cranky Peaches that he lost his position?

*The Baron von Rottweiler conned his business partners.*

That I could believe. But which players were the baron's business partners and might have wanted to kill him?

*The Baron von Rottweiler drank Scotch from his flask every evening.*

*Zelda York cheated a neighbor out of $1,000.*

Uh-oh. I hoped that wasn't true!

*The poison in the Baron von Rottweiler's flask is an overdose amount of acetaminophen with codeine.*

Aha! So that was what the faux bottle of poison contained. That was a significant clue.

One of the women, who had brought a sleek ruddy-colored Abyssinian with her, stopped to ask if cats could find clues. I directed her to the indoor agility center and The Cat's Meow.

Robin Jarvis stepped up to the desk. She handed me three clues in red envelopes. "Am I doing this right? I don't recall seeing any mention of fake clues in the handout you gave us."

Val groaned and answered with a snap in her tone. "They weren't in the original plan."

Robin recoiled a little and seemed surprised.

I interceded fast. "It appears that someone in town is playing a little prank on us by adding clues. But the game is still on." I read her clues quickly, hoping Val wouldn't rant.

*The Baron von Rottweiler left his first wife so destitute that she had to live in her car.*

*The Baron von Rottweiler accused an innocent man of murder.*

*Liesel Miller is a busybody who pokes her nose where it does not belong.*

Hey! Now I was offended. That was my Oma they were talking about. Okay, I had to admit that Oma had a natural curiosity but it stemmed from her inclination to want to help other people. I feared I leaned that way, too. But that was no reason to call her a busybody!

I handed Robin the two real clues about the baron. "Only one fake clue," I said with a smile. "Please select your prize."

Robin chose a piece of paper from the bowl and read it aloud. "*Free teatime at the Sugar Maple Inn!* That sounds wonderful."

The second Robin walked away, I turned to Val. "You know, there was an easier way to do this. I haven't seen one fake clue that mentioned the Baron von Rottweiler."

Her eyes narrowed. "So it was probably someone who wasn't fully in the loop when we were planning Murder Most Howl." Val's mouth pulled into a bitter line. "All I can say is that the perpetrator is a dead man if I ever figure out who it was."

"Val!" I'd never seen her so upset. "You don't mean that."

"Don't I? I haven't been so angry since . . ."

"Since what?"

"I haven't been so upset in years."

Another player rescued her from having to explain. I stared at the little red envelopes he presented to me.

*The Baron von Rottweiler's third wife's mother recently had an upper respiratory infection.*

*Holly Miller was fired from her last job.*

That wasn't exactly correct. Whoever wrote the notes about local people was taking liberties and presenting information in the worst possible light. Still, it was highly annoying. And some, like the one about Peaches and Larry, could have serious consequences. Larry's marriage could break up because of it.

When the man left with his prize slip in hand, I asked Val, "Where did you buy the red envelopes?" I fervently hoped she wouldn't say she purchased them online. If that was the case, we'd never figure out who wrote the ugly clues.

"At Pawsitively Decadent. They have a section in the back with wrapping paper and stationery. The red envelopes are meant for gift enclosure cards. I thought they were just the right size. And the red color would make it easier for people to find them."

Val jumped up. "What am I thinking? I have to open the pub!" She shot out the door in a rush.

Half an hour later, Holmes showed up. "Val sent me over. I hear I can be useful checking clues."

Perfect. I explained to him how it worked. As soon as he was up to speed, I retrieved my jacket and Trixie's from the kitchen. Back in the lobby, I looked around for her. "Trixie?" I called.

"When I came in, she was heading upstairs with the little black and tan dog," said Holmes.

I trudged up to the stair landing and called Trixie again. She appeared at the second-floor railing and looked down at me like a little kid who had been interrupted at play.

"Let's go! Walkies!"

She scampered down to me. Back on the main floor, I helped Trixie with her jacket and called Gingersnap, but she was thoroughly engaged in a petting session with Robin. Her tail swished across the floor in delight.

As I walked by Holmes, I said, "Thanks for manning the fort."

"Where are you going?" he asked.

"To Pawsitively Decadent. I bet they don't sell those little red envelopes in bulk to many people."

On the porch, I ran into Blanche and Charlotte. For once she wasn't carrying Ella Mae.

Charlotte stopped me. "Look what we had done!" She flitted her fingers in front of me like a new bride showing off her ring. Her fingernails had been painted with a glittering snowy white background. On alternating fingers were dog bones, dog paws, and tiny paintings of Ella Mae.

Blanche seemed subdued. At Charlotte's prodding, she showed off her fingernails. A glittery blue background was perfect for miniature paintings of her saluki.

"We had such fun!" Charlotte said. "Our husbands have been obsessed with the clues, but we're having a great time."

They hustled into the inn, and I took off with Trixie. Dusk was moving in fast. The cloudy skies probably didn't help. I wondered if more snow was headed our way.

The sidewalks of Wagtail brimmed with visitors. Dogs in a variety of sweaters and coats plunged through the snow with glee, Trixie among them.

She tired of it soon, though, probably because it was up to her chest. She ran along the sidewalk, stopping occasionally to sniff things that I couldn't see.

At Pawsitively Decadent, I held the door open for her, and she readily ran inside. I was greeted by two unfriendly faces. The owner of the store and my own Aunt Birdie glared at me.

"I'm surprised that you dare to show your face around town, Holly," sniffed Aunt Birdie. "It's a good thing your grandmother isn't here to see this mess you've made. You and Val are just spiteful and mean. You've libeled everyone in Wagtail."

I tried to overlook her hatefulness, but I couldn't help tweaking her just a little. "It's not libel if it's the truth." Hah! That ought to shut her up.

I hadn't thought Aunt Birdie could look more enraged, but I was wrong. Maybe I shouldn't have said that. Somewhat more meekly I added, "Besides, neither Val nor I wrote those clues."

The store owner grumbled, "I should hope not. They say that I drink!"

"A dipsomaniac!" exclaimed Aunt Birdie.

He frowned. "There's not a thing in the world wrong with a little Scotch at night."

I tried to soothe him. "Of course not. Actually, the offensive clues are why I'm here. Val said she purchased the red envelopes from you. Do you remember anyone else buying some recently?"

"Only the people involved in your disastrous game."

My breath caught in my throat. Shelley? Zelda? Surely not. They wouldn't do anything to ruin Murder Most Howl. Could it be Hollis Hobbs, Shadow's dad? "Oh?" I tried to sound casual but my heart was beating like a chugging train. "Who besides Val?"

"Not very organized, are you? Norm, obviously."

Aunt Birdie reached over and shook my arm. "Are you okay, Holly?"

I could barely breathe. In the frenzy about the fake clues, I had almost forgotten about Norm's death. Even worse, I had foolishly dismissed Val when she said Norm wanted to make trouble.

"Do you remember when he bought them?" I choked out.

"Sure. Yesterday around noon. He asked me if they were the same type of envelopes Val had bought. I recall precisely because I joked about it being very last minute. Val bought plenty of envelopes weeks ago. I couldn't believe she ran out."

I wanted to kick myself. He had seen the clue envelopes on our table at the restaurant. That must have given him the idea.

"Did he say anything else?"

"Just how much he was looking forward to the game. He even came back later on and left some clues in here, which I thought was surprisingly nice of him."

"Don't be too impressed. He's the one who left all those gossipy clues about you drinking, and about Aunt Birdie—"

She cut me off. "Nonsense! I will not have you speaking ill of the dead. Did my sister teach you no manners whatsoever?"

I almost giggled. She didn't want me to say that she was stalking Max. Well, I couldn't blame her. Especially if it was true. That kind of revelation was very embarrassing.

"Do you still have the clues he left here?"

His mouth swung to the side in irritation, but I could see a grin developing. "Now that you've gone and dragged my name through the mud, I don't want to say anything nice, but you girls must have done something right. Folks barreled in here first thing this morning. Best day I've had since the holidays. This is the only lull I've had all day long. Those clues flew out of here like they were written in gold."

"I'm glad to hear that! If you figure out anyone else who could have made up those fake clues, you let me know. Aunt Birdie, dead or alive, I fear Norm is our culprit."

No sooner had the words left my mouth than I wondered if his ugly stunt had resulted in his death. I had to talk to Dave.

"Trixie!" I called. Her nails clicked along the floor as she raced full speed to the front of the store with a giant carob-iced cookie in the shape of a squirrel in her mouth. The tail had already been consumed.

I had no choice but to buy it now. "I'd better take one for Gingersnap, too." As I walked away to find another one, I overheard the store owner chuckle and say, "I sell those cookies like crazy since I put them down low where dogs can help themselves."

I paid for my purchases, including a new catnip-filled white owl toy for Twinkletoes.

I stepped outside, wary about which Wagtail residents might be angry with me next. Everyone seemed to be going about their business as normal, though. Hours had passed since Dave said he was off to the pharmacy. I punched his number into my phone. When he answered, I asked, "Where are you? I have information."

"Just headed back to Norm's house. Why don't you meet me there? It's number four Oak Street."

I agreed, called Trixie, and we cut across the park toward Oak Street, thankful for the lights along the paths, which were growing increasingly dark after the early winter sunset.

Norm's house turned out to be an adorable Cape Cod that I had admired many times when I walked by. They had put an addition on the right side with a perpendicular roofline and a Palladian-type arch in the porch roof over the front door. The house nestled in the embrace of old trees. Every light in the house was on, and spotlights mounted on the roof illuminated the outside, too. Under a black roof, the brick facade had been painted taupe with fresh white trim and adorned with black shutters. But someone had painted the front door the color of fresh leaves in the springtime.

Her nose to the ground, Trixie ran up to the front door.

Dave waited for me on the porch. "I thought we'd better talk out here. This has been a blow to Savannah. I don't know if she should hear everything yet."

Trixie faced the front door and yelped.

"Hush, sweetie." I filled Dave in on the ugly rumor-type messages about Wagtail residents and the red envelopes. "Savannah probably won't be happy to learn that it was Norm who was so malicious toward his neighbors."

Dave took a deep breath. "Oh man. That changes everything."

"You mean because it could have been anyone in town who was afraid Norm would spill their secret?"

"Exactly. The pool of potential suspects just grew."

Trixie yelped again, and a dog inside the house barked in response.

The front door opened and a corgi trotted out, happy to see Trixie.

The attractive young woman holding the door threw me for a loop. "Y'all must be freezin' out here. Come on in. Are you hungry? Folks have been droppin' food by all day."

Surely she couldn't be Norm's wife? She had to be twenty years younger than Norm.

She held out her hand to me. "I've seen you all over town but we've never really met. I'm Savannah Wilson."

"Holly Miller," I said to the woman I'd overheard talking on her cell phone the day before.

# Thirteen

I stepped inside the house, thinking back. What exactly had she said on the phone?

A fire blazed in a comfortably furnished living room with a vaulted ceiling. They must have knocked down some walls because the house had the open floor plan that was so popular. As she had claimed, food in everything from fine china to aluminum foil covered the dining table.

"Look at that." Savannah pushed loose blonde curls off her shoulder. "Isn't it darling? Bingo is giving Trixie a tour of his home."

It certainly seemed that way. I was slightly amused that she knew Trixie's name but not mine.

Bingo led the way to his plaid bed and then to a box overflowing with dog toys. Trixie followed along, investigating everything thoroughly.

"Bingo is going to miss Norm." Savannah tilted her head and watched Bingo. She carefully patted the corner of her eye, which was rimmed in heavy black eyeliner. "I used to tell Norm that Bingo thought he was a dog treat dispenser. He always had cookies in his pockets for his little Bingo."

"I'm so sorry for your loss," I mumbled. "How are you holding up?"

"Everything has just been such a rush since Dave woke me up this morning that it really hasn't hit me yet, you know? My parents came straight over and—" tears welled in her eyes "—I imagine tonight when it's quiet, and Norm doesn't come home . . ." She let the rest hang in the air.

We all knew what she meant. I sought something to say. "You have a beautiful house. I've always admired it."

"Thank you. Norm hated this house. It was too plain for him. And he really hated my green front door." Savannah chuckled and shook her head at the memory. "But he lived here to make me happy. He had bought a fancy place on the other side of town. It's called Randolph Hall. Do you know it? A huge white monstrosity with columns all over the front porch. In the middle they even go up two stories. You know the house I mean?" She waved her hands. "It's historical and all that but it's just gigantic. Eleven bedrooms! It should be a museum or something. I said no way was I going to live in that hulking thing. Can you even imagine rattling around in a place like that? Not to mention the ghosts. Norm got it for a steal, and I thought he should sell it but he insisted he would live there one day." Savannah stopped chattering and looked at her hands. Speaking softly, she said, "I guess he won't now." She looked away. "'Scuze me. Y'all help yourselves." Savannah hurried down a hallway.

"How awful for her." I felt so sad. A scrapbook lay on the table. A picture of Savannah and Norm on their wedding day was centered on the front cover. I picked it up and peeked inside. It began with photos of Bingo as a puppy. The next pages contained pictures of flower arrangements identified by little labels like *From Norm for my birthday*. She'd kept everything, including scraps of candy bar wrappers and paper napkins. They were interspersed with handwritten notes from

Norm. In one photo, Savannah held pom-poms on a football field. A note beneath it said, *You were the prettiest girl out there tonight.* I felt a wave of revulsion when I realized that he was courting her while she was still in high school. Ugh. I slammed the scrapbook closed and set it down.

Dave drifted over to the dining table. "People certainly have been generous." He popped a miniature ham biscuit into his mouth. "Mmm. I'd know Delta Hobbs's biscuits anywhere." Dave turned and looked out the large bay window. His shoulders straightened, and the fingers of his left hand curled into a fist.

I walked over to him. "What is it? What's wrong?"

He didn't say a word but it wasn't hard to figure out. Someone had run through the snow in the backyard. The spotlights shone on one set of tracks and they sure didn't look like dog tracks to me. They didn't meander. And they only went in one direction, from the back door away from the house.

I stared at the footprints. They hadn't filled in with snow so that meant the person ran out of the house after ten or so in the morning. The snow had been coming down fast before that. "What do you think it means?" I asked Dave.

"Holly, would you mind if I talked to Savannah alone?"

"Of course not." I could take a hint. I called Trixie. When I opened the front door, Dave was still staring at the footprints in the snow.

Trixie trotted happily along the sidewalk, but I was in a melancholy mood. Someone had either been in the house during the heavy snowfall and left out the back when it had ended, or had entered the front door and departed from the back door.

Why? The only reason I could imagine was to avoid being seen. The bounty on the table was proof that Savannah had been receiving visitors all day. Had someone been caught in her house when others arrived? Who would slip out the back door to remain unnoticed? And why would anyone be concerned about that? Unless it had something to do with Norm's death.

I strained to remember what Savannah had said on the phone. Her eyes had been rimmed in red as though she'd been crying. I stopped walking and tried to put myself back in that moment mentally. Blanche! She had mentioned that Blanche was in town. And something about *doing it this weekend.*

Dear heaven. What had she done?

Once again I needed to talk with Dave. I didn't think he would appreciate being interrupted while he was questioning her, though. Trixie and I headed back to the green, which was now covered in white.

A small commotion was taking place at the front stairs to the inn. I ran as well as I could in my boots.

A cluster of people appeared to have cornered Myrtle, who had backed up to the second step. She held the poison bottle high over her head.

"What's going on?" I cried.

Ten people turned toward me, including some of Myrtle's book club friends. They all talked at once. I caught bits and pieces as they spilled their ire. "Annoying . . . demanding . . . can't stop and drink for fear of her . . . no peace . . . spoiling our fun."

Before I could intervene, Geof Tredwell walked up behind Myrtle and snatched the bottle from her hand.

Myrtle screamed as though he'd stabbed her.

With a big grin, Geof held the bottle up like a trophy and the others cheered.

Myrtle shouted in protest, "That's not fair." She caught sight of me. "Is he allowed to do that?"

I shrugged. "I don't see why not." We would all be relieved that she didn't have possession of a weapon anymore.

"That's stupid." Myrtle shoved her way through the little crowd to me with Geof on her heels. "You mean if I tackle him, I can have it back?"

"No physical violence, please, Myrtle. He just swiped it from you."

Under the porch lights, Myrtle turned a shade of red that frightened me for her health. "How many weapons are in circulation? That's the only one I've seen besides the candlestick."

"There are four in all. The poison bottle, a cleaver, a candlestick, and a gun."

Geof smiled. "I had the candlestick at one time but someone stole it from me. You can bet I'm going to sleep with this thing. Now, Myrtle, perhaps we could have a little talk about your connection to the Baron von Rottweiler."

Myrtle's mouth opened and closed like a fish gasping in air. I gathered she didn't much like having the tables turned on her. I tried not to laugh or smile as I passed them on my way inside.

Holmes still manned the desk and was accepting Norm's gossipy clues from participants. Twinkletoes sat on the desk like an Egyptian cat, her tail wrapped around her front paws.

"How's it going?"

Holmes smiled at me and my heart fairly melted. "Pretty well but some of these clues are plain mean. Did you find out who's revealing secrets about Wagtail residents?"

Promising that I would be right back to tell him all about it, I removed Trixie's jacket. After stashing it in the private kitchen along with my own, I gazed at a bottle of wine. It had been a long day. I really wanted a glass of wine but that would put me to sleep in about two minutes. Instead I nuked milk for two hot chocolates and added Nutella and hazelnut liqueur. Maybe that wouldn't put me right to sleep. I added a dollop of whipped cream to each one, carried them over to the desk, and pulled up a chair next to Holmes.

"Uh-oh," said Holmes. "I'm being buttered up."

"Would I do that to you?"

Holmes snorted. "You're just like our grandmothers." He handed me a slip of paper. "Can you believe this?"

I unfolded it.

*Val Kowalchuk sleeps in the buff.*

"Who would care? Isn't that her own business?" asked Holmes.

"Hardly scandalous. Even our grandmothers wouldn't be shocked by this." I stared at the slip of paper. "Why would Norm think this was important to spread around? Such a harmless thing, really."

"Norm?"

I filled Holmes in about Norm and the red envelopes.

"But why would he do that? It's as though he intended to upset everyone in town."

"I don't know. Maybe they're not all from the same person . . ." I snatched up another one of the scurrilous clues and compared them. They looked exactly alike except for what they said. "How would Norm know what Val wears when she sleeps?"

Holmes drew back, away from me. "Noooo. Not Norm and Val. I can't see them together. No, definitely not. Maybe she was kidding around at the pub and told someone she sleeps in the buff. Norm might have overheard."

That was possible. "He was really reaching if he thought her lack of sleeping attire would upset anyone. What do you know about Savannah and Norm?"

"I barely know either of them at all. He moved here after I left. I gather he put off quite a few people with unsavory business tactics. My mom said Savannah grew up on Snowball. Very pretty, very popular. Homecoming court, cheerleader, that kind of thing."

"She must be twenty years younger than Norm was."

Holmes nodded. "Yep. Twenty-four. Even I heard that gossip. Apparently, her folks were thrilled that she was marrying a well-to-do businessman who would give her the good life."

"Do her parents still live here?"

"Over on Snowball, I think. Savannah hasn't been married to Norm very long. Seems like there was another wife before her."

"Know of any connection she might have to Blanche Tredwell?"

Holmes kicked me gently under the table.

Blanche, so pale that even her makeup couldn't hide it, was saying good-bye to Charlotte not five feet away from us. Blanche left with Robin.

Ella Mae in her arms, Char walked over to Holmes and me. "Holly, could you be a dear and let me into our room? Geof is out looking for clues, and he walked off with our room key."

"Of course." I excused myself and started up the grand staircase with her. "I saw Geof earlier. He's really into the game."

"He and Ian are in their element. Actually it's nice seeing them work together. They've been terribly competitive their whole lives."

"Is that what you meant when you said 'it's the story of his life' last night?"

"Yes. Ian is a brilliant scientist. Internationally known with all sorts of papers and books and awards. He's something of a superstar in his field. And then to marry someone like Blanche Wimmer! Ian sure trumped Geof in his choice of wives. I'm always reminding Geof that he's better looking and taller than Ian."

"Is Blanche okay?" I asked. "She seemed so pale."

"She lost her husband."

"You mean lost as in couldn't find him?"

"Oh no, dear. He died."

How could she be so calm about it? "Ian died?"

"Did I say husband again? I've been calling him that all day, which probably didn't help a bit. Ex-husband. Norman was her ex-husband."

"Norman Wilson? Of Wagtail?" I stopped in the middle of the hallway.

Char blinked at me and grimaced. "How utterly thoughtless of me. You probably knew him. I'm so sorry."

Surely I had misunderstood. "Norm Wilson, who resided in Wagtail and died last night or early this morning, was once married to Blanche Wimmer Tredwell?"

"That's right. I don't know why she's so broken up about it. The man was odious to her. He was very possibly the worst thing that ever happened to her."

Char reached her door and waited for me to unlock it.

"So you knew Norm?" I swung the door open.

"Me? Oh my, no. I didn't meet Blanche until she was engaged to Ian. Thanks for letting us into our room."

Char closed the door behind her.

I ambled back toward the stairs in a bit of a daze. That was the connection between Savannah and Blanche. Blanche had been the first wife and Savannah the second. In the dog playground, Savannah had said to someone that Blanche was in town. And then something about not being able to wait? Now or never? What were her exact words?

A shudder rippled through me. Had Savannah murdered Norm in the hope that Blanche would be blamed? Shaking out of my funk, I scrambled down the stairs to Holmes.

"Blanche was Norm's first wife!" I whispered.

Holmes drew back and eyed me. "For real?"

"Apparently."

He whistled softly. "They're the same type. Not now, of course. But doesn't Savannah remind you a little bit of Blanche when she was young? The long blonde hair, the knockout figure. They both go a little heavy on the makeup."

He was right about the similarities. In spite of myself, I giggled.

"What's so funny?"

"I think one of the clues about the Baron von Rottweiler said he left his first wife for a younger woman."

"That scum!"

The two of us laughed together, releasing the tension.

I reached for the phone. "I have to let Dave know about this."

The number rolled over to the police department headquarters on Snowball Mountain. The woman on the other end asked if it was an emergency. It wasn't really. She told me Dave and half the force were out rescuing stranded motorists and to call back. Only emergency calls were being taken at the moment. I relayed the news to Holmes.

"You look dog-tired," said Holmes.

"I am. Looks like things are pretty quiet. Have you had dinner? We can poke around in the magic fridge."

"I love that refrigerator. There's always something good in there."

We packed up the clues and carried our drinks to Oma's kitchen. Twinkletoes ran ahead of us. I called the dogs for their dinner.

Holmes opened the fridge and poked around. "Looks

like chicken stew was the lunch special. There's even one for the dogs. And another one for cats."

He set the containers on the counter, and I pulled out three pots to heat them. "Is there rice in the fridge for the dogs?" I asked.

Holmes nodded. "Should I nuke it?"

"Please. Thanks for helping out. I never imagined anyone would make up fake clues about the people of Wagtail."

"No problem. I love hanging around the inn. Besides, I've been going through the list of clues. I'm still not sure who murdered the baron, but I have some ideas. Listen to this." He leaned over and read off the clue list.

*The Baron von Rottweiler's third wife is afraid he'll kill her like he did his second wife.*

I chuckled at him. "No fair. You have all the clues in front of you."

"In spite of that I don't have it completely figured out. There are one hundred clues! By the way, you can be glad I spared you the drama of Charlotte and Geoffrey Tredwell."

"What drama?" I set Twinkletoes's food on a counter, out of reach of the dogs.

She smelled it carefully, as though she wasn't sure it was worthy of being eaten. Apparently, it passed the sniff test because she began to eat with gusto.

"While you were out gallivanting around, Charlotte nearly filed for divorce because Geoffrey was supposed to be dog-sitting Ella Mae, and he forgot all about her."

I couldn't help chuckling. "Char's a little bit clingy with poor Ella Mae." I checked the temperature of the dog stew. Perfect. I spooned it into their bowls over the rice and set them on the floor.

"They couldn't find her. You can imagine the scene, with Char yelling at Geof and racing up and down the stairs in search of her."

I laughed as he described it. I could just imagine Char's panic. I ladled our stew into deep bowls while Holmes set the table. He added a loaf of fresh sourdough bread and sweet butter.

When we sat down to eat, he went on. "They finally found her in the Dogwood Room. Seems Ella Mae hopped up on the lap of a book club lady and the two of them took a nap together. It was actually pretty cute. The lady had stretched out on the sofa and little Ella Mae was stretched out beside her in exactly the same position."

"So Char forgave Geof?"

"Nope. I'd say he's in the doghouse for a while."

The wall phone rang. I got up to answer it.

Old Mr. Wiggins, the vice mayor who was filling in for Oma during her absence, said, "We just got a call from the highway department. They're closing down the highways because conditions are so rotten. Over in Snowball, too. He said the roads look like bumper car rides. And there's supposed to be another big storm tonight, so there's a good chance no one will be going home tomorrow."

I was glad I didn't have to call everyone. I guessed that came with the territory of the mayor and vice mayor in a small town like Wagtail. I thanked him and hung up.

"The roads are closed. We're in for another whopper tonight."

"I can stay over and give you a hand," said Holmes.

I swear my heart picked up an extra beat.

"You won't mind if I bunk in your guest room. Right? Or is there a new beau I don't know about? Wouldn't want to cramp your style."

I swallowed hard. A romantic evening by the fire with Holmes on a snowy night? But I knew that was wishful thinking. Pretending to be calm and cool, I said, "Of course you can stay over. Thank you for offering to help. And there are no new beaus, so you needn't worry about that."

We washed up the dishes and returned to the lobby.

The dining area was empty. Myrtle, Sylvie, and some of their book club friends had gathered in the Dogwood Room with a couple of bottles of wine.

Zelda walked in, bundled up head to toe. "Have you seen Leo? He didn't come home, and I'm worried about him being out in this weather. Word around town is that we're in for a big storm tonight."

I shook my head. "I haven't seen him at all."

At that exact moment, someone screamed like she'd found a corpse.

# Sixteen

She screamed again.

I dashed to the little crowd that was forming at the Dogwood Room. "Excuse me. Coming through! Excuse me!"

Sylvie wobbled precariously on top of a sofa and pointed toward the floor at either her shoes or Leo, who sat below her watching her antics as though she was fascinating.

I glanced around. Nothing was out of place. "What's wrong?"

Before she responded, I noticed that Gingersnap and Trixie, still a respectable distance away from Leo, had pointed their noses in his direction, and their little nostrils twitched.

"That cat put something in my shoe."

"Like a toy?"

"Like a mouse!" she screamed.

Zelda matter-of-factly picked up a shoe. "Leo does that when he likes people. It's a huge compliment to have him bring you a gift."

"Well, you tell him that I don't care for dead mice!"

I peered into the shoe. The poor little gray mouse was a goner. Leo must have carried him around for hours.

"I'm so sorry, Sylvie." I hissed at Zelda under my breath, "Get that mouse out of here."

She smiled up at Sylvie. "I'll bring your shoe right back."

"Good heavens, don't do that. It had a dead mouse in it. Are you nuts? I don't ever want to see that shoe again."

"We'll reimburse you for the shoes, Sylvie," I assured her. "May I help you down?"

Holmes stepped up from behind me and assisted Sylvie in dismounting the sofa, undoubtedly much more adeptly than I would have.

"Just let me know how much the shoes cost, and we'll take care of it," I said.

Sylvie shuddered. "I hate mice. *Hate* them! They're filthy little germy creatures." She flicked both hands in the air rapidly. "Ugh. That was disgusting." Sylvie gazed at Leo, who hadn't budged. "What's wrong with that cat?"

One of her book club friends laughed. "Haven't you ever had a cat? They love to bring you their catch. It's a big honor to have them give it to you."

"I guess I haven't known many cats. Why is he watching me?"

"Clearly, he likes you," said her friend. She picked up Leo, no small feat given his size, and held him in her arms. "Here, pet him."

Reluctantly, Sylvie touched Leo's forehead with one finger.

"He's purring! He likes you!"

Sylvie didn't appear convinced. To Leo she said, "If you'll excuse me, I think I'd better find some other shoes to wear."

Her friend laughed and set Leo on the floor.

The little crowd dispersed, and Sylvie hobbled off wearing one shoe.

I hurried to the reception area, where I found Zelda. "What did you do with the mouse?"

"Poor little guy. I wish cats didn't kill mice. They're so sweet."

"Where is he?"

"I found a little box for him. I'll bury him in my backyard."

I didn't mention that her backyard was under a foot of snow. Zelda was resourceful. She'd think of something.

She glanced around before whispering, "So Holmes is staying with you tonight!"

"Where did you hear that? Honestly, Wagtail is just a gossip mill."

"Holmes told me. I thought you might need some help tonight."

"Don't go getting excited. He's still engaged. But maybe he'll tell me more about what's going on in their relationship."

"My mama always told me engagements were made to be broken."

"Zelda! I have no intention of anything like that. But it will be fun to have him around."

"Uh-huh." She winked at me as though she knew better.

The truth was that I wouldn't want to break up his engagement. Not that I thought I ever could. But that was a decision Holmes had to come to on his own. And he might never decide to break it off. Maybe his fiancée was the right woman for him. I had no business butting in, no matter how much I might want to. "Now you behave." I shook my finger at her in a teasing way. "He's just being nice."

"Uh-huh."

Upstairs, via the open stairwell, I could hear people calling Ella Mae. I looked up to see Weegie trotting down the stairs with Sylvie.

"Are you okay, Sylvie?" I asked. "I'm sorry you had such a shock."

"I'm fine, thank you. Leo sure got my heart racing. I'll consider that today's aerobic exercise!"

"How much do we owe you for the shoes?"

"Shoes? Oh, forget about it. They weren't anything special. Old, worn-out walking shoes that probably needed replacing anyway. But Weegie did want to talk with you about something else."

"What can I do for you?"

Weegie seemed reluctant to speak but Sylvie motioned to her. "I'm not one to point fingers at other people. But I thought you should know that my lucky shamrock pendant has gone missing."

"Are you sure?"

"Quite. I've turned my room upside down." She rested her hand on my arm. "It's not worth much. It's not real gold or anything. I really shouldn't have even mentioned it."

Sylvie's mouth skewed. "It sure looks like it's real gold. What you need to know, but Weegie is reluctant to tell you, is that you have a thief on your staff."

Zelda's wide eyes met mine.

"Weegie last saw it on her dresser just before that young man replenished the firewood in the bedrooms."

"Shadow?" I asked.

Weegie cringed. "He was very nice."

Sylvie tilted her head at her friend. "Was it nice of him to take your necklace?"

"I do so hate to blame anyone . . ." muttered Weegie.

Sylvie scoffed. "It had to be him or the housekeeper. No other strangers were in your room, were they?"

"Please don't fire him because of this," said Weegie.

"Now you leave that up to Holly." Sylvie shook her head. "Today he's nabbing a worthless necklace but tomorrow it might be something valuable. She can't afford to let that happen."

"I'm so sorry," I said for the millionth time, wishing there was something more that I could say. "Could I help you search for it?"

"Thank you but that's really not necessary. I wouldn't have said a word about it if Sylvie hadn't seen me looking for it. I'll give the room one more good sweep before we leave tomorrow."

I waited until they had vanished from sight before whispering to Zelda, "Do you know anything about Shadow being a thief?"

She seemed surprised. "Not a thing! I like Shadow. And you know Marisol wouldn't have taken it."

That was true. We loved Marisol, the housekeeper. She was totally dependable and aboveboard.

Maybe that ugly clue about Shadow having a criminal record wasn't true. But then what had happened to the not-so-lucky shamrock necklace?

I looked into Zelda's sweet face. "Honey, you know the fake clues? There was one about you." My heart pounded. This would be a good test of their veracity.

"Me? Hah! My life is so boring that they'd have to make up something juicy."

"It said you borrowed a thousand dollars from a neighbor, that you didn't repay."

The color drained from her face. "Now that's just not fair. It wasn't me. It was my good-for-nothing ex-husband. I had nothing to do with it. Besides, if you ask me, it was all a con anyway."

So it was true. Sort of. I shuddered. "What happened?"

"That stinking Norm had some kind of business gimmick going and got my ex all excited about it. We didn't have two dimes to rub together, so Norm offered to lend my husband money to invest. Then, when it was a big disaster, Norm had the nerve to come to me and ask me to pay him! With interest!" Her tone grew shrill. "The divorce was already in progress, and I had kicked my husband out the door. I didn't even know where he was. I never signed anything, I swear! Norm never even talked to me about it until that day. My idiot husband had run up a ton of credit card bills that I had to pay. So I told Norm if he wanted his money, he ought to go find my husband and get it from him."

It was a convoluted story but I couldn't blame Zelda for refusing to pay when she wasn't involved. It didn't make me feel any better about Shadow's possible criminal record, though. It seemed that while Norm had put a twist on a lot of the clues, so far, it appeared that there was always a little truth behind them.

Zelda returned to the lobby to collect Leo.

I grabbed a spare key to my apartment and locked up the reception entrance and office.

Most of the book club ladies were still gathered in the Dogwood Room. I walked over to them. "I hope you're enjoying yourselves."

There was a chorus of cheers, and I noticed that one of them was wearing a lampshade like a hat. Someone had had too much wine with dinner. "I wanted to let you know that the roads have been closed. They're too dangerous right now. The good news is that we're extending Murder Most Howl, so you have another day to figure out what happened to the Baron von Rottweiler."

"We're not going anywhere tonight!" said one of them.

"Good to know because they're expecting another big blast of snow."

"Will we be able to go home tomorrow?" asked Sylvie. Her dimples disappeared and a worry line formed between her eyebrows.

"Is your husband all right?" asked Weegie. She leaned toward me and whispered, "He has a heart problem."

"I'll phone our neighbor. Maybe she can check on him." Sylvie rose and walked past me toward the grand staircase.

The woman wearing the lampshade must not have been as drunk as I thought because she asked, "We're gonna be snowed in?"

"I can't say yet, but if I had to guess—"

"Yeehaw! Another night away from my husband, and I get to play hooky from work. Where's that wine? I'm celebrating."

"Oh my gosh, it's like that book. Hitchcock made a movie where they're all stuck at the inn and everyone gets murdered!"

"That's not Hitchcock, that's Agatha Christie."

"No, it's Clue, the board game. I am Miss Scarlet, in the Dogwood Room with—" she looked around "—where's the candlestick?"

I figured that could go on all night. I waved in case any of them were paying attention and took my leave.

Myrtle followed me. "Do you mean we can't leave?"

"Not until they open the roads."

"There's no way off this mountain? That's not safe. What if there's an emergency?"

"I guess they could load a person into a snowmobile."

"Then I want to go down the mountain by snowmobile tomorrow. I have to go home. I have to be at work on Monday morning."

"I'm sorry Myrtle, but if the roads are closed, it won't do you much good."

"This is an outrage. What kind of place is this? You're detaining us against our will. That's a crime. What's it called? Oh yeah, false imprisonment."

I was tired of trying to be nice to her. Still, I smiled sweetly. "You are free to check out anytime you like, Myrtle."

A howling wind rattled the front door.

Myrtle scowled at me. "You know perfectly well that I can't leave here in this weather. I'd die trying."

It wasn't like I'd suggested she camp outside. I'd had a very long day, so I just said, "Have a good night, Myrtle," and walked away from the nutty woman.

I found Holmes in the dining area, next to the fire. He sat at a table with Geof and Ian.

"Excuse me." I handed the key to Holmes. "I didn't mean to interrupt."

Holmes checked his watch, a fancy number his fiancée had given him. "You're so beat. I can keep an eye on things for the next couple of hours until Casey gets here if you want to go on up to bed."

My visions of a romantic night by the fire with Holmes fizzled. The truth was that I was too tired to think let alone sit up by the fire. "Thanks. I'll take you up on that. Did you tell Ian and Geof about the roads?"

"I will right now."

"Call me if you need anything." I said good night and trudged up the stairs. Trixie and Gingersnap followed without being called. I thought they were probably as tired as I was. I changed into a nightshirt that said *Sleeps with Dogs*, and when I walked into my bedroom, I found Twinkletoes curled up and waiting for me.

I slid under the fluffy down comforter, ruing the fact that I had missed my chance to hang out with Holmes and get the scoop on his fiancée. Trixie and Gingersnap jumped up on the bed and staked out their corners, and I closed my weary eyes.

I awoke fully recharged and sat up. The world outside my window was white. Snow adorned the railing of the balcony. Trixie and Gingersnap still snoozed, with Gingersnap snoring softly. No sign of Twinkletoes, though.

Mindful of the fact that Holmes was in the apartment, I slung on the Sugar Maple Inn bathrobe that Oma had had embroidered with my name. I tiptoed toward the kitchen and heard Twinkletoes hissing.

Had someone's cat gotten loose and made its way up here?

I peeked into the living room and found a rollaway bed with bare feet sticking out at the closest end. Why wasn't Holmes sleeping in the guest room? Why was Twinkletoes sitting on a table near his head hissing at him? She loved Holmes!

I walked closer to remove her and discovered my former boyfriend, Ben Hathaway, was the owner of the bare feet jutting out from under the covers. He was fast asleep, and didn't even notice Twinkletoes.

But when I picked her up, she acted like I had offended her, hissed louder, glided through my hands, bounced squarely off Ben's abdomen, and flew through the apartment in a huff.

"Hi, Ben." What else could I say?

He grunted and rubbed his eyes. "Did you just punch me?"

Uh-oh. I couldn't admit that it was Twinkletoes. He wasn't keen on animals as it was. "Would I do that?" I teased.

"Must have been a dream. I'm glad to see you're back in the world again."

"What does that mean?"

"It means I went in to say hello last night and you were out of it."

"I was pretty tired. What are you doing here?" I blurted out. I should have been nicer, but I hadn't expected him to show up on a weekend when I had to work because Oma was away. And it struck me as odd and somewhat uncomfortable to have Ben staying with me at the same time as Holmes.

"Since your grandmother is away, I thought I'd come help out. I meant to be here sooner, but my car got stuck coming up the mountain."

Holmes emerged from the guest room. "Dave had to rescue him."

"*Rescue* is a strong word. *Assist* would be more accurate."

"Is your car damaged?" I asked.

Ben flushed purple. "We, uh, won't know until they get it out of the snowbank. But, hey, I made it. Good thing I came, too. Holmes filled me in about the guy who," he whispered, "was murdered."

I was ashamed of myself. Ben had done something nice by coming to the Sugar Maple Inn but all I could think was that he had ruined my chances for a romantic moment with Holmes, who probably wouldn't feel it necessary to stay over now that Ben was here. In fact, he might think he was in the way.

Before I moved to Wagtail, during a particularly trying time in my life, Ben had proposed to me. Twice actually. Once by text, and once in a pity proposal that made me realize we were through. I didn't need his pity, nor did I want to spend the rest of my life with a man who saw marriage as a practical arrangement. I didn't want to live that way. I had never thought of myself as a romantic, but rather level-headed, sensible even. To my surprise, I realized that if I was going to marry, I wanted it to be because someone loved me. I would have appreciated a single rose or a declaration of adoration. Even now I cringed a little to think that I felt that way. But I did.

What I did not understand at all were Ben's repeated visits to Wagtail. He loathed the mountains and wasn't fond of dogs or cats. He itched in the great outdoors. Maybe he just needed to get away from the city for some reason.

We heard a key in the lock, and Mr. Huckle shoved in a room service cart loaded with tea, coffee, a basket of assorted muffins and croissants, and a smaller basket of dog and cat treats.

Ben sat up. "Ah, my favorite part of staying here."

"Good morning, Mr. Huckle." He handed me a mug of tea. "How's the weather?"

He stared at me in shock. "You didn't hear it?"

"Hear what?"

"The storm, Miss Holly. The wind was frightful."

I walked to the window overlooking the lake. Everything was covered with snow, even some parts of the lake that must have frozen.

"How are the guests taking it?"

"Most of them are still in their quarters." He smiled at us. "Cook and Shelley made it, though."

I flicked a light switch. "And we have power. It's a good day!"

I grabbed a chocolate croissant and practically inhaled it. While the guys talked and enjoyed their prebreakfast treat, I hopped in the shower. I dressed in black jeans and a white cashmere sweater that would keep me warm without a lot of bulk. It was the perfect day for the dangling snowflake earrings Oma had given me. They caught the light and sparkled when my head moved. I slipped on my faux fur–lined lace-up boots and carried moccasins with me for indoor wear.

Ben and Holmes seemed to be getting along well. From the looks of the goody basket, and the way Trixie and Gingersnap focused on Holmes, I had a feeling they'd been given bits of banana muffins or plain croissants.

I fed Twinkletoes flaked cod, called the dogs, and left the guys to enjoy their leisurely morning. We trotted down the stairs, put on the coats I had left in the private kitchen, and walked through the inn to the reception area. Zelda hadn't arrived yet. I unlocked the doors and let the dogs out.

They played in the snow with fresh enthusiasm. But poor Trixie had to work hard at jumping like a bunny. Every time she hopped, she disappeared in the snow again. I finally rescued her, and placed her where the snow wasn't as deep.

I heard scraping and peered around the corner. Shadow waved at me. He had already made a significant dent in clearing the walkways for our guests.

At that moment, I despised Norm. If he hadn't made up those horrible clues about the residents of Wagtail, would I be less suspicious of Shadow? I would have to talk with Shadow sometime about the missing necklace, but for now, I was just grateful that he was cleaning the walks!

By the time we returned, Zelda had arrived. "There you are. Officer Dave is looking for you. He said to tell you he's at Café Chat."

In my opinion, the inn had the best breakfasts in town. I had been fortified by that chocolate croissant, though, and Dave had to know what I had learned, so Trixie, Gingersnap, and I left, however reluctantly, and headed out in the cold to Café Chat.

In better weather, people always lounged at the outdoor tables. Some habits must die hard because one couple sat outside in spite of the weather. Steam rose from their mugs and their two Saint Bernards looked very comfortable lounging in the cold air.

I held the door for the dogs, who scampered inside. Dave sat at a table in the corner, eating scrambled eggs. A portly man sat across from him, leaning over the table a bit. As I drew closer, I could see that it was Larry, the chef who allegedly had an affair with Peaches Clodfelter.

I hesitated for a moment, not wanting to interrupt their conversation. But Trixie had no such qualms and ran straight to Dave, planted her feet on his thigh, and cocked her head at him, clearly pleading for a bite of his food. Not to be left out, Gingersnap followed, sat down, and lifted a paw for Dave.

Dave glanced at them and looked up. He waved me over.

Apparently, their bad manners were rewarded. When I reached the table, both of them were chewing something. "Trixie! Gingersnap!" I scolded. They didn't look one bit ashamed. In fact, they had the nerve to turn pleading eyes on Dave again.

"My new best friends," he said, grinning at the dogs. "Have a seat."

I pulled out a chair and greeted Larry.

He grunted and gazed at me with a swollen face and a whopper of a black eye.

"That looks so painful. What happened?" I asked.

"Val!"

I glanced at Dave, who continued to eat calmly. "I'm sorry, I don't understand. Val slugged you?" Larry must have done something awful. Val wasn't the type to haul off and punch someone.

"My wife coldcocked me."

Dave tried to hide a smile.

"How is that Val's fault?"

"You're to blame, too!" A red flush crept up Larry's jaw. "All of you who were involved in this misbegotten mystery weekend."

It took more than a little bit of willpower on my part not to suggest that it might be his own fault for having an affair with Peaches in the first place.

Dave shook his head at Larry, conveying what I was thinking. "I can't imagine what you see in Peaches anyway."

Larry glared at him. "Really? As I recall, you thought her daughter was pretty hot."

Dave almost choked on his toast.

These stupid rumors were making people turn on each other!

I took two deep breaths before I said, "It was Norm who spread the ugly rumors about local people."

Dave stopped eating. "You're sure?"

I explained about the envelopes.

Larry's jaw dropped. "Confound that man. I never did him a dirty turn in my life. Too bad he's dead. I'd have spit in his food if I'd known what evil lurked in his heart."

Dave spoke in a monotone. "You better not be doing that to anyone. Evil heart or otherwise."

Larry didn't react to Dave's advice. "No wonder somebody put that pestiferous louse out of his misery. More like out of our misery. He had it coming!"

He spoke so loud that Myrtle jumped from her seat and scurried over to our table. That woman was definitely an early riser. "Are you talking about the Baron von Rottweiler?"

Larry turned angry eyes on me before looking up at Myrtle. "The Baron von Rottweiler conned me into investing in one of his businesses, and I lost every last penny."

Myrtle gasped. "Did you want to kill him?"

"Nope. But I'd like to kill Norm Wilson."

Myrtle dug a tiny notebook out of her pocket. "Who's that?" she asked as she wrote.

Larry sulked. His head seemed to sink between his shoulders, and he appeared to be done with Myrtle.

"I'm so sorry," I said to her. "Larry's being a little bit grumpy. Norm has nothing—"

"Wait a minute." Myrtle stopped scribbling. "Norm's the guy who was murdered!"

"Right." I nodded at her. "But that has nothing to do with Murder Most Howl."

Myrtle narrowed her eyes and leaned to the side a bit to get a better look at Larry. She raised her eyebrows, turned, and hurried back to her table. When she sat down, she leaned in and appeared to confide something to Sylvie and Weegie.

"What's wrong with you?" I hissed. "I'm sorry that Norm let the cat out of the bag about your affair with Peaches, but you can't go being a jerk to visitors."

Larry leaned his forearms against the table. "I don't think you understand. My wife has kicked me out. My entire life has turned upside down. If somebody hadn't already done Norm in, I'd be doing it myself right now."

With that, Larry stood up and disappeared into the kitchen.

My eyes met Dave's. "Is he diabetic?"

Dave wiped his mouth with a napkin and fed Trixie the last morsel from his plate. "He hasn't bought any insulin."

"So he's off the suspect list. Lucky for him. But he shouldn't go around saying things like that."

Dave avoided my eyes.

I frowned at him. "You'd make a terrible poker player."

That brought a smile to his face. "I figured that out a long time ago."

"You think Larry murdered Norm?"

Dave sucked in a deep breath. "You know I can't tell you everything."

I didn't much care for this game. I couldn't read his mind. All I knew was that he hadn't crossed Larry off his suspect list for some reason.

Dave drank coffee from a Café Chat mug.

"Norm was married to Blanche Wimmer."

Dave spewed coffee. Luckily, most of it landed on his plate. "Thanks a lot!"

"It's true. Apparently, she was his first wife."

Dave dabbed at his shirt with the napkin. "Who'd you hear that from?"

"Her sister-in-law."

"I guess I know who I'll be meeting in the flesh today. Are they staying at the inn?"

"Her sister-in-law is but Blanche and her husband are somewhere else." I shrugged. "And I have one other little bit of information which I may not share now that you're playing games about Larry's involvement."

Dave relaxed in his seat, still wiping off coffee spots. "Holly, I appreciate your help. More than I can tell you, actually. But this isn't a game. This is my job. There are laws about what I can reveal."

I felt more than a little bit ashamed. "Yesterday morning I overheard Savannah talking on her cell phone. I can't recall exactly what she said, but she mentioned that Blanche was in town and that she was going to do something this weekend. She was crying, Dave. And I'm pretty sure she said 'the sooner the better.'"

Dave let out a low guttural groan. He winced.

I didn't know, and now I didn't dare ask, what he found out about the footprints behind Savannah's house. I had a feeling he was sorry that my information put her in a bad light. I was trying to figure out how to weasel the information out of him, when his phone beeped at him. Maybe I should ask him about Shadow's criminal record first.

He rose from his chair with the phone still at his ear and quickly left money on the table. When he hung up, he said, "Sorry, gotta go. What is it about signs that say *Road Closed* that people don't understand? Including your boyfriend, by the way. Blanche will have to wait."

"He's not my boyfriend," I pointed out.

"Really? Then why does he keep coming here?"

That was a good question. It worried me. I thought I had made it clear that we were through. But at the moment, I had more urgent things on my mind.

We left at the same time as Weegie, Myrtle, and Sylvie. I found myself walking back to the inn with the three ladies.

"Tell us what you know about the Baron von Rottweiler," Myrtle demanded.

I laughed. "I think you know much more about him than I do."

"Come on," prodded Weegie. "Myrtle won't give up until you tell us."

"Let's see. He aggravated a lot of his business partners. Apparently he had several children, but I haven't met any of them yet."

"I'm one!" Myrtle sang with pride. "Illegitimate, of course."

"Of course. He left his first wife for a younger woman. And I believe the first wife was destitute and had to live in her car or some such."

Weegie gasped and stopped walking. "Just like Blanche!"

# Seventeen

It was my turn to be surprised. “Blanche?”

Weegie nodded her head. “Blanche Wimmer was a mess after her divorce. She had to sleep in her car until she could make enough money to get back on her feet.”

“How do you know that?” I asked.

Weegie blushed. “Don’t you read gossip magazines?”

Myrtle’s mouth dropped open. “I most certainly do not!”

“Well, everyone else does. You’re just a stick in the mud.” Weegie strode ahead with Puddin’.

Myrtle and Sylvie complained about Weegie all the way back to the inn. But I had other things on my mind.

As soon as I helped Trixie out of her coat, I hustled over to Holmes, who was eating breakfast with Ben.

“Where’s the list of clues?”

“Hi. Nice to see you, too.”

“C’mon where’s the list?”

He handed me a sheet of paper. “What’s up?”

I sat down in the chair next to him and scanned the clues.

"I don't know. The good baron is beginning to sound an awful lot like Norm Wilson."

Holmes snorted. "That's ridiculous."

"Really? Listen to this." I read them aloud.

*The Baron von Rottweiler left his first wife for a younger woman.*

*The Baron von Rottweiler left his first wife so destitute that she had to live in her car.*

Holmes elbowed me. "C'mon, Holly. You're not that naive. A lot of men leave their wives for younger women."

"Do a lot of exceedingly successful women have to live in their cars when they divorce? That's what happened to Blanche."

"It doesn't say the baron's wife was successful. And what about this one?" He pointed at a clue.

*The Baron von Rottweiler poisoned his second wife.*

"Obviously that one didn't happen. Savannah's alive and well."

"Maybe you're right. I just never heard of anyone having to live in her car after divorce. Well, not when she was making buckets full of money. Talk about a motive for murder. He must have run off with every penny she made."

"And yet she didn't kill him."

"Not then anyway."

Holmes shot me a doubtful look. "Really? You think Blanche would have waited all these years?"

"Maybe her anger festered. Maybe she was waiting for the day she could get her revenge. Maybe that's why she came here."

"I can't deny that's a possibility, but I think Blanche has moved on. Besides, she's not the killer type. She's way too sweet."

"Why, Holmes Richardson! You have a crush on Blanche!"

His face turned the color of rosé wine. "Every guy my age did. She was a big star when we were teenagers. Didn't you have a thing for her, Ben?"

Ben pierced the yolk of a fried egg with his fork. "I was more of a comic book nerd."

I stifled a giggle. This was a side of Holmes I'd never seen. Not that there was anything wrong with it, I just never thought about him having crushes on models. It was sort of sweet, actually. "Maybe you can meet her while she's here."

"Why do you think I've been sitting at the clue desk?"

I burst into laughter. "I thought you were pitching in to help us." I mimicked him. "'I love being at the inn.'"

Shelley walked up to our table. "I think you'd better order for Trixie and Gingersnap. They've been following me around since you walked in."

"Sorry about that. What's the special this morning?"

"Ham steaks with fried eggs and hash browns."

"Sounds good. Is there a dog version?"

"Thin rounds of pork tenderloin with a fried egg and hash browns."

I didn't need Zelda's powers to know they would snarf that up. "Sounds great, Shelley."

She had barely moved away when Sylvie approached our table. "May I have a word with you?"

"Of course."

She smiled at me and her cute dimples pierced her cheeks. "In private?"

"Yes. Of course." I rose and walked to the front desk with her. "How can I help you?"

"Darlin', I love this inn. It's just enchanting. But these days, with social media and all, it only takes a second for a place to get a bad reputation."

"Oh? Is something wrong?"

"That young man is still working here. The one who stole

Weegie's necklace. I'd hate for it to get around that you have a thief on your staff."

I looked her in the eyes. Oma's coaching over the years was as loud in my ears as if she were standing beside me. Always make the guest happy. Never argue with a guest. "I appreciate your concern. And I'm so glad you told me about this issue." I thought fast. "We'll have someone with him the entire time he's inside the inn."

"Really? That's the best you can do? Honey, if I owned a beautiful inn like this, I would sure fire anyone who stole from the guests. But if the reputation of the Sugar Maple Inn doesn't matter to you, well, then there's not much I can do about it."

I yearned to say, *Hey, lady! There's three feet of snow on the ground. Did you want to walk through it to get to Café Chat this morning?* But I knew better. What could I say to calm her while I got to the bottom of the stolen necklace issue? I whispered, "I met with the police this morning. That's what I was doing at Café Chat."

"The police? Oh my word. I thought you would let him go, not send him to jail."

There was no pleasing this woman.

"I'm glad to know that you're taking it seriously." Sylvie walked away, looking distressed.

It was too early for Marisol, the housekeeper, to arrive. As soon as she came, I planned to have a word with her about Shadow.

I returned to my breakfast, a knot in my stomach about the problem with Shadow. But I tried to put on a happy face for the benefit of the guests.

After breakfast, Holmes and Ben volunteered to man the clue return desk in case anyone else came by to check their clues. I wasn't at all sure I liked them becoming friends. On a completely logical level, I thought it was nice. But to my surprise, there was an impish side of me that kept thinking, *No good can come of this.* At least Ben was being entertained while I worked. I decided to see the bright side and hope for the best.

I hustled to the office to take care of some things, and at the dot of ten, when Marisol arrived, I jumped from my chair, startling Twinkletoes, who had been lounging on the desk.

Trixie had already reached Marisol, who just happened to have miniature treats in her pocket. She fed one to Trixie.

"Did you have trouble coming in?" I asked.

"It's not bad in Wagtail. But I wouldn't want to try going down the mountain."

"Marisol, yesterday a guest complained that a necklace was missing from her room—"

"You think I took it?"

"No, no! I'm worried that Shadow did. But you were with him the whole time he was in the rooms, right?"

"Ay, this is trouble. I could have had my back to him sometimes. I opened the rooms for him, waited while he fixed the fireplaces, and then locked the doors behind him. He was never alone. But you know, a necklace—" she shook her head "—this is easy to take." She made a swift motion with her hand as though she were grabbing something.

She was right. A necklace could be easily concealed in a hand or a pocket.

"He was very nice. So worried about getting the floors dirty. I don't think he would steal anything."

"Thank you, Marisol."

"Which room was it? I'll look around. Maybe it's tangled in the sheets or it fell on the floor."

"I would appreciate that. In fact, I'll help you." We walked up the stairs to Swim and knocked on the door. Happily, neither Weegie nor Myrtle happened to be in.

"You take the bathroom," said Marisol, "and I'll run the duster over the hardwood floors. Maybe I can catch it."

The bathroom was unremarkable. It wasn't on the floor or in the tub or among the toiletries on the counter. I walked toward the closet. Maybe it had snagged on clothing. No such luck. The closet was nearly empty.

I turned around to Marisol. "Anything?"

She held up the candlestick. "No necklace, but I find this under the bed."

"Oh, that's funny. It's a weapon for Murder Most Howl. Weegie or Myrtle must have hidden it there. We better put that back."

"It belongs to the game?" Marisol smiled. "For the next few days I will be careful to leave what they hide under the beds. I'll keep looking for the necklace when I clean."

"Thanks, Marisol. Geof in Stay has misplaced his money clip. Keep an eye out for it, please?"

"Of course."

I walked down the stairs thinking about Shadow and the necklace. Instead of getting more gossip, I decided to go straight to the truth of the matter. I would speak to him and see what he had to say for himself. Wasn't that usually better than getting misinformation from third parties?

I grabbed my jacket.

"Where are you going?" asked Holmes.

"Outside to talk to Shadow."

"He went home to grab some lunch," said Ben.

"Miss Holly!" Mr. Huckle sounded like a reprimanding schoolteacher. He hurried toward me. "Was that young Shadow I saw cleaning snow off the porch? I thought we decided that your grandmother should hire someone on her return."

What could I say? I had done what I thought was best and had stepped right into a big steaming mess. "I know that's what you advised."

I couldn't put the Shadow problem off any longer. "Where does Shadow live?"

"Not too far from here. I'll go with you." Holmes stood up.

"Think you could fill in for Holmes a bit?" I asked Ben.

"Why can't I go with you? Holmes can stay here."

"Do you know where Shadow lives?" I asked.

He frowned at me. "All right. I'd rather eat lunch anyway. Did you know the cook will make me a grilled cheese and prosciutto sandwich if I want? Hey, wait a minute. This

Shadow fellow must have a phone. Why don't you just call him?"

"I'd rather speak with him in person."

"And you need an escort because you can't find the place?"

Why was he stalling and quizzing me? I was squirming under Mr. Huckle's scrutiny.

I lowered my voice to a whisper. "It seems he committed some kind of crime, and I need to ask him about it. I . . . I might have to let him go."

Holmes grabbed his jacket, and Gingersnap jumped to her feet, ready to go for a walk.

I bundled up Trixie, who was the first one out the door.

Behind me, Holmes said, "I'd forgotten all about Shadow killing that woman."

The cold air hit my face at the same time as Holmes's remark knocked the breath out of me. "I hope you're joking."

"Nope. It really happened. I didn't live here then but I recall Grandma Rose talking about it. It was four or five years ago."

We walked along the sidewalk at a brisk pace.

I didn't know whether to be relieved or horrified. At least he wasn't a thief. "Was it . . . self-defense?" I held my breath in hope.

"I really don't know the details. I didn't spend much time here back in those days."

I told him about Sylvie and Weegie's accusation.

We walked quietly for a few minutes, watching the dogs race ahead and double back.

"This probably sounds stupid," he said, "but I don't think stealing is necessarily equivalent to killing. I guess some people start out stealing and then get on a downward spiral and end up murdering someone to obtain money or valuables. But I'm not sure it works in reverse."

"He was so excited that I hired him. I can't imagine that he would have taken anything the first day." I sighed. "But being a murderer is even worse! I should have checked him out before bringing him on the staff." I was kicking myself mentally.

We paused and looked both ways along one of the two streets where cars were permitted. There wasn't a sound. No engines humming, no children shrieking as they played.

Holmes looked up at the sky. "There's more snow coming."

We crossed the street and walked toward a small log cabin. Snow clung to the roof, but I could see green edges here and there. We walked past pine trees laden with snow and dormant rhododendrons that would surely be stunning when they bloomed in the spring. We stepped up to the front porch.

Holmes knocked on the door while I admired it. Green trim ran around the edges, but in the middle, a glass pane the length of the door was partially covered by a wood carving depicting a deer standing by a tree and drinking out of a stream.

The door swung open exactly as I was saying, "This is the most incredible thing I have ever seen!"

Shadow grinned. "You like it?"

Holmes ran a hand over the wood. "You really ought to sell these. I bet a lot of the people with cabins around here would buy them."

"Aw, shoot. It's nothing special." Shadow bowed his head but I could see he was delighted by our praise.

"That's where you're wrong. It's very special. It's art!" I gushed.

Shadow smiled. "Y'all come on in." The dogs trotted inside, pausing for Shadow to pet them and wagging their tails in acceptance of him, which made me feel like the bad guy.

The living room, dining room, and kitchen were all clustered in one room with a gently vaulted roof. Giant windows on the other side of the room overlooked a valley and the mountains beyond as though the house sat on top of the world.

"Holly," said Shadow, "I noticed that the door to Swim is closing too tight. If you want, I could shave it down a little . . ." His voice faded along with his smile. "I guess I know why you're here. Gosh, I'm forgetting my manners. Could I offer you a cup of coffee?"

Holmes jumped at it like Shadow had offered him something truly special.

At Shadow's bidding, we sat down. A stone fireplace dominated the interior. Except for the sofa, the furniture was made of wood, hand-crafted no doubt. Each piece was decidedly original.

It was very tidy for a young guy. The glossy wood top of the dining table was neatly set with two woven placemats.

Trixie pawed at something under the sofa.

"Stop that," I hissed.

Nothing doing. She was determined. She lay on her belly and tried to wedge her head under the sofa to reach it. Still no luck, but she had gained Gingersnap's interest.

When Shadow brought us steaming mugs of coffee, both dogs had their rumps in the air and their noses crammed under the edge of the sofa.

Shadow chuckled at them. "What's going on, guys?"

He knelt and in a nanosecond stood up with the elusive item in his hand—a dog cookie in the shape of a bone. "I had a dog visitor last night. He must have left this under the sofa. Can they have it?"

They were looking at it the way I look at doughnuts. "Sure."

Shadow broke it in two and gave Trixie the smaller piece. He finally sat down with his shoulders hunched forward. "Every time I think that nightmare is behind me, something happens that brings it up again. I guess I'll always be tarnished by it." His eyes met mine and didn't waver. "It's okay, Holly. You can fire me. When I told my mom about the job, the first thing she asked was if I told you about my problem. I kinda figured it was all too good to be true."

I thought I must be an idiot. He seemed so genuine and

nice that I wanted to keep him on the staff! I sought the right words to ask him what happened. "I hear someone . . . died?"

His head drooped. When he lifted it, he said, "That's exactly what happened. Someone died. I didn't kill anybody. I stood right up in court and said so. I never would have done anybody any harm."

He paused a moment. When he had gathered himself, he continued. "I worked for The Doggy Bag."

It was a simple statement. From the way he said it, I gathered it was supposed to mean something to me. I didn't have a clue what The Doggy Bag was.

"I remember that place. They worked out of Randolph Hall," said Holmes.

Randolph Hall? The place that Norm bought and Savannah disliked.

Holmes continued, "Takeout for you and your dog. It was very popular. Set to go big with franchises, right?"

Shadow nodded. "Up until that lady died. The idea was that dogs are part of the family. So, instead of getting a bucket of chicken or whatever and bringing it home for the kids, you could get lunch or dinner from The Doggy Bag and feed the whole family, including the dog. They didn't cook with onions or garlic or things dogs can't eat."

"Interesting concept. So what happened?" I prompted.

"It was my job to do the dishes, and mop the floors, and throw stuff in the laundry. When we were super busy, I would pitch in filling the orders or whatever they needed. So, this one day, Mike was out somewhere and Michelle was busy taking orders on the phone, so I was packing the food in containers. Juliana, one of our regulars, came to pick up her order. I was the one who filled the order and handed it to her. She went home and ate it and died."

"The dog, too?" asked Holmes.

Shadow shook his head. "The dog got really sick but they think he could smell the . . . the poisonous stuff in it, so he didn't eat much." He ran a hand over Gingersnap's head. "Dogs can smell like a million times better than we can."

His story was missing something. "You didn't cook the food, right? So why were you blamed for Juliana's death?"

"Because she was poisoned by laundry gel packs. You know, the ones that are so colorful? A bag of them was out on the counter, next to where the food was being packed up, and they said I must have put them in Juliana's food."

I shot a glance at Holmes, who looked as confused as I felt. "Why would they blame you?"

"Because I was the one who set the laundry gel packs on the counter." He wrung his hands like he wanted to wash the taint off them. "I was the one who was packing the food. Nobody else's fingerprints were on the bag of dishwashing packs. Just mine." Shadow winced and fell silent. "I never would have killed anybody. And even if I wanted to, I sure wouldn't have done it that way! Who would have ever thought you could kill a person with laundry detergent?"

"So it was an accident." Holmes spoke gently.

"I guess." Shadow sucked his upper lip into his mouth so he resembled a bulldog. "I don't have a better explanation. All I know is that I didn't put that junk in her food. I'm not stupid!"

"That's why you have a criminal record?" I asked, just making sure it wasn't the only reason.

"I was arrested and charged with manslaughter. That's when you kill somebody but you didn't mean to do it."

"Have you ever stolen anything?" I asked.

"Shoot, no." He grinned. "My mama and daddy would have tanned my hide!"

"Did you do time?" I asked.

"Not much. My folks bailed me out, and then I got ten years' probation."

I could see the problem with hiring him. If something did go wrong, if Shadow had another accident, the inn would be blamed for hiring him in the first place. No wonder he couldn't find a job. The trouble was that I didn't see a malicious person when I looked in his face. He didn't shy away from looking me in the eye. I guessed that psychopaths were capable of doing that, but somehow, I felt that Shadow wore his emotions openly. What you saw was what you got. He didn't strike me as a devious killer or a tricky thief.

I decided to be blunt. "One of the guests is missing a shamrock necklace."

"I'm right sorry to hear that." His eyes widened. "Oh! You think I took it?"

"Did you?"

"No, ma'am. No way! I told you, I don't do things like that."

I believed him. I watched Gingersnap and Trixie. They had sniffed around a bit, then settled near us. True, Gingersnap liked everyone, but I wondered if she would be as fond of him if he weren't really a good person. Besides, he would be outdoors half the time anyway, shoveling snow and cleaning up outside. "Okay, how about this. You're not fired—"

Shadow beamed at me. "For real?"

"For real. But for two months you're in a test period."

"What does that mean?"

"If you goof up, or you don't come to work, or you don't do your job well—" I paused, pondering whether I should say it or not "—or things go missing, then you're out."

He gulped. "You think I took the necklace."

"Actually, I don't. Holmes and I have been around long enough to know that guests like to blame the inn when things disappear. It's probably on the floor somewhere, or in a dark corner of a suitcase. But for the next few days, I don't want you in or near the guest rooms unless Zelda or I am with you. Got it?"

"No. If you believe me, why would you make that a condition?"

"Because the two guests who reported the missing necklace won't be happy if they see you near the rooms."

He thought for a moment. "Yeah. Okay, you're on!"

I felt relieved when we left. I would check with Dave to make sure that there weren't any theft allegations against Shadow. And if he didn't work out, I could still let him go.

When we stepped off the porch, Holmes slung an arm around me. "You're such a big softy!"

"You think that was a mistake?"

"No, I think you did exactly what Oma would have done. She'd be proud."

Trixie and Gingersnap dug in the snow near a rhododendron. They buried their noses, but their tails wagged like crazy.

"C'mon, girls," I called. "Trixie, Gingersnap, come!"

They pulled their noses from the snow and raced toward us.

The sun glinted on something hanging from Gingersnap's mouth. "What is that?" I muttered. "Gingersnap!"

She trotted over to me, but held her head to the side as though she didn't want me taking the prize she'd found. I grabbed her collar with one hand and gently took the thing in her mouth, offering a treat from my pocket in exchange for it.

I held it out so Holmes could see. Gingersnap had found a gold chain with a shamrock on it.

# Nineteen

What had I done? "Shadow lied to us!" I groaned.

"You think that's the missing necklace?" asked Holmes.

"It was described as an inexpensive gold necklace with a shamrock. How many could there be? It was her lucky necklace."

"There must be a million necklaces like that. Of course, the odds of one of them happening to be at Shadow's house aren't very good." He snorted a laugh. "Doesn't seem like it's bringing anyone luck. She lost it, and now it looks really bad for Shadow."

"I feel like such an idiot. I believed him!"

"I did, too. Maybe there's a reasonable explanation."

"Tell me one logical reason that this necklace might have happened to be here."

"It belongs to his girlfriend, and she lost it." He looked at the little gold necklace with a green shamrock pendant and took it from my hand. "Wait here. I'll be right back."

"Don't confront him, Holmes!"

He ignored me, loped back to the spot where the dogs

had found it, and hung it from a branch of the rhododendron where Shadow would have to see it.

He jogged back to me.

"What are you doing?" I asked, incredulous.

"This is a test to see what Shadow does. I'm giving him a chance to save face."

"You expect him to return it, thus proving—what?"

"If he brings it back, he'll prove his good intentions. If he tries to sneak it into a room or never says anything about it, that will prove his guilt."

"I think his guilt is pretty well established. That necklace didn't get to his house by accident."

"Give him a chance. I find it hard to believe that he could lie so convincingly."

I was having the same problem. Was he that adept at lying? Somehow, I didn't think so. But there wasn't a good explanation for the necklace turning up at his place. I met Holmes's hopeful eyes. I had nothing to lose. At least if he showed up with it, I could fire him on the spot. He might even quit. "Okay. I can't believe that I'm going to have to fire Shadow." I moaned. "I thought I was doing the right thing. After all, it didn't sound like he meant to kill Juliana. Of course, if I had known her, I probably would feel differently. Do you think he poisoned her intentionally and lied through his teeth to us just now?"

Holmes shrugged and steered me along the street on a different path home. Before we crossed the street back into the heart of Wagtail, we stopped for a moment to watch children sledding on a hillside. They screamed and laughed, even when they fell off their sleds.

Trixie and Gingersnap joined the fray, barking and running along behind the kids.

One little boy, about eight I thought, slammed his sled into his mother's legs and stomped off a short distance. Naturally, all the adults watching the fun turned their attention to her. "I'm sorry," she said to no one, yet everyone. "He's usually not so—" she raised her voice "—ill-tempered. His sled blew away in the storm last night, and he doesn't like the new one I just bought because it's not red."

The little boy shouted back at her, "I don't like the new one because it's not slick and fast like my old one."

Holmes grinned. "Can I try it?"

Oh no. We really needed to get back to the inn. What was he doing?

He grabbed my hand. "C'mon, Holly."

He raced up the hill tugging me along behind him. In seconds, he sat on the sled. It was big enough to hold two, but barely.

I tottered as I stepped on it behind him and eased into a sitting position.

"Hold on!" he shouted as he pushed the snow with his hands.

I wrapped my arms around him, thinking more about the fact that my face had accidentally brushed his hair as I boarded than the fact that we were about to take off.

The sled flew downhill at an incredible speed. That little boy was nuts. Gingersnap and Trixie barked alongside us until we turned over in a tangled heap. Holmes and I laughed like kids. I could have sworn there was a moment when he looked into my eyes. Just the flicker of a connection before the sled took off without us, commandeered by Gingersnap and Trixie, who rode to the bottom of the hill on their own.

"Did you see that?" I asked. "It was like they understood how to sled."

Holmes laughed. "Man, that was fun! I haven't done that in years." He reached toward my face. "Hang on, you have snow in your hair."

He grinned as he brushed it away.

My heart beat faster. No question about it—snow, fireplaces, cuddling up close—winter was definitely romantic.

Holmes seized my hand and didn't let go when we walked the rest of the way down the hill. I savored the moment, knowing there wouldn't be many more like this when he finally tied the knot.

Aunt Birdie waited at the bottom, her arms crossed, and her eyebrows raised. Oh no!

"Having fun while your grandmother is away? I would think you would be more concerned about Murder Most Howl, the lies being spread about the good people of Wagtail, and . . ." She lowered her voice and hissed, "Norm's death."

I was mortified. What could I say to mollify her? If there was one thing she liked, it was being needed. "Aunt Birdie, why don't you drop by the inn for high tea today. Maybe you could help me with a little problem."

Holmes gave me an are-you-nuts glance. He grabbed the sled and towed it over to the little boy. "Thanks! This is the fastest sled in Wagtail. I'll give you twenty bucks for it."

Aunt Birdie took that opportunity to whisper, "Holly! He's engaged."

I was more painfully aware of that fact than anyone else on the planet, except maybe for his fiancée.

The little boy's sour expression changed. He took the rope handle from Holmes. "No, thanks. I think I'll keep it."

Holmes nodded. "Good choice. But you call me if you decide to sell, okay?"

The boy's mom mouthed "Thank you" to Holmes. She beamed as her son started the trek back up the hill.

Holmes joined us, still brushing snow off his trousers.

"We'll see you later, then?" I asked Birdie.

She nodded, but the critical look on her face told me she was still thinking about Holmes and me. I called the dogs, who were all too ready to walk home.

A couple of blocks later, a little Yorkie wearing a fluffy pink jacket that matched the bow tying her hair up out of her cute face ran down her sidewalk to greet Trixie and Gingersnap. I recognized GloryB, who had stayed with us at the inn in the fall.

Her mom, Lillian Elsner, wasn't too far behind. "She's not home," she said, laughing.

"Who?" I asked. I thought she lived alone with GloryB.

"Blanche. Isn't that why you're here? There's been a steady parade of looky-loos on the sidewalk since word got out that Blanche is staying at Randolph Hall." She nodded at the mansion across the street. "GloryB has been glued to the window, watching everyone. She's seen a lot of her friends from the park, too. Bingo dropped by Friday morning and now Trixie and Gingersnap are here."

"Oh, is this where she's staying?" asked Holmes.

I shot him a nasty look. I recognized the feigned surprise in his tone. I bet he knew perfectly well where Blanche was staying. It wasn't a coincidence that we were walking by. "Oh, please! Like you didn't know?"

Randolph Hall was worthy of a supermodel, but it seemed a bit gaudy to me. What had Savannah said? Too many columns across the front? The architect had gone overboard. I read once that the definition of elegance was "just enough, but not more." Too bad the person who built the house hadn't learned that. Multiple columns in two different sizes were a bit much.

In the center of the house, four columns soared to the top of the second floor, holding up a roof, a portico of sorts. I mused that without that massive structure, the house would look very much like a large white farmhouse. On each side of the portico, the front porch bowed outward in large curves held up by more columns, and on each side of those curves, the porch continued, then extended back along the sides of the house. The front door was painted black.

"It's massive," I said.

Lillian leaned toward us. "She's very nice."

"She must have rented the house from Norm," I mused. It made sense that she would have contacted her ex-husband about a place to stay.

"Norm!" Lillian shook her head. "That's a sad business. Imagine freezing to death on a bench."

Lillian hadn't lived in Wagtail very long so she might not have clashed with Norm yet. On the other hand, she was an attractive and well-to-do widow, who surely hadn't gone unnoticed by him.

"Did you know Norm well?" I asked.

A slight smile wavered on her lips. "No. He was always after me to invest in his harebrained business ideas. I told him I sank every penny I had into the store. I lived in Washington, DC, too long not to recognize a blowhard full of hot air."

She smiled at GloryB, who appeared to listen to Lillian instead of sniffing around like Gingersnap and Trixie. "I know one doggy who won't miss Norm. GloryB is nice or at least polite to everyone, except Norm. You always growled at him, didn't you, sweetie? Wouldn't you love to know what they're thinking? Dogs are so perceptive about people."

I gazed at GloryB's innocent face. What had she picked up on about Norm?

"He paid Blanche a visit after the meeting about Murder Most Howl. I left the inn right behind him. I couldn't figure out where he was going, and without power, it was very dark on this end of town. But it was definitely him. I think he had to get up his nerve to knock on the door. He waited outside for a bit before he was ready to go in."

Lillian clasped a hand over her mouth. "I sound like an old Wagtailite, gossiping about the neighbors! Actually, it was GloryB who sat by the window and growled. I wouldn't have looked out otherwise. I'm glad I ran into you, Holly. Thanks for helping out with Murder Most Howl. We've been swamped today. Our first great sales day since the holidays!"

"I'm relieved to hear that. We've had a few glitches, so it's good to know that part of it is working out."

"The visitors have been just great. I've been asked a lot of questions about the Baron von Rottweiler. I was his mistress. I knew his deepest darkest secret."

"Which was?" prompted Holmes.

Lillian threw her head back and laughed. "Now, honey,

I can't give that away. But the oddest thing happened. Two women came into the store and asked about Norm. They were pumping me for information on him as though he was the victim in the game."

"Did one of them bring her apricot poodle?" I asked.

"Weegie! She came by and bought a whole wardrobe for her dog, Puddin'. But the one doing most of the asking about Norm was petite. She had a short haircut. Gray with dark streaks, not much humor. Her pudgy friend was a hoot, though. Darling with dimples that showed when she laughed."

"Sounds like Myrtle and Sylvie. Maybe I should have a little talk with them."

"I'd better get going. At least the shop didn't lose power last night. What a storm! GloryB is always so well behaved but even she got up and barked at the howling wind."

We said good-bye, and she walked toward her house with GloryB scampering ahead of her.

"Well," I said to Holmes, "are you satisfied or are we going to wait here all day in the hope you'll get a glimpse of Blanche?"

He nudged me with his elbow in a kidding way. The dogs trudged on and so did we. They no longer sprang through the snow or raced ahead of us, though. They were ready for a long snooze by the fire. I wouldn't have minded that myself.

But when we walked into the inn, Holmes and I stopped dead.

Aunt Birdie was waiting for us beside a rather large suitcase.

"*Hmmpf.* I didn't expect to see Ben here. Holly, perhaps Mr. Huckle can take my luggage up to my room."

"Your room? Oh, Aunt Birdie. I believe you misunderstood me when I said we'll see you later. We're full up. There's not an unoccupied room in the entire inn."

"No matter. I'll stay in your grandmother's apartment."

"We could probably fit a rollaway bed in the living room if you don't mind sharing with Mr. Huckle." It was a little audacious of me, but I couldn't help myself.

Ben and Holmes snickered.

"There's nothing amusing about that. I believe you have a guest room? I don't mind sharing your suite." She removed her faux leopard print coat and held it out to me.

"Ben and Holmes are staying with me."

Her mouth dropped open. "I see I'm not a minute too soon. The moment your grandmother leaves town, this place turns into a den of iniquity. Mr. Huckle is not doing his job properly. I shall have a word with him."

"Aunt Birdie, there's nothing to be agitated about. You can sleep in the comfort of your own home knowing that they're here to help me if we get another big blast of snow."

Her expression and tone changed. "I thought you needed *my* help."

"Is that pine in your hair?" asked Ben.

No wonder Birdie was giving me that look. Ben reached toward me, but I backed up a step and felt my hair for pine. Sure enough, I pulled a pine needle out.

Mr. Huckle toddled up to us. "Miss Holly, if I am not mistaken, you haven't had time for lunch. Perhaps you, Miss Birdie, and your gentlemen friends would like to take tea while I man the desk for a bit."

So this was how it would be. On Oma's return, she would hear that Trixie had found another corpse, I had hired a murderer who stole a guest's necklace, and instead of working, I had entertained gentlemen callers.

I raised my chin and summoned every ounce of dignity I had left. "Thank you, Mr. Huckle. That's very thoughtful of you. I believe I'll just stop upstairs for a moment to fix my hair."

As I walked toward the stairs, I ignored Ben's question, "How did you get pine in your hair?"

Five minutes later, I joined them at a table by the fire. I needn't have worried for a moment about Mr. Huckle's comment about my gentlemen friends. They appeared to have bonded over Blanche. They had taken seats from which they could see her enjoying teatime with Ian, Geof, Char, and Robin.

Blanche wore another off-the-shoulder sweater and tight leggings that matched the color of her saluki's fur. The sweater was trimmed in rhinestones, and she looked every bit a star.

"If you don't stop staring at Blanche, I'm going to make you change your seats."

Holmes and Ben sputtered excuses.

"Seriously. How would you like it if every woman in the room was watching you? Get up!"

With about the same level of happiness as the little boy who had lost his favorite sled, the guys changed their seats and shifted their drinks so that I was looking in Blanche's direction and Holmes's and Ben's backs were to her.

"Thank you," I said.

We had just taken our seats again when Aunt Birdie joined us.

Shelley showed up with tiny, single servings of mac and cheese and set them before us. "Cook is trying out Mac and Cheeselets as an alternative to cucumber sandwiches in the wintertime." She set two bowls on the floor for the dogs. "Mac and Tease for Trixie and Gingersnap."

I peeked in the bowls. They were eating fast but I could make out macaroni, hamburger, and just a tease of cheese. "Thanks, Shelley." I helped myself to a Mac and Cheeselet.

"Since when is mac and cheese served for afternoon tea?" sniffed Aunt Birdie. "This isn't proper at all."

"We haven't had time for lunch. You don't have to eat it. Maybe Shelley could bring you cucumber sandwiches."

"No need. I'm rather fond of mac and cheese. A pedestrian dish, yet curiously satisfying."

Shelley made a face but returned to the kitchen and brought us a pot of tea.

We all dug into the savory dish, perfect for those who had been out in the cold. The Parmesan on top crunched ever so slightly—the best part if you asked me. But no one was asking or talking. We ate like we were starved.

Twinkletoes and Leo stretched out by the fire, making for a charming scene.

At the next table over, I could hear Myrtle and Sylvie.

"How long do cats live?" asked Sylvie.

Myrtle put down her cucumber sandwich. "About the same as a dog, I guess. Twelve, fourteen years?"

"That long? I had no idea."

"Are you thinking about getting a cat?"

"No. There are just so many cats and dogs around here that one can't help wondering about these things."

"I'm far more interested in murder. It had to be the wife," said Myrtle. "The age difference is staggering. He had to be as old as her parents."

I smiled to hear her speculation on Murder Most Howl. But I noticed that Weegie and Puddin' were enjoying tea at a different table, not with other members of their book club.

"Don't they always look at the spouse first in a murder investigation?" asked Sylvie. "I bet she married him for his money. She probably got tired of the old coot and knocked him off."

"There was a huge age difference. What could they possibly have had in common?"

"I have never understood that," said Myrtle. "I know why men like younger women, but what could that girl have been thinking?"

"Now those are sensible women," muttered Birdie. "They probably never invited two young men to share their sleeping quarters."

"What do you bet he already had a mistress?"

I tried to hide my smile. Once they discovered that Lillian was the baron's mistress, Myrtle and Sylvie would suspect her instead of the wife.

"I think we have to make another trip around to see the merchants. Some of them probably know the scoop. Like the fellow in the bookstore, he seemed to know everyone." She paused to take a bite of a smoked salmon pinwheel. "What we need is an excuse to visit the wife."

Aunt Birdie shot me an appalled look.

Holmes muttered, "Visit?"

Everyone except Ben stopped eating and listened rather openly.

"I wonder where she lives," said Myrtle. "We could take her some flowers."

Under my breath, I said, "Am I the only one who thinks they're talking about Norm?"

"Myrtle," said Sylvie, "I don't think that's a good idea. You'd be appalled if someone in your family had died and some stranger dropped by to question you."

Yikes! I jumped to my feet before I thought about what I should say. My abrupt movement alarmed little Ella Mae, who raced over to me. Trixie opened one eye but Gingersnap didn't budge from her snooze by the fire.

I bent to pick up Ella Mae, buying myself a little time to think of something that wouldn't sound like I was scolding our guests. Clutching the lively little dog, I approached the table where Myrtle and Sylvie sat.

"Are you enjoying teatime?" I asked.

"Everything is so delicious," raved Sylvie. "I don't know that I'll have room for dinner tonight."

"I'm so glad." I lowered my voice. "I'm afraid I couldn't help overhearing your conversation, and I wanted to be sure you understand that the prizes are only for solving the murder of the Baron von Rottweiler."

Myrtle flapped her hand in disgust. "There's no way anyone can win that. Those two brothers—" she flipped her hand toward Ian and Geof Tredwell "—have made it impossible to get information from any of the other players. They stole my weapon from me in broad daylight, right in front of you, and you didn't do a thing about it. Then somehow they stole the candlestick, too. They cheated, and what's worse, you helped them." She glared at them with open contempt. "Besides, there's a much bigger prize in solving Norm's murder—bringing a real killer to justice. That's far more important than any ridiculous game."

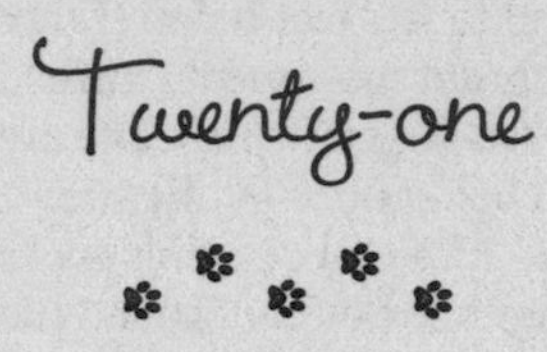

# Twenty-one

I froze at her words. "Myrtle, the local police are working on Norm's murder. I don't think it's wise to interfere."

Myrtle drew her head back and stared at me as though I was being outrageously insulting. "My, my. Says the woman who hired a criminal to go into people's rooms and steal from them. If the local police are anything like you, they'll never solve the case. A killer wouldn't have a thing to worry about here."

Her words stung, but I had to keep my cool. "I'm pleased to assure you that the local policeman is very competent."

Myrtle stared straight ahead and jammed a giant bite of the salmon pinwheel into her mouth. She intentionally avoided looking at me, and acted as though I weren't there. I knew when I had been dismissed.

I smiled at Sylvie, who gave me an apologetic look.

I sucked in a deep breath of air and moseyed over to the Tredwells. Char reached up, and I handed her Ella Mae. "How are you enjoying your stay?"

"Everything is just delightful," Char assured me. She

turned to look at Blanche. "Blanche didn't want to come on this trip, but I think she's even enjoying herself now."

Blanche nodded. "After tea, Charlotte and I are taking the dogs for massages."

Geof snorted.

"You're not going?" I asked Robin.

"Please. I can get a massage anywhere. I'd rather walk around and enjoy the scenery while I'm here."

"Holly, Geof has lost his money clip. Has anyone turned one in?" asked Ian.

My throat closed up. *Shadow*. What else had he taken? "Oh no. I'm so sorry, Geof," I choked. "I'll tell the staff to be on the lookout. Where did you last see it?"

Char beat him to a response. "Holly, don't worry about it. I'm certain he left it in a restaurant or a store."

Geof looked a little miffed. "I could swear I saw it in our room yesterday morning."

I smiled but goose bumps rose on my arms. What else had disappeared from the inn?

I promised to keep an eye out for it, wished them a lovely afternoon, and returned to my own table, where Shelley had replaced the platter of Mac and Cheeselets with a three-tiered server loaded with tiny sandwiches and fabulous sweets.

Sylvie and Myrtle had left, hopefully not to pester Savannah.

"Can you believe her?" Holmes licked cream off his finger. "She's acting like Norm's death is the game."

Aunt Birdie plucked a slice of apple Bundt cake off the server. "Really, Holly. You should find a better quality of guest. Has she no sensitivity for anyone? Imagine the nerve!"

"I have a feeling she's somewhat disagreeable by nature." I finished the few remaining bites of my mac and cheese, ready to dig into the pastries. Near my feet, I heard muffled snorting. Gingersnap's eyes were closed, and her paws twitched like she was running in a dream. I smiled when she barked in her sleep again.

At that moment, Weegie approached our table. "I'm sorry to interrupt you, but I was wondering if you might have another room I could move into for the rest of my stay."

Given the issues with Shadow, I hoped she didn't have a plumbing issue. "Is something wrong with your room?"

"Yes. Myrtle is staying there."

"Weegie, I'm so sorry. We're booked solid. I don't have anything that isn't occupied."

Aunt Birdie piped up. "She doesn't even have room for me. And I'm her only living blood relative."

Holmes's eyes met mine, and it was all I could do not to burst out laughing. My mother, Birdie's sister, was alive and well, not to mention their parents, my half siblings, my father, and Oma.

Weegie's entire body sagged. "I can't stand another night with that woman. Honestly. Isn't there some little corner? An office maybe?"

"If some of your friends will take you in, I could put a rollaway bed in their room."

She brightened up immediately. "Oh, thank you!" She scuttled back to the table where she'd been eating, chatted for a moment, and returned. "It sounds like Fetch is a pretty good size. Would that work?"

"Absolutely. I'll bring up a bed shortly."

"What a relief. I have learned a powerful lesson this weekend. You don't know a person until you travel with her. I always liked Myrtle but the woman is a nut. Spending an hour with a person once a month can be so misleading. Almost anyone can act sane for an hour or two. Here we are in this beautiful resort, and all she can do is complain. That woman was born with a glass half-empty. Now I know why none of the others would room with her."

"I'm glad you were able to work things out."

She thanked me again and returned to her friends. I could hear them agreeing to help her move her belongings immediately.

Ben set down his fork and observed me. "You handled that very well. Does it happen a lot?"

"It's not uncommon."

Holmes reached for a scone and laughed. "When it's a married couple, then you've got real problems."

The dining area had begun to empty out. I sipped my English breakfast tea and slathered a scone with cream and blackberry preserves.

"I certainly am enjoying this. You have most interesting guests. Do you need my help with one of them?" Birdie looked at me over the edge of her teacup.

"Our handyman quit."

Birdie choked on her tea. "Gracious, I hope you're not going ask me to be the handyman!"

"I needed to hire a new one. I happened to meet Shadow Hobbs—"

Birdie interrupted me. "Oh dear."

"I was hoping you could tell us what happened when Juliana died."

"That was a terrible tragedy. Somehow those gel packs of laundry detergent landed in Juliana's takeout. Apparently they're quite deadly. I had no idea. They say the package was on the counter where Shadow was packing food, and he must have slipped them into Juliana's order. Some sort of stew or chili, I think it was. It's so caustic that it didn't take much."

Ben's eyes grew round. "That's despicable." He placed his hand on his throat like he felt the terrible poison.

"There are those, including me, who never believed that Shadow did it. They had him, no doubt about it. His fingerprints on the package condemned him."

"Why did you think he was innocent?" I asked.

"I've known Shadow since he was a baby. His real name is Hollis Junior, after his dad, but they called him Shadow because he followed his father everywhere. If you saw Hollis, you knew little Shadow couldn't be far behind. He was the sweetest boy. Why would he go and murder Juliana? He testified in court that he barely knew her."

"What about the owners of the business? Did they have a beef with Juliana?" I asked.

"Not that I ever heard about. It was a tragedy all the way around. Norm lost his wife—"

I interrupted her. "Norm? Juliana was married to Norm?"

"Yes, of course. He was devastated."

Norm kept turning up like a bad penny. Of course, in that case he had been a victim.

Birdie continued, "The owners lost their business and everything they owned. Such a shame. They were a cute young couple. Things were going so well for them. They had bought Randolph Hall and had done such a lovely job of fixing it up. As far as I know, they didn't have any issues with Norm or Juliana. Wagtail was just on the cusp of turning into a dog and cat resort. Of course, no one would eat anything they cooked anymore. They went out of business and moved away. We all thought it horribly ironic that Norm bought Randolph Hall at auction—" she paused for effect "—with the money he got from suing them."

"And it all happened because of Shadow," I muttered. I shuddered at the thought of losing the Sugar Maple Inn that way. "I have to let him go."

"Don't do that!" Aunt Birdie seemed surprised. "It was several years ago, and if it was his fault, it was an accident. Doesn't he deserve a chance to redeem himself?"

"Where has he been working since then?" I asked. "He has that cute cabin. He must be making some money."

"Odd jobs." Holmes sighed. "He cobbled that cabin together with discarded building material."

"Even those huge windows?" I was doubtful.

"You'd be surprised what builders will discard. They ordered the wrong size and gave them to him for free just for hauling them away. He helps clean snow off the highway down the mountain with his truck. Things like that."

I was so torn. I wanted to help him. Shadow was clearly industrious and talented. He'd already proven that he was a hard worker. "I don't know what to do."

I told Aunt Birdie and Ben about the missing necklace.

"That doesn't sound like him at all," protested Birdie.

I watched her. She'd steered me wrong once before. Way wrong. The trouble was that I liked Shadow. I liked what I had seen of him. I was only scared because of something that had happened a few years ago. "He wouldn't be in the kitchen or involved with the laundry . . ."

Shelley and the cook had put in a long day. They stopped by our table to say good-bye.

"We'll be here in the morning," promised Shelley. "You should still have gas to warm food, even if the power goes out. Buckle down and stay safe."

Aunt Birdie looked frightened. So that was the reason for bringing her suitcase. She was afraid to be alone in the storm.

"Aunt Birdie, maybe you should stay over to help. You know how to waitress, don't you?" I teased. "We can put another rollaway bed in my apartment. It'll be like a slumber party."

She sat up straighter. "Well, if you need me . . ."

The next couple of hours passed quickly. Holmes, Ben, and I delivered rollaway beds to Fetch and to my apartment. I gave my bedroom to Birdie, despite her protests. As we worked, I notified everyone to keep an eye out for Geof's money clip.

We brought the lanterns and candles back to all the public areas, just in case we lost power, and stashed a variety of board games in the Dogwood Room to entertain guests who didn't care to venture out if another storm hit.

Just after five o'clock, the moment I had dreaded arrived. Shadow marched through the door and headed straight toward me. His father followed, right behind him.

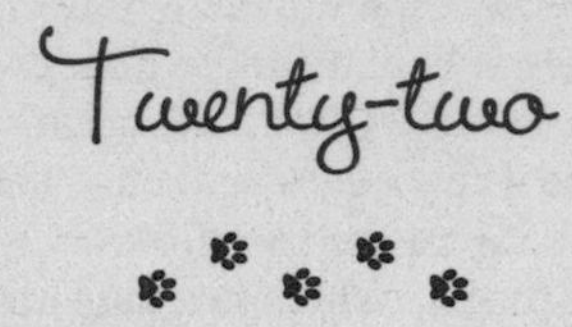

Hollis Hobbs was a bear of a man. Tall and robust, he reminded me of a mountain man who could probably live off the land, hunt, track, and defend his women. He had always been very nice to me and had been an enthusiastic participant in the planning of Murder Most Howl. But the scowl on his face told me this wasn't a social call.

Shadow appeared to be sad and, true to his name, was but a mere shadow in his father's presence. I expected Shadow to quit his new job now that we had caught him with the shamrock necklace. I still had mixed feelings. I wanted to follow my gut instinct and hire him but didn't know if I should risk it.

He held the necklace out to me. "You didn't have to pretend a necklace was missing and then plant it at my house. I would have understood if you had just asked me to quit. I know no one wants to hire me. My dad says the best thing for me would be to leave Wagtail and go someplace like Washington, where no one will know what happened at The Doggy Bag."

I could feel my face flushing. Why was my first instinct to

apologize? What was it about him that made me want to believe him? I should be turning the tables on him. After all, he must have taken the necklace. How else could it have gotten to his cabin? Unless someone planted it there. But that was unlikely. Not impossible, but I feared it was wishful thinking on my part.

Hollis stood behind him. For moral support?

"Shadow," I said gently, "one of the dogs found the necklace under a bush at your house. You must have dropped it."

A crease formed between his eyebrows. "I don't understand how that could be. I didn't take it." His head turned down like he felt the weight of the world.

Why, oh why, did I want to hug him and make him feel better?

Hollis spoke softly. "I realize that Shadow had a problem in his past, but he isn't a liar, Holly. If he says he didn't take it, then he didn't."

I glanced back as I felt Holmes move in behind me, like it was a standoff between the Hobbses and the two of us.

"Then how did it end up at his house, Hollis?" asked Holmes.

"If you found it, why'd you leave it there?" Hollis replied.

He didn't answer the big question but he threw the ball back in our court.

"Look, Hollis," I said. "I want Shadow to work here. We need a handyman, and Shadow did a great job for us today. I was very pleased. Holmes and I left the necklace as a test. We figured Shadow would know he had been caught and his reaction would prove . . . something . . ." My voice faded since I wasn't exactly sure anymore what it would have proven.

Hollis sighed. "Seems to me it's not a very good test. How do you pass? No matter what, you're still going to ask how it got to his house. He can't win."

"That's because it shouldn't have been there. It should have been upstairs in a guest room with the rightful owner." As I spoke, it dawned on me that I ought to check to be one hundred percent sure that it was the missing necklace.

Hollis started to speak, but Shadow stopped him. "I don't know how it got to my house. I've heard of crows stealing shiny things. Maybe it fell off the lady's neck, and a crow picked it up. But I know one thing. If I was a thief, and I got caught like this, I probably would have tried to sneak it back into the room it came from. 'Cause then, you'd have to think I never took it in the first place. You wouldn't know if it was the same necklace or not, or how it got back there. That would be a sneaky thing to do. I can't do it because I don't know which room it came from, 'cause I didn't take it. I've done the right thing by coming here and returning it. I can't do no more than that." He looked me straight in the eyes. "I didn't take that necklace, and I didn't kill Juliana. I don't know what happened to her. But now that Norm has gone to his maker, he knows the truth."

I swear Hollis growled. “Good riddance to that man. If it wasn’t for him—”

Shadow jerked around and held up his hand like a cop. “Dad, stop it! I knew it was a bad idea for you to come with me. I’m not a kid anymore, and I can stand up for myself. Norm is gone, Dad. He had nothing to do with that stupid necklace. You can’t keep blaming him for every bad thing that happens to me.”

Ben edged up behind me and whispered, “He’s right, you know. You set him up in a no-win situation. No matter what he did, you would still think he took the necklace.”

“I don’t think it was delivered to his house by a crow,” I said with irritation.

“Maybe not, but where’s your evidence that he took it?”

“Ben,” I muttered, “he was in the guest rooms.”

“Holly,” he muttered back, “who else has access to them? The housekeeper? Casey? Zelda? Mr. Huckle? Friends of the guests?”

“Which one of them would have dropped it off at his house?” I hissed.

"The one that doesn't like him."

I hated it when Ben played his lawyer games with me. I hated it even more when he had a point.

It made no sense. None. The necklace had magically vanished and flown to Shadow's house. I considered asking about Geof's money clip, but in my mind, I heard Ben saying, *You have no evidence. His own wife thinks he left it somewhere else.* For that matter, Char might have swiped it for some reason.

I winced. I was my own worst enemy. A stronger person would have fired him and that would have put an end to the mess. Why did I believe Shadow? And then, Oma proved just how much she influenced my life. "Truth gives a single reason," she'd told me many times, "while a lie offers many." If he had stolen the necklace and got caught, wouldn't he make up a better story?

"Shadow, how about we wipe the slate clean?" I asked. "We'll go back to hiring you for a trial period and see how it works out. Okay?"

The smile on his face was like a ray of sunshine. Shadow stuck his hand out to me to shake. "Deal. I'll make you proud. They say wicked winds and more snow are coming tonight. I'll go home and catch a nap, then I'll be back with nontoxic ice melter, and a snow blower so your guests won't have trouble getting back after dinner."

He turned to his father and said, "I told you I didn't need your help."

Hollis gave me quick nod, and I knew he was grateful to me for giving his son a chance. Deep in my heart, I wanted to believe Shadow. The way he spoke and acted, it was hard for me to imagine that he was lying about the necklace. But the core question hadn't been answered. How did it get to his house?

Relieved to have that behind me, I walked upstairs to Fetch and knocked on the door.

Ella Mae charged down the hallway toward me. The second Weegie opened the door, Ella Mae shot inside.

I handed Weegie the necklace.

"You found it! I can't believe it. I thought it was gone for good." She clasped it on her neck. "The member of our book club who gave it to me died a few months ago. I know it's not worth anything, but I'm sentimental about it. It makes me feel like she's with me in a way. Isn't that silly of me?"

"Not at all," I assured her.

"I'm not taking it off until I'm home. Thank you so much. Where was it?"

"Let's just say it took a trip across town and back."

"This is turning out to be a pretty good day. Maybe I should have another look at the Murder Most Howl clues now that I have my lucky necklace back." She leaned toward me and whispered, "When I moved my stuff, I stole two of Myrtle's clues!" She tittered like a kid. "Listen to these. I think they're key, or she wouldn't have hidden them."

*The Baron von Rottweiler's mistress is having a secret affair with the owner of the bookstore.*

*The Baron von Rottweiler's third wife's older brother owns a bookstore.*

Ella Mae dashed out of the room with a large toy of some kind in her mouth and Puddin' running behind her.

"Aren't they adorable playing together?" gushed Weegie. "I was worried that Puddin' wouldn't have fun, or that I would end up having to leave her in my room but she's had a blast. I love that I can take her to restaurants. It should be like that everywhere. Which restaurant do you recommend for dinner? We want to dress up, go someplace classy, and toast the book club members we lost last year."

"Then it's The Blue Boar that you want. Very elegant and the food is superb. Tell them I sent you. It's a short walk from the registration entrance."

"Thanks!" She called Puddin', who tried to wrestle the

toy from Ella Mae but tiny Ella Mae was determined to keep her prize.

Puddin' was obviously well trained because she came running when called.

I walked down the hallway to see what Ella Mae was carrying. She shot me a wild look, as though she was afraid I would take it from her. The little rascal had the candlestick weapon in her mouth. The tiny dog could barely carry it. Someone must have opened the door to Stay because she raced inside, half dragging the candlestick along with her.

I paused for a moment. Wasn't that curious? Geof and Myrtle both claimed someone had stolen the candlestick from them. I couldn't help wondering how Weegie ended up with it. Was she the one who stole it from Geof? Or had she stolen it from Myrtle when she moved? Val had said the game participants would lie and trick one another. It looked like she was right.

I walked down the grand staircase, and Ben called out to me. He and Holmes sat at a table with Mr. Huckle and Aunt Birdie in the otherwise empty dining area.

Ever the perfect butler, Mr. Huckle asked, "May I pour you a cup of tea?"

I sank into a chair. "Yes, please!"

Gingersnap and Trixie still snoozed by the fire with Twinkletoes. Leo had left for parts unknown. Maybe he had followed Zelda home.

Holmes held the list of clues in his hand. "Remember how you said the Baron von Rottweiler was beginning to sound a lot like Norm?"

I nodded and smiled gratefully at Mr. Huckle, who handed me an oversized cup of steaming tea. "Thank you."

"Something bothered me about the wives. When Shadow was here, I realized that it was the time period between Blanche and Savannah. I don't know exactly when Blanche divorced Norm, but it seemed like there was a long gap. Now we know that he was married to Juliana in between."

He excitedly pointed at the page of clues.

Aunt Birdie stiffened. "I hope those are clues about the game and not lies about local people."

I wasn't following Holmes, but I'd had a thought of my own. "You think Hollis murdered Norm?"

All four of them blinked at me like I'd lost my mind. "Didn't you notice? Hollis seems to blame Norm for Shadow's problems."

Ben sat back and contemplated me. "Shadow cut him off. Too bad. I'd have liked to have heard more."

Holmes flipped the page and wrote something on the back. "That fits right in. You were right, Holly. Listen to this." He read aloud.

*The Baron von Rottweiler left his first wife for a younger woman.*

"Norm probably left Blanche for Juliana."

*The Baron von Rottweiler left his first wife so destitute that she had to live in her car.*

"You said that happened to Blanche."

*The Baron von Rottweiler poisoned his second wife.*

"Juliana was poisoned."

*The Baron von Rottweiler accused an innocent man of murder.*

"Shadow was accused in Juliana's death."

Val! Val had written the clues. I had heard of a person's blood running cold and felt like it just happened to me.

I sat up straight. "What about the other clues?"

Holmes scanned the list. "There have to be a lot of red

herrings in here. Like the ones about the baron's many children. Here's one I don't know about."

*The Baron von Rottweiler kept a mistress.*

"Mr. Huckle," I said, "would you know anything about that?"

"Please, Miss Holly, I'm not in the habit of gossiping, but if I were, I wouldn't be aware of any romantic dalliances outside of marriage on Norm's part."

I tried to bite back my grin. The man gossiped plenty. I'd heard him talking with Oma and Rose.

"Aunt Birdie?" I asked.

"You know I don't stoop to gossiping. But at Pawsitively Decadent today, I saw two of your guests who are not married to each other purchasing some items together."

Really? To her that wasn't gossip?

"Who?" asked Mr. Huckle. "Miss Robin and Geof?"

"How did you know?" Aunt Birdie leaned toward him, her eyes bright with anticipation.

"They have caught my attention. I fear a bit of hanky-panky there."

I rubbed my face with my hands. I hated to imagine that Robin and Geof were up to no good while Char doted on little Ella Mae, but that wasn't my problem.

"Why would Val do that? Why would she structure the entire game around Norm's life?" I asked. "I know she didn't like him but this is a little scary."

"He made a pretty good villain." Ben stretched his arms. "She never names him, of course, very shrewd on her part. I wonder if he could make a case for libel? Probably not."

"He's dead, Ben."

Mr. Huckle raised one eyebrow. "I believe we can thank Miss Val. She has done a rather remarkable job of laying out Norm's potential murderers, hasn't she?"

"I think you'd better call Dave." Holmes sat back. "He needs to know about this."

I knew Holmes was right. I knew that was what we had to do. But Val was my friend. The clues didn't mean she had killed Norm. Did they? Had she made up the game as an elaborate cover for murdering Norm?

Silence fell upon us. I looked from face to face but found no help for my position on the matter. Moving slower than molasses, I headed for the telephone on the desk, and with a heavy heart, I changed my mind. "I'm going to talk to Val face-to-face. This isn't something I want to discuss on the phone."

Trixie awoke and ran to my side, looking up at me and whimpering as though she understood my distress. She probably did.

I wasn't in the habit of turning friends in to the police. Maybe this was all coincidence. Maybe Val just dreamed up nasty things the baron might have done and didn't even realize that she had painted the picture of Norm's life. That part about his first wife having to live in her car couldn't be a coincidence, though.

I bundled up Trixie and donned my jacket, leaving the others to handle whatever came along while I was gone. They offered to come with me, but I thought Val would be more forthcoming if it was just me.

In the darkness, snow had started to drift down again. Leo sat on thc front porch, watching something.

Just beyond the little plaza in front of the inn, I could make out a woman alone, holding her arms out, her face turned up to the sky. She twirled slowly, like a child enchanted by the snow.

I watched her carefree enjoyment of the weather. She wobbled a bit and fell backward, landing on the soft cushion of snow.

Trixie shot down the stairs, wagging her little tail.

I hurried after her. "Trixie!" I ran as well as I could through the snow. To my utter horror, Trixie playfully pounced on the woman.

Making matters even worse, Leo jumped on top of them. "I'm so sorry. Are you okay?" I lifted Leo and reached out a hand to none other than Blanche.

She laughed so hard that tears rolled down her cheeks. "I'm fine. Just clumsy." She grasped Trixie's little head between her hands and planted a kiss on her forehead. "You're such a cutie pie!"

Leo squirmed. When I set him down, he stepped into her lap as though he was demanding equal time. "You too, Leo!"

I could hear him purring. Blanche gently lifted him and deposited him in the snow.

"Leo seems to like you." I helped Blanche get up on her feet.

"He was waiting on the steps of our rental house when we arrived, like he was the official welcome committee. When we unlocked the door, he walked in as though he owned the place!"

"Wagtail friendliness. It even extends to the cats and dogs."

"I love Wagtail. I love everyone!" she shouted.

Maybe she'd been drinking.

I tried to find the right words. Ones that wouldn't be construed as offensive. "Can I help you get somewhere?"

"No. Thanks for offering. I like being outside. The snow has started again. Everything is so crisp and clean. I feel . . . I feel like . . . No. I *know* that my troubles are over. I never have to be afraid again. You can't imagine what a liberating feeling it is to be free of torment." Blanche gazed at me. "I hope you never have to know."

"Does this have something to do with Norm?"

"It has everything to do with Norm. I'm sorry, you were probably under his spell like most people are. You only saw the candy-coated outside and never knew what he was really like."

"I didn't know him well at all." What a remarkable difference from the sad Blanche I'd seen the day before. It was as though she was glad to be alive. "I have to walk over to Hair of the Dog for a minute. Feel like walking with Trixie and me?"

"Sure! It's probably better than twirling in the snow and getting dizzy anyway. Though I still want to make a snow angel. Did you do that when you were a kid?"

"I did! Not in years, though. Maybe I'll join you." We started walking toward the other end of town.

"That would be fun. I'm sorry. I'm a little giddy. I've been on an emotional roller coaster this weekend. Ian, Geof, Robin, and Char think I'm off my rocker."

"I'm sure they understand. Norm's death must have hit you hard."

"Hit me. Yes, that's a good way to put it. I was stunned. There was a time when I thought he was charming. He had that delicious Southern accent and exquisite manners! Oh, gosh. He had manners that no one teaches their sons anymore. He swept me off my naive little feet. We married, and he acted as my manager. He took care of everything for me. At the time I thought it was marvelous, but it turned out to be my big mistake. I was making a lot of money back then." She sighed. "I never expected him to take everything. The day I left him, he reported our credit cards stolen. I couldn't even check into a hotel. He cleaned out the bank accounts. I had nothing. You cannot imagine the horror. And New York City is so expensive! I slept in my car. It was terrifying. I will never forgive him those nights of terror. Really, I was worried about moving the car because I might run out of gas, and I had no cash to pay for more, and if it got towed, then I wouldn't have a safe place to cower." She paused. "I never hated anyone so much in my life."

"Then why did you come here?" I asked. "Didn't you know that Norm lived in Wagtail?"

"Of course I knew. I didn't want to come. But Geof and Char were all excited about adopting a dog. And then Geof told Ian about Murder Most Howl, and the two of them pushed and pushed me. They love games. Don't get me wrong, Ian has always been wonderful to me. I think Ian, Geof, and Char never met anyone like Norm. They didn't mean to dismiss me and my fears, but they tended to think I was a bit of a drama queen when it came to some things—like Norm. They just didn't have a frame of reference and thought I was embellishing."

She stopped walking and turned toward me. "Oh, look! Leo's following us. I love that crazy cat. Holly, I'm sorry I didn't want to stay at your inn. It's lovely. I've been in Char's room and in Robin's. So quaint and charming." She reached over and placed her hand on my arm apologetically. "I had so many stupid men follow me to my hotel room when I was a model. Men who worked for hotels and inns used to bring me things I hadn't ordered, just as an excuse to get into the room and meet me. It was awful."

We started walking again. "Ian found a house for rent in Wagtail. The kind of place I've always wanted to live. Big and beautiful with a history." Blanche pulled her hair back off her shoulders. "Every time we drive by one of those places that's for sale, I bug Ian about it. So he found one in Wagtail to lure me. 'All the glamour, none of the upkeep or cost,' he said."

Blanche took a breath and looked me in the eyes under a streetlamp. "To be honest, Ian, Geof, and Char thought it would do me good to see Norm. That it would give me some kind of closure to know that he couldn't hurt me anymore. That I am in control of my own life, and he is nothing to me."

She adjusted her glove. "I can't tell you how much I dreaded this trip. I thought maybe they were right. Maybe I needed to face Norm and take control. I never expected to be so sad when he died. There's something so final, so irreparable, about death. Dear heaven, how many times did I wish that man a hideous death? And now I find myself in the oddest conundrum of feeling both sorrowful and shamefully giddy at the same time. Freedom from Norm is engulfing me in huge waves. At long last, he truly is in my past. I never expected it to happen like this, though." She stopped talking for a moment. "Thank you for letting me dump my troubles on you. Hey, would it be a big imposition to stop by our rental house? I'm a little damp from the snow, and I probably ought to change for dinner anyway."

"Sure, no problem. Where are Geof, Ian, and Char?" I asked.

"Upstairs in Geof and Char's room. They're studying the clues about the Baron von Rottweiler. I slipped away by myself." She smiled. "I just needed a little time enjoying the fresh air and the falling snow, and proving to myself that I have nothing to fear anymore."

"Is that why you asked to leave the inn by a back door?"

"Thank you for showing us the way. I was terrified of running into him in the dark. That was probably silly of me."

"What did you think he would do to you?" I asked.

"Call me a cow. Berate me. Make me feel ashamed. Lock me in a closet. Norm could make an angel into a devil just by twisting words. When I think about it now, I don't understand how he had so much power over me when all the while he is the one who lived off of me and took the money I made. Ian thinks he felt entitled because he was raised in a mansion with cooks and housekeepers. I certainly wasn't. I worked hard for every penny I ever made."

We walked up to the black front door of Randolph Hall and Blanche unlocked it.

Given Blanche's horrible past with Norm, I couldn't help wondering why they were staying in a house that belonged to him. Even if Randolph Hall was a fancy mansion, why would they have anything to do with Norm?

She switched on a light in the entrance hall, which wasn't at all what I had expected.

The black and white marble floor suited the grandeur of the house. But the switchback stairs could have been in any house. They led upward on the right, with white pickets and a black handrail.

I assumed stairs to the basement must have been located beneath them. A small table to my right held a tasteful arrangement of winter greens and bright red berries.

"I'll just be a minute," said Blanche.

"Do you mind if I look around?"

She headed up the stairs and called, "Make yourself at home!"

I used my hand to wipe Trixie's feet. Just in time because she tagged after Leo, who strolled into the living room like he thought he lived there. I wiped my boots on the mat. Who knew when I'd get another chance to see the mansion? I peeked into the living room. It was massive and decorated with beautiful antiques and old-fashioned seating upholstered in faded velvet. I noted that someone had truly loved columns because there were more inside the house.

I walked through it and found myself in the dining room. A bay window gave it charm. The brass chandelier strung with chains of hundreds of crystals took my breath away.

The kitchen on the other side of the house was a strange mix of ultramodern stainless steel and old-fashioned cabinets. With a start, I realized that this was the room where Shadow had allegedly poisoned Juliana's food.

Leo startled me by jumping onto the breakfast table next to me. He purred and rubbed his big head against my sleeve. I ran my hand over his head and back.

Things had probably been changed around since that terrible day but my guess was that the commercial-looking stainless steel–topped table in the middle of the room was where the packing had probably taken place.

I peered out the window in the back door. A long garden, now covered in snow, stretched to the rear of the property.

Trixie raced into the kitchen, which excited Leo. He leaped to the floor and darted in and out of the kitchen in a kitty frenzy. Trixie stopped cold, not sure how to play that game. Suddenly, she barked and chased Leo.

"Trixie," I hissed. "Stop that. Behave yourself."

She reluctantly returned.

But I noticed that Leo came back, searching for her.

Trixie's entire body tensed, ready for more fun.

"No!" I said it firmly.

But Trixie still watched Leo's every move.

And then in one swift motion, Leo batted a toy out from under a pie safe so hard that Trixie's pent-up readiness finally exploded.

She barked and raced after it.

I followed her. "Give, please."

Trixie shied away from me.

"Trixie . . ." I warned.

She dropped it on the floor. I picked it up in a hurry before she could change her mind or Leo could bat it again. It was nothing important. Just a blue plastic top to something. I set it on the kitchen counter in case anyone was looking for it.

"Holly?" called Blanche. "Ready to go?"

I whistled for Trixie and hurried back to the foyer. "This is a fascinating house. The chandelier in the dining room is incredible."

"You know what I like about it? These stairs could be in a farmhouse. There's an odd mix of country casual and mansion chic in this place. Leo! Here, kitty, kitty!"

Leo came running.

When Blanche opened the door, he seemed to understand that it was time to go and stepped outside. But this time, when we turned toward the pub, he must have had other plans because he scampered in the opposite direction.

We strolled quietly for a moment. "How did you meet Norm?" I asked.

"He came to New York to find his fortune. I just didn't realize that he thought he'd found it in me. Norm's family lost everything when he was fifteen. His father had a gambling problem and squandered their money. He went from being the kid who lived in the fancy house and attended private school where he was king, to being the kid in a small apartment with his mother. Suddenly, he was the new kid in public school. That's where he learned to get by on charm."

"I had no idea. Must have been hard for him."

"He kept that part of his life to himself. He tried to cultivate the image of the rich kid."

"No wonder he bought Randolph Hall. Savannah said he wanted to live there."

Blanche stopped cold and looked at me, her mouth open. "He owned Randolph Hall?"

"You didn't know?" I asked.

"I did *not*. I don't think Ian knew that, either. We never would have stayed there. We picked up the key from a real estate office here in town. Well, well. Isn't that interesting? It's a beautiful place. I can see why he would have wanted to live there. It would have been as though he regained the mansion his family lost." She closed one eye suspiciously. "Wonder how he could afford it. Probably stole money from some other unsuspecting schnook like me."

Aunt Birdie had said something about a lawsuit. I wasn't sure I should repeat it. It was probably idle gossip.

"But you were never afraid of him."

"Physically? Yes, I was. Funny thing—we had been in town about an hour before his current wife showed up. Have you met her? Darling girl."

"Savannah?"

"That's the one. The poor child wanted to leave him. Do you know what she said to me?"

I couldn't imagine. I was stunned that she wanted to leave him.

"She said, 'You're the only one who got out alive. How did you do it?'"

"What did you say?"

"Run. I told her to run. She thought that was a joke, so I told her the truth about how I left him. I guess I'm not a very good role model."

"What did you do?" Illegal ideas flashed through my head.

"When I wasn't on top of my game anymore, someone turned me down for a shoot because I was too old—sadly still in my twenties—and too fat. I weighed a lot less then than I do now. Norm locked me in the bedroom for three days with nothing but bottled water. I'm lucky I was his meal ticket. He had to let me out because he needed me to work. That was the day I left him. He went with me to a shoot. When I spotted him flirting with some young girl, I took the opportunity to run like crazy. I'll never forget the panic when I was waiting for the elevator. I thought he would walk out and nab me any second."

"That's awful!"

"All those feelings came right back. We saw him standing outside of Randolph Hall while Savannah was there with me. Ian had gone out for a run with the dog, so it was just Savannah and me, cowering inside the house. Well, I was cowering. Savannah seemed a lot braver than me."

"Did you confront him?"

"No! It wasn't too long before Ian returned and that coward, Norm, gave up on lurking in a hurry. Will you listen to me? The man is dead and gone, and I'm still talking about him."

"I guess you always will. He put you through terrible times."

"And stole all the money I made."

"But surely you recovered some of your money in the divorce."

"Not one penny. He had spent every last dime and tried to convince the judge that I should pay back the money he borrowed and conned from other people. It was a hot mess."

"But you still felt sad when he died."

"You know, I'm beginning to think it was more shock than sadness. I really hated him. That relationship has haunted me since the day I left him. And now that he's gone, it's as though someone opened a window and let in fresh air and sunshine. This will sound corny, but I feel like someone finally lifted a burden off my soul."

I held the door open for her at Hair of the Dog. Trixie scampered inside, followed by Blanche, and I had one of the weirdest experiences of my life.

Everyone, every single eyeball in that pub, turned to stare at us. The chatter stopped. People whispered and pointed. I'd never been through anything quite like it.

Blanche acted as though it was perfectly normal. I guessed it was for her.

Val hurried toward us. "Ms. Wimmer, er, Tredwell! What a pleasure."

"Thank you."

I introduced her to Val, who promptly asked if she could take a picture for the wall of the pub.

Blanche was gracious and funny. She didn't seem to mind the swarm of people who formed to meet her and have their pub napkins signed.

"We should have a Blanche Wimmer dish," said Val. "What's your favorite sandwich or pub food?"

Blanche thought for a moment. "How about a good old-fashioned American hamburger, Blanche-style? Can I come back there and show you? I'll need some onions . . ."

Val hustled her to the grill.

Blanche shed her jacket and gloves and, with the ease of a TV chef, set about explaining how to make her favorite burger.

Val whispered, "I'm taking the camera in the back to print out the picture so she can sign it."

Blanche performed in front of a rapt audience, so I followed Val.

While she focused on printing out the photo, I wandered around her back office. I had never been in there before. We usually talked in the bar area, or met at a restaurant or the inn.

She had decorated the walls with framed diplomas and family photos. I recognized her as a child in one of the pictures. She posed with her arm around a taller blonde girl about her age. "You have a huge family!"

"That was my grandparents' anniversary. All the aunts and uncles and cousins came."

I smiled at a mock-up photo where Val and the blonde girl pretended to be mermaids. Their young faces had been inserted into voluptuous mermaid bodies. "Is this your sister?"

"That was a vacation in Florida with my cousin, Juliana, and her folks. She and I were like sisters. We did everything together. I miss her so much."

My heart skipped a beat. Juliana?

I tried to sound casual but red warning flags were jumping up in my head. "The same Juliana who was married to Norm? Why didn't you tell me?"

The printer whirred and a picture emerged. Val didn't look at me or respond.

"Val, did you intentionally base the Murder Most Howl clues on Norm?" I blurted it out, not at all the way I had meant to approach the subject.

She focused on the picture in her hands. "I don't know what you mean."

I walked over to her. "I think you do. Why would you have done that?"

Val sighed. "It's harder than you'd think to write one hundred clues. I kept writing evil things the baron had done, and before I knew it, he sounded a lot like Norm. I figured I'd go with it. I mean, if you have to avoid everything anyone has ever done, then you'd never have any clues."

She sounded breezy, as if it were no big deal. "You didn't think you were hitting a little too close to home?"

"There were plenty of clues that didn't apply to him at all. The baron had a ton of children. As far as I know, Norm didn't even have one."

That was probably true. But I was seeing a side of Val that was making me uncomfortable. Would I feel that way if Norm hadn't died? Surely Val's clues hadn't triggered his death. I tested her. "Or maybe you wanted to aggravate him?"

"What's the big deal, Holly? You're making it sound like I did something despicable. So I yanked his chain with a few of those clues. It doesn't matter anymore now anyway. It's not like he's going to complain about it."

Maybe not. Then why did it bother me so much?

She'd never answered whether her cousin was the same Juliana. "So you were related to Norm."

"Bite your tongue! Only by marriage and that was an appalling choice on Juliana's part. I don't know what she was thinking."

A cheer went up out in the bar. The two of us hurried back in time to see Blanche mugging for cameras and joining people in selfies. She was a good sport.

Blanche signed the picture, and we were on our way back to the inn. While we walked, I worked up the nerve to ask her an important question where she might have special insight. We were almost back at the inn by the time I was brave enough to utter the words. "Who would have wanted to murder Norm?"

Blanche chuckled wryly. "Besides me, you mean? Let's see. His wives, the people who love them, the people who made the mistake of investing their money in his schemes, the people he took advantage of. There was a long line of people who would have liked to do him in, Holly. I might have been at the front of the line, but somebody else did the dirty work for me."

I froze at her words. Surely she didn't mean that literally? Ian? Ian and Geof?

The front door of the inn opened.

Ella Mae, dressed in a fuzzy white coat, raced toward us, followed closely by Charlotte. "There you are! We couldn't find you anywhere. The boys are hungry again. Are you ready for dinner?"

Blanche turned toward me and gave me a hug. "Thank you for listening to me ramble. It was . . . cathartic for me."

She wrapped an arm around Charlotte's waist as they walked away, and I heard her say, "Isn't it peculiar that spilling your guts to a stranger can feel more cleansing than telling people you know?"

Charlotte responded, "That's because the people who know you already know your problems and don't listen anymore."

I wondered if that was true.

The inn was quiet. It was the time of day when most people were out to dinner or getting dressed to go. I wondered where Aunt Birdie, Ben, and Holmes had disappeared to. Had they decided to take naps? I wouldn't have minded a snooze.

Trixie knew exactly where they were. She dashed over to the door of Oma's private kitchen and through the pet door.

I followed her, except I opened the big door. Sure enough, everyone had gathered there. Twinkletoes sat on the hearth, glaring at Ben, for whom she had no fondness. The feeling was mutual on Ben's part. He didn't grow up with animals and had never felt the bond of love with a cat or a dog.

Aunt Birdie nursed a large glass of wine, supervising Mr. Huckle as he warmed something on the stove. From the annoyed look on his face, and her comments, I gathered she was instructing him on how to do it correctly.

Holmes seemed thoroughly at home, relaxing in a big chair with his feet up on the hearth and Gingersnap by his side.

Altogether a charming scene. It wasn't just the warm kitchen and the heavenly scent of dinner on the stove, but the togetherness of people who cared about one another.

"Wine, Holly?" asked Holmes.

I declined. I had no reason to imagine anything else would

go wrong, but between the business with Shadow and the news that Juliana had been Val's cousin, I felt the need to be alert.

"A good bracing cup of tea, Miss Holly?" asked Mr. Huckle.

He wasn't British. I smiled at his firm faith that a cup of tea would make the world right again. "Thanks. I'll put the kettle on. What are you cooking? It smells delicious."

"Beer-braised pork chops. I hope you'll enjoy them."

Behind his back, Aunt Birdie waved her hand doubtfully. "There are entirely too many onions in it."

"Perhaps you should taste it before you opine, Miss Birdie."

Their banter was silly but it soothed my rattled nerves. There, in the warmth of Oma's kitchen, the rest of the world seemed to melt away.

"Onions? Do we have something for the dogs?"

Ben showed me a pot. "It's called Rodeo Roundup. I thought it was for people. It's not bad."

"You tried it?" He was eating dog food?

"A little bland, but all it needs is a dash of salt."

I peered into the pot. Ground beef, kidney beans, corn, and brown rice. I'd had worse.

Holmes groaned and stretched. "We had quite an interesting conversation in your absence."

I poured boiling water over a tea bag. "Oh? What about?"

"Norm!" they all chimed together, ruining my fantasy that the rest of the world had disappeared.

Mr. Huckle announced that dinner was ready.

"Sit next to me," said Holmes, pointing to a chair.

Aunt Birdie nudged me with her elbow.

She needn't have worried. Holmes flicked out a notepad and sat down. "We've made a list of all the people who might have wanted to kill him."

"Our number one suspect is Blanche." Ben spooned sauce over his pork chop. "Lillian saw him enter Randolph Hall. And we know he was terrible to her, taking her money and causing her to have to live in her car."

I nodded my head and helped myself to salad. It was worse than they knew. Still, I liked Blanche. She'd been through the wringer with him. "Poor Blanche. I hope she didn't kill him. Who else?"

"Don't forget Blanche's current husband and his brother." Holmes made a notation on the pad. "They might have killed him to protect her. Or out of love for her."

"You won't like this, Miss Holly, but I'm afraid we must consider your friend, Miss Val. Her behavior has been so odd. How could she know all those things about Norm?"

I looked at Mr. Huckle. "She was related to him. His second wife, Juliana, was her cousin."

Forks clanked to plates.

"Well, that moves Val to number one on the suspect list." Aunt Birdie drank from her wine glass.

"To tell the truth, it sounded more like she was being lazy. After all, as Ben said, he made a great victim. He had done so many terrible things to people. It was easy for her to make up clues based on him."

Ben shot me a pleased smile. "Aunt Birdie, why would that make Val the number one suspect? If anything, she would have wanted to murder Shadow for killing Juliana, not Norm."

"Shadow." Holmes cut into his pork chop. "I don't know what to think about him. I feel like he's telling the truth when he insists that he didn't poison Juliana. Holly, did he give you the impression that he blames Norm for anything?"

"No. Norm lost his wife. He was the hapless victim of that sad saga."

"How about Shadow's dad, Hollis?" Aunt Birdie was gobbling up the pork chop and sauce that contained too many onions. "I was there when Shadow said his father had to quit blaming Norm for everything that went wrong for Shadow."

"It was clear that he blames Norm for something. Mr. Huckle, this is so good I want to lick the pan," said Ben.

Mr. Huckle offered him another chop and spooned more of the sauce over top of it.

Aunt Birdie placed her knife and fork on her plate and sat up straight. "I might be able to shed some light on this. I'm told that Shadow's legal fees cost his parents a great deal of money. And then to add insult to injury, Norm sued everyone involved. Of course, that didn't extend to Shadow's parents, but it meant more legal fees for a civil trial."

Ben ate like he'd never seen food before. Maybe he was living off cereal and milk now that I wasn't around. He swallowed a bite. "Ah yes. When all else fails, blame the lawyers."

"C'mon, Ben. You can see how Hollis would have been resentful." Holmes speared a carrot slice in his salad. "Holly, who do you think it was?"

"I don't know. I feel like we're missing something. All we know for sure is that the night he was killed, Norm left here and Lillian followed him. She saw him hanging around outside of Randolph Hall, then she saw him go inside."

"And that's where the trail ends until he showed up on the bench, frozen. I'd say that's fairly incriminating. Wouldn't you?" Holmes gazed at me hopefully.

"Who does that incriminate? Blanche? Her husband? I know that killers don't wear horns on their heads and carry pitchforks, but I like Blanche. I haven't talked to Ian much, but Char and Geof seem like nice people. I'm having trouble imagining that they would have come here planning to kill him."

"It's worth noting," said Ben, "that unless the killer is diabetic and had to have insulin on hand, the killer planned this in advance. Who would Norm have been willing to meet at a park bench in the middle of a blizzard?"

"Blanche or any young blonde." The words slipped out of my mouth.

"Is there a mistress after all?" asked Aunt Birdie. "Someone he promised to marry perhaps?"

"Why would he stray when he can go home to Savannah?" Holmes sipped his wine.

"Excuse me," protested Aunt Birdie. "There's a lot to be

said for women his age . . . and older. Maybe he got tired of young things who fill their heads with frivolity."

We all stared at Aunt Birdie.

"It's possible."

I could see the men at the table were doubtful about that. And to be honest, so was I.

Gingersnap sat down next to me and pawed at me. "Are you still hungry?"

She whined. Not at all like Gingersnap.

"What's wrong, sweetie?" She ran to the door, but instead of going through the doggy door, she looked back at me expectantly. It was my rule to make sure the dogs went out to do their business before they ate. But I'd forgotten about Gingersnap. "Did anyone take Gingersnap out?"

Somewhat sheepishly, they all shook their heads.

"We'll be right back." I rose from my seat, grabbed my jacket, and followed Gingersnap through the inn to the sliding glass doors in the reception lobby. Trixie trotted along for fun.

Once outside, Trixie bounded off somewhere, but Gingersnap headed for the doggy potty. Snowflakes floated gently from the sky. The peaceful stillness of snow surrounded us. I strolled in the direction of The Blue Boar, enjoying the wintery moment.

"Shadow," sang a female voice. "Shaaadow."

I looked around but couldn't see her. Ground-mounted lights brightened the walkway but not much more.

"*Shh.* You're not supposed to be here." I recognized Shadow's voice. "You're going to get me in trouble."

"I miss you." Sweet, sincere.

"Baby, we talked about this. We can't be seen together for a while."

"I know. But it's been so awful. I need you."

Silence followed.

And then Gingersnap, the dog who loved everyone and never made a fuss, growled. It was a gentle growl that meant

*I want your attention right now.* I knew what was coming. Yup. The plaintive barks. Not mean, not vicious. They were insistent little pleas. Shadow wasn't paying attention to her.

Trixie returned to me and brought along a corgi wearing a quilted winter jacket. He looked an awful lot like Bingo.

I heard rustling through the bushes and fully expected to see Gingersnap but a person crashed through them.

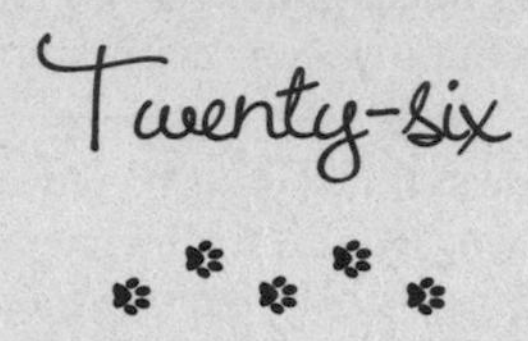


Flailing her arms, she staggered backward right at me.

Just as she keeled over, I reached out and stopped her from falling.

She screamed, and someone else rammed through the bushes, calling, "Savannah? Savannah, are you okay?"

She yanked away and turned to look at me. "Oh, it's you."

I was face-to-face with Norm's widow, Savannah.

She finger-combed her hair. "It's all right, Shadow. It's just Holly."

He emerged from the bushes, followed by Gingersnap. Even in the dark, I could make out the pain on Shadow's face when he saw me.

"It's a beautiful night for a walk," I said.

"I just started spreading the ice melt," Shadow responded. "Savannah, weren't you on your way to pick up takeout from The Blue Bear?"

"I was! Bingo and I are starving."

Right. Like she didn't have a fridge full of food that

people had dropped off? "I'd better get back. I was just letting the dogs out for a bit." I called Trixie and Gingersnap, and headed toward the inn.

Savannah giggled, and I heard Shadow say, "I love you crazy bad, Savannah, but if you're not careful, the only place we'll see each other is at the county jail when you come to visit."

I knew from the moment Savannah stumbled into my arms, but Shadow's words confirmed the worst. I was crushed. Shadow was in love with Savannah.

I'd had such hopes for him. I had wanted to believe him. Now bits and pieces fell into place. He had probably taken the necklace intending to give it to Savannah. And worse, might have killed Norm so they could be together.

I shed my jacket and dragged back to Oma's kitchen.

"What happened to you?" asked Holmes.

"You're pale as a ghost." Aunt Birdie dashed over to feel my forehead. "Are you sick?"

Mr. Huckle hurried to the stove and put the water kettle on.

I collapsed into my chair at the table and heaved a great sigh. "Shadow may have murdered Norm."

They stared at me in silence and then they all spoke at once.

I raised my hands to shush them. "Shadow is in love with Savannah and the feeling is apparently mutual."

"Maybe Savannah killed Norm," suggested Ben.

"Nonsense," scoffed Aunt Birdie. "She could have just divorced him."

"Just because they're in love doesn't mean either of them murdered Norm." Holmes frowned at me. "It's a powerful motive, though. I'll add Savannah to our list."

I heaved a great sigh. "Shadow said they couldn't see each other or the only place she would see him was at the county jail when she came to visit."

"My word!" Mr. Huckle sat down quickly as though he'd lost all his strength.

I thought it was noble of him not to point out that I shouldn't have hired Shadow. This would teach me not to listen to his advice. "You knew all along about Shadow's criminal record. Why didn't you just tell me?"

Mr. Huckle appeared surprised. "To be honest, I thought it a most unfortunate accident. I have always been fond of young Shadow. I just felt that your grandmother would *not* be pleased to come home and discover a new employee."

Ben narrowed his eyes. "You went out to the dog bathroom and you came back with this revelation?"

"They're out there necking in the dark, Ben. I overheard their conversation. Don't you see? It all fits together. Shadow took the shamrock necklace to give to Savannah. And I bet the footsteps in the snow that I saw in Savannah and Norm's backyard were Shadow's. He was probably there when people started dropping by with food."

Holmes headed for the door.

"Where are you going?" I asked.

"To bring them in here and find out what's going on."

Clearly appalled, Ben jumped up and shouted, "No! Have you lost your mind? You want to bring a killer in here and question him?"

"What do you think he's going to do, Ben? There are five of us."

I glanced at Aunt Birdie and Mr. Huckle. I didn't imagine they would be much help if Shadow was aggressive. "I'll call Dave. Maybe it's better not to alert Shadow. He might try to make a run for it."

"No one can get off this mountain, Holly. But I'm all for calling the law. A much better idea." Ben took his seat again.

Holmes reluctantly returned to the table. "Okay, maybe you're right. Shadow could make his way down the mountain."

"How?" Ben seemed dumbfounded.

"Toboggan. Four-wheeler. Snowmobile. Skis. He grew up here like I did. He might have to steal some of those things to get away, but he'd know how."

I stood up and trudged to the wall phone but only got Dave's voice mail.

There was a knock on the door.

I was in the middle of leaving a message when Dave leaned his head in. His cheeks were rosy from being out in the cold. "I thought I might find you here."

"Officer Dave, what a pleasure. Would you care for a bite of dinner?" Mr. Huckle retrieved his jacket and laid it on top of mine.

"No, thanks. I grabbed a Blanche Burger over at Hair of the Dog."

"Perhaps I could interest you in dessert? Cook has left us gingerbread cupcakes with chocolate frosting." Mr. Huckle pulled a serving tray from a back corner of the kitchen and brought it to the table.

"Now that is irresistible. Got any coffee?"

"Coming right up."

I scrambled to my feet. "Ben, clear the table, will you? Mr. Huckle, I'll make the coffee. You've been working all day long."

"Why, Miss Holly, this isn't work. It's family."

That sentence almost broke my heart. We were probably all the family he had. At least in Wagtail. I gave him a hug on my way to the stove.

Meanwhile, Holmes was filling in Dave about Shadow.

Dave listened carefully but didn't seem surprised.

"You knew," I said. "You've known since the day we saw the footprints in the snow behind Norm and Savannah's house."

"Let's say I've had them on my radar."

"But you haven't arrested them," Aunt Birdie mused.

I poured tea and coffee for everyone, and brought cream and sugar to the table.

"No evidence." Ben slumped a little in his chair. "All I have is a motive. No murder weapon. No witnesses. No confession."

"It breaks my heart to think that sweet child could have

murdered Norm." Aunt Birdie sipped her tea. "The things people do for love. They should have just waited. Someone else would have knocked off Norm sooner or later."

"It's possible that someone else did. Birdie's right," said Dave. "A lot of folks in this town had reason to be angry with Norm."

"But I heard Savannah's conversation with someone saying she couldn't wait. That she was going to do it this weekend."

Dave nodded. "You want her convicted of murder on the strength of that?"

"She might have been talking about getting her hair cut," said Ben.

Somehow, I didn't think so, but I could understand their point. "You may never solve Norm's murder then. If he died because someone gave him an insulin injection, the murder weapon will be impossible to find. Syringes are tiny. It could be hidden anywhere."

Officer Dave bit into a gingerbread cupcake. "Mmm, these are good. Don't worry about not finding the syringe. There is no perfect murder. Something always goes wrong."

The bell in the front lobby rang again. I excused myself and stepped out to see who needed help.

Weegie and Puddin' were waiting for me. Weegie gazed around before whispering, "I think I solved the mystery."

"Really? Who?"

She pulled her head back and looked at me with suspicion. "I thought I was supposed to tell Val."

"Oh, that mystery." In all the commotion about Norm, I had momentarily forgotten about the Baron von Rottweiler. "Good for you! Yes, you're quite right. You need to tell Val."

"Where can I find her?"

"At Hair of the Dog." I pulled a map of Wagtail out of the desk and drew a circle around the location of the pub.

"I'm on my way."

"Alone?"

"That man was murdered but I assumed that was a fluke or a local thing. Are you saying it's not safe?"

"It's perfectly safe. I was just surprised that you don't have an entourage. You're usually with some of your book club friends."

"I'm not telling them! No way. If Myrtle finds out that I have the solution, it won't be safe for me!" She laughed hysterically. "C'mon, Puddin'. We might win!"

I walked out on the porch with them. A frigid wind blew, the kind that made your fingers feel half-frozen.

Weegie wrapped a scarf around the bottom of her face and took off at a brisk pace.

I hurried back inside. Since Mr. Huckle had been kind enough to cook dinner, I insisted that he put his feet up by the fire and enjoy an after-dinner drink.

Holmes jumped to his feet. "I know just the thing."

"No coffee, please, Holmes, or I won't be able to sleep."

Holmes busied himself with butterscotch schnapps. Meanwhile, I rinsed the dishes and stacked them in the dishwasher.

"Is it usually so calm around here at night?" asked Aunt Birdie. "I always imagined that it would be intolerably noisy."

"It depends on the guests. Most of the rowdy ones hang out at Hair of the Dog," I explained. "It will probably pick up when the book club ladies come back from dinner. They were a hoot the other night."

"Really?" Aunt Birdie shook her head. "I would have expected them to be sedate and retire to their beds with books."

"Not these women!"

"They're just kicking up their heels a bit to be away from home. One does that on vacation." Mr. Huckle accepted a drink from Holmes. "It's good for the soul to let loose once in a while."

That was funny coming from him! I had never seen him act the slightest bit loose or improper.

Dave scrambled to his feet. "I'd better get out there and make sure everyone is behaving. Thanks for dessert."

I walked to the front door with him. "Feel free to stop back by here if you need to warm up."

I hustled to the reception lobby to lock up the office and found Shadow sitting on the love seat in his stockinged feet. "Hi. Is everything okay?"

"Nothin' is okay."

# Twenty-seven

Shadow sounded like he was carrying the weight of the world. He slumped forward and appeared miserable. "I've been sittin' here trying' to get up the nerve to talk to you. You were so nice to hire me, but I think we didn't get off to a good start."

I pulled up a chair and sat opposite him. Twinkletoes bounded onto the love seat and reached her paw out to him. He turned his head toward her and ran his hand over her back.

"I wanted to explain about Vana—"

"Vana?"

"Savannah. I don't want you thinking poorly of her. We, uh, we've been in love since high school. Her mom and dad had bigger plans for her, though. A few years back, her dad took me aside and told me to leave her alone. That I didn't have any prospects, and a girl like Vana could do better'n me."

I winced just hearing him talk about it. "That must have hurt."

"Yeah. Well, I've got two eyes. I knew Vana was special. They didn't want me around. And then the whole thing with

The Doggy Bag happened and all they could do was tell her 'we told you so' and 'we knew he was no good.' I about died the day she got married to Norm. Something inside me broke."

He finally looked up at me. "I'm not a fancy guy. I only wanted a few things in my life. Vana and some kids running around. Lost that. A job. Nobody wanted to hire me after the problem at The Doggy Bag." He smiled at Trixie, who watched him intently like she was listening. "And a dog. I was afraid I might have to move to the city, so I didn't get a dog either."

"You have a wonderful cabin."

"When you're unemployed, and your girlfriend is married to somebody else, hammering is a real good way to vent."

I smiled. "And you didn't lose your sense of humor."

"On Friday morning, Vana said she was going to leave Norm. She was finally going to do it. I thought things were looking up. Then you hired me, and I thought my streak of bad luck had ended. I volunteer at the shelter. There's a dog there that I'd like to adopt. I thought I finally could. And now it's as if God is playing a bad joke on me. It all came crashing down. Vana doesn't really get it. She doesn't see how bad this looks for us. Officer Dave has already been by to question both of us. It won't be long before he comes to arrest me. I wanted you to know."

He was doing his best not to cry, and so was I. Now all I wanted was for him to work for the inn, marry his beloved Vana, get a dog, and have a baby. Didn't seem like too much to ask out of life. This sweet fellow surely couldn't have killed Norm. If only he had an alibi. "I guess you were home alone the night Norm was killed?"

He turned guilty eyes up to meet mine.

I didn't know what that meant. "What's wrong?"

"I wasn't alone."

It all clicked into place. Savannah must have stayed the night with him. "It was Bingo who lost his dog bone under your sofa?"

"Norm scared Vana. She went to see Blanche. I guess Norm must have followed her because he hung around outside waiting for her to leave. She called me, and I told her to go to my place. It was a pretty bad night what with the blizzard. Every time the wind banged a branch against the cabin, we thought it was Norm coming for her. But he never showed up. Of course, we knew why the next morning."

It was possibly the lousiest alibi in the history of man. Savannah could have killed Norm, and then gone to Shadow's place. Or they could have murdered Norm together. Or Shadow could have done the dirty deed to protect Savannah. It was no help to either of them at all. There was one constant, though. Blanche had said that Norm watched them from outside of Randolph Hall. Savannah had a reason to be fearful. Blanche had told her to run from Norm. Maybe she had. Right into Shadow's waiting arms.

"Why do you think they'll arrest you?"

"'Cause of my history. They'll think if I killed once, I'll do it again."

"Who do you think murdered Norm?"

Shadow shook his head. "I wish I knew. My dad says Norm did so many people wrong that they were lined up for a chance to do him in."

"Did your dad ever try to kill him?"

Shadow grinned. "If my dad had ever tried, Norm woulda been dead."

A chill ran down my spine. In a weird way, he was bragging about his dad, but it made me wonder if his dad had finally accomplished it. "Hey, Shadow, is your dad diabetic?"

"How'd you know that?"

"Just a hunch." A very terrible hunch. "Why did your dad hate him so much?"

"Norm ruined my life. It's because of Norm that I have so many problems. He thinks Norm murdered Juliana and pinned it on me. Only nobody was ever able ever prove it. He came by to get Juliana's order after she had already picked it up. Then he went to a local football game that night. Everybody saw him there."

"Is that what you think happened?"

"All I know is that I'm not stupid enough to put laundry detergent into food. I shoulda moved out of town like my dad told me to do. Then I wouldn't be in this mess. But this is my home. Everyone I care about is here. I couldn't leave Vana."

He was breaking my heart—like a lost puppy. What was it about this guy that made me want to believe him? I wanted to hug him and tell him everything would be all right. But that would be a lie. Juliana's death would plague him for the rest of his life. And now it looked like things might get worse for him if he or his dad had murdered Norm.

"Don't give up hope yet. Maybe everything will work out." I didn't add, *Now that Norm's gone*, but that's what I was thinking.

Shadow thanked me and trudged back outside. Watching him walk like a broken old man made me sad.

When I returned to the table, Holmes had started a new list, and Mr. Huckle had poured me another cup of tea. It was going to be a long night.

An hour later The Thursday Night Cloak and Dagger Club members began to return. Once again the second floor sounded like a sorority house. I was glad they felt at home.

A few of them trickled downstairs to the Dogwood Room. Ben, Holmes, and I loaded a cart with pitchers of Holmes's fabulous drink, gingerbread cupcakes, and for those who didn't care for sweets, cheese puffs fresh from the oven. We added baskets of dog cookies and dried fish cat treats to the cart as well.

Holmes rolled it into the Dogwood Room, and we set the goodies out for them along with glasses, plates, and Sugar Maple Inn napkins.

Two cat owners brought their kitties with them on leashes. Twinkletoes, who hadn't always been the best cat ambassador by hissing at some of the feline guests, strolled in and took it all in stride. She even chirped at the other cats, which I hoped translated to a feline welcome.

Weegie and Puddin' returned from their walk over to Hair of the Dog. There was a chorus of "Where have you been?" from her friends.

Weegie appeared to relish the attention. "I'll confess. I went over to Hair of the Dog to make my official guess about who killed the Baron von Rottweiler."

I glanced around to see how Myrtle was taking it but she wasn't there. "Did Myrtle go up to bed?"

One of the women said, "No wonder we've been having so much fun!"

"She must have gone out with some of the others," said another. "After dinner, we broke up into groups because some wanted to go out and some of us wanted to come home and get warm."

Sylvie joined them. "Brr. I took a long hot shower. The Blue Boar was so lovely, but this was no night for being out and about in a dress and pantyhose."

I offered her one of Holmes's drinks.

"Just what I need," she said. "I hope we can go home tomorrow. My husband is asking when I'll be back. Apparently he ate the entire casserole of mac and cheese that I left for him."

"Wait a minute, girls," said Weegie. "I just did a nose count and everyone is here except for Myrtle. Who saw her last?"

Before anyone could answer, there was a loud clunk that I recognized and the lights went out.

The members of The Thursday Night Cloak and Dagger Club groaned. Gingersnap ran to my side and leaned against my legs, trembling.

Happily, the fire gave off some light. Enough for me to locate matches and light candles. Of course, the first thought that came to my mind was that Mr. Huckle had pulled the switch again.

I carried a candle to light my way, but when I passed the

front window, I realized that none of the other buildings within sight had lights on, either. Even the streetlamps were out. What a pain.

With the help of Holmes, Ben, and Mr. Huckle, we brought out candles and lanterns again. Aunt Birdie busied herself complaining and telling us the inn would surely burn down and that it would not be her fault because she had told us not to light all those candles and lanterns.

"Would you rather break your ankle?" I asked.

"Everyone should just go to bed."

I figured most people would do exactly that but some of them might find comfort in being with other people. And I did notice that Aunt Birdie migrated to the Dogwood Room, where she poured herself a drink and chatted with the book club members.

Weegie and another member of The Thursday Night Cloak and Dagger Club approached me. "I never thought I would say this considering how annoying Myrtle has been, but we're getting a little bit concerned about her. We've called her room and her cell phone but no one is answering."

"She's probably asleep. Did you try knocking on the door?"

Sylvie ambled up. "Who was the last to see her?"

While they sorted out who went where after dinner, I grabbed two lanterns. Weegie accompanied me upstairs to Myrtle's room. Puddin' and Trixie bounded ahead of us but Gingersnap stayed right beside me.

"I'm sure she's fine." I knocked on the door gently at first. When there was no response, I banged on it as hard as I could. "Myrtle?" I tried one more time before unlocking the door.

I swung it open. "Myrtle, it's Holly." Raising the lantern to illuminate the room, I headed for the bed. It was empty.

# Twenty-eight

The bed was made. It appeared that no one had slept in it since Marisol made it in the morning.

Weegie strolled around the room. "No sign of her purse or phone."

I hoped she hadn't fallen in the bathroom. The lantern illuminated it quite well. She wasn't there either.

"She must not have come back from dinner. Or she returned and went out again." Weegie followed me to the door.

I called the dogs and locked the door. There was no hurrying in the dark. We carefully made our way down the stairs. In the Dogwood Room, I raised my voice a little. "May I have your attention, please?"

The chatter subsided just as the front door opened and a gust of freezing air blew in with Geof, Char, and Robin. Char carried a bundle that she set on the floor and unwrapped. Ella Mae shook her entire body and raced up the stairs, chased by Trixie and Puddin'.

I asked Holmes to give Robin and the Tredwells lanterns, then turned back to the book club ladies.

"Myrtle is not in her room, and we didn't see her purse or cell phone. I'm going to call the police. It would be helpful to know where you last saw her so he'll know where to start looking."

I felt Geof, Char, and Robin move in behind me, their lanterns bringing more light into the room.

"None of us remember seeing her after dinner in the restaurant," said one of them.

I turned to go to the phone.

Geof asked, "What's going on?"

"Myrtle is missing."

"I hope she's not outside." Robin shivered and rubbed her arms. "You could freeze to death on a night like this."

"I'll go out and check between the inn and The Blue Boar," said Holmes. He had already fetched his warm jacket.

"I'll help," said Geof.

When I dialed Dave's number, I noticed that Ben accompanied them and wondered briefly if he even had gloves.

Luckily, Dave answered right away. "On my way. You call Hollis, Shadow, Larry, Max, and anyone else you can think of."

When I hung up, I called Val. "Have you seen Myrtle?"

"The short obnoxious woman? She hasn't been in here all night." I explained briefly and asked her to call Dave if Myrtle showed up at the pub.

Mr. Huckle had donned a heavy winter coat and gloves. Oy! All I needed was for him to slip and fall outside. I passed along Dave's instruction. "Could you make the phone calls and then walk through the inn? We'd better make sure she's not inside somewhere. I'll bundle up and go out with the dogs. Maybe they'll find Myrtle faster than we can."

He was still saying, "Certainly, Miss Holly," when I patted his arm and dashed into the Dogwood Room, where I asked Aunt Birdie to keep the guests supplied with drinks and food. Several of them had already headed upstairs for their coats so they could help search.

I called Trixie and wrapped two coats around her. "Gingersnap?"

Surely Oma must have some kind of coat for Gingersnap for frigid temperatures. I swung by the office on our way out. I flicked the flashlight on items in the closet. On the top shelf, I located a quilted dog coat with a fluffy faux lamb fur lining. Gingersnap wasn't pleased when I fastened it on her. But she raced to the door and waited as if she knew we were on a mission.

We stepped into an eerie night of darkness. Lanterns flickered and voices called, "Myrtle! Myrtle!"

I intended to follow the dogs. They weren't tracking dogs but their noses might lead them to her anyway. I carried the lantern low to see the walkway. Bitterly cold air stung my face. I wrapped my scarf over my nose and mouth.

Trixie and Gingersnap made a beeline to the doggy potty. That wasn't very helpful. When they were done, I walked all the way to The Blue Boar. They sniffed around nearby but didn't show an interest in veering off the walkway.

I didn't know quite where to go. Where would Myrtle have gone by herself? To Hair of the Dog to report her Murder Most Howl findings to Val? I started along the sidewalk. Mr. Huckle had done a good job. I could hear people calling Myrtle's name all around me and well into the distance. Lanterns bobbed along in the green as though they floated by themselves.

Gingersnap and Trixie acted like they usually did. They were just happy to be out for a stroll. Giving up any hope that they would find her, I walked fast. If Myrtle had fallen, I would surely notice her body. *Oh no!* Myrtle had been outraged that she had to stay on Wagtail Mountain an extra night. Surely she wouldn't have tried to ski out? That would be sheer folly unless she was an accomplished skier. It seemed unlikely, though. She would have packed her belongings, wouldn't she? Or would she have relied on other members of

The Thursday Night Cloak and Dagger Club to pack them and bring them home to her?

I heard barking. Insistent barking. Trixie perked up her ears. Where was Gingersnap?

The barking wasn't angry or fearful. It was a high-pitched dog-SOS-style sound.

Trixie turned and ran. I was worried about slipping in the dark but I hurried behind her as fast as I could.

Trixie disappeared from view. Where had she gone? I stopped again and listened.

Gingersnap still yelped. To my right, I thought. I turned down the next street. I could still hear Gingersnap. But where were they?

I walked at a fast clip, swiveling from side to side with my lantern so I wouldn't walk by them. I reached the end of the block and realized that the barking was now coming from behind me. And then it stopped. The silence was alarming. Had something happened to Gingersnap?

Hurrying back, I spotted her. She ran into the street, did a U-turn, and dodged back behind a house.

I followed her to a black stair railing that I assumed led to a basement. In the moonless night, I couldn't make out anything. I squatted and held out my lantern, lowering it as far as I could. Trixie's white face and body glimmered faintly at the bottom. On my end, all I could make out were the soles of a pair of boots.

# Twenty-nine

I sat down and lowered myself one step on the icy concrete stairs. It was definitely a body. It lay facedown, so I couldn't make out who it was. But it was a good bet it was our missing Myrtle. My heart pounding, I eased back up to the top, my gloves slipping on the slick railing.

I pulled my cell phone out of a pocket. Wagtail was known for dead spots and poor cell phone connections. I hoped I would be able to make a connection. I almost cheered when I heard the sound that meant Dave's phone was ringing.

"Did you find her?" he was breathless.

"I think so."

"Where?"

I held up my lantern. "The side yard of a little white house on Redbud."

"Is she okay?"

"I don't know. I think we need an ambulance."

The line went dead. What would happen if she needed medical care? I wondered if I should wait in the street to guide him, or if I should see if I could help Myrtle. The latter won.

If she was alive, helping or comforting her was the least I could do.

I returned to the stairs and sat down on the top one as I had before. I lowered my feet, then my bottom one step at a time. I sat next to her boots. Then by her side. It seemed an eternity passed before I was firmly on the bottom. Trixie was licking Myrtle's face.

"Myrtle?" No response. "Myrtle?" I said louder.

She didn't move. I slid off my glove and touched her shoulder. "Can you hear me?" I shouted.

She still didn't move.

She wore gloves but no hat. The wind whistled above us.

I took off my hat and slid it onto her head. I knew better than to turn her over. If she had broken her neck or back in the fall, moving her could result in paralysis. If she was alive at all.

Relief flooded through me when I heard Dave's voice yelling my name. "Back here!"

The strong beam of a flashlight blinded me briefly. I raised my hand to shield my eyes.

Dave took care coming down the steps. "The ski patrol from Snowball is coming."

"How?"

"Snowmobile." He said it as though it happened every day.

"Do you think she's alive?"

"Can't tell. All we can do at this point is wait. They'll have to stabilize her on a stretcher before they can pull her out of here." He flicked the beam of the flashlight at the steps and upward.

"Whose house is this? What would she have been doing here?"

"It's a summer home. The owners live in Florida during the winter."

He hadn't answered my second question. I figured he couldn't know what Myrtle had been up to either.

"Treacherous," was all he said.

I followed the light. It was evident even to my untrained

eyes that she had fallen from the top and slid down the snowy stairs. "The displaced snow along her right side is from me, trying to get down here without slipping."

I heard him sigh.

"Wait, I thought I saw something. Go back."

Dave retraced the route the light had taken.

"There! What is that?"

Hidden halfway under Myrtle, something gleamed in the light. Dave pulled it out.

"The gun from Murder Most Howl!" I felt slightly sick. "What kind of demented person would go around killing people and leaving the fake murder weapons near their bodies?"

"Let's hope she's not dead." Dave walked up the steps. The beam of the flashlight danced along the snow. Gingersnap accompanied him. "You and your dogs made a fine mess of the tracks but I think someone else was with her."

From the clicking sound I heard, I guessed he was trying to take some photos. I didn't think he would have much success.

It wasn't a moment too soon, though. People began to cluster at the top of the stairs. Holmes made his way down to me.

"Is she alive?"

"Don't know."

An emergency medical technician pushed his way through and joined us at the bottom of the stairs. "Did you move her?"

"No."

"Good. Thanks. Hop on out of here so we can work, okay?"

I climbed up the way I came down, backward on my bottom, one step at a time. Trixie had no such problems. With her four-paw drive, she raced past me. Holmes walked up like a normal human, putting me to shame for being overly careful.

I waited with Ben and Holmes while the rescue squad fastened Myrtle to a board and flipped her. Shivering in the cold, I realized that my fingers were going slightly numb. We had to get the dogs back. They didn't have shoes to keep their paws warm.

The EMTs brought her up out of the stairwell. "We have a heartbeat. Faint, but it's there."

With that good news, I asked Dave to keep me posted and hurried back to the inn as fast as I dared to go. Ben and Holmes remained behind.

Gingersnap limped up the stairs to the inn, which worried me. As soon as we walked through the door, I dropped to my knees and reached for a front paw to massage it. I scooted the lantern closer. No wonder she was limping. Hard balls of ice were stuck to the fur between her toes.

I helped her remove them, leaving a watery mess on the floor. I needn't have worried, though. Just like magic, Mr. Huckle appeared with a mop.

With both dogs walking normally, I shed my jacket and hurried to the fireplace to warm up.

"We heard they found her?" asked Char. She sat with Robin and members of The Thursday Night Cloak and Dagger Club. Ella Mae pranced around from person to person.

Even in the firelight I could see the worry on their faces.

"Gingersnap did. Myrtle is still alive."

"Woohoo!" Cries of joy resounded through the Dogwood Room. "Where is she?" They gazed around as if they expected Myrtle to walk in at any moment.

"They're taking her to the hospital. I don't know much about her condition. She fell down concrete stairs, facedown. I think she was unconscious. At least, she didn't respond to me." I could see their initial excitement waning. "I don't want to upset you, but it didn't look good."

Holmes, Ben, and Geof joined us, along with other members of the book club who had been out searching. I moved away from the fire to give them a chance to warm up.

Mr. Huckle and Aunt Birdie had been busy in the kitchen. Mr. Huckle rolled in a cart with hot chocolate and homemade pizza, fresh from the oven. They didn't really go together but anything warm and comforting was welcome.

Those who had been outdoors pounced on the hot food. Geof offered Char a slice but she declined.

"Is this dog pizza?" I asked, just to be sure before giving some to Gingersnap and Trixie.

Mr. Huckle nodded. "Indeed. Cook had it clearly marked in the freezer."

I checked it out. It looked like thin pizza dough, sprinkled with hamburger and cheese.

Ben picked up a slice. "This looks more my style. Can people eat it?"

Mr. Huckle assured him that it was perfectly safe for human consumption but he might find it a little bit bland.

After Ben had eaten half of a piece, I couldn't help teasing him. "Aren't you worried that you might get the urge to bark?"

"I don't understand this," said Weegie. "One minute Myrtle was driving us batty at dinner and the next moment, she disappeared."

Another member said, "I guess we were so eager to get away from her that none of us noticed. I feel terrible. We should have been better friends."

"What was she doing at dinner?" I bit into another piece of mushroom and olive white pizza.

"She was always complaining about something. Anyone remember?"

"I think her wineglass wasn't clean enough."

"She thought the prices were too high and the menu too exotic—" the speaker looked toward Geof and Char "—I'm sorry, but she also groused about you and your brother, claiming the game was stacked for you to win."

Geof sputtered, "That's just not true. I know she's your friend but—"

Char deftly slid her hand onto his knee and squeezed. He stopped midsentence.

One of the club members spoke softly. "She said something

about that man who died. Not the baron, the real man. I just humored her. I wish I had paid attention."

I wished she had, too. I couldn't imagine what would have possessed her to go to that house.

The front door burst open, and Dave walked in. He left his boots and outerwear at the door and strode to the fire. He must have been freezing.

"Do any of you have next of kin information on Myrtle?" he asked.

A couple of them gasped.

"Doesn't mean anything. We just need to notify her family, that's all."

The members gazed at each other.

"She's divorced."

"Her children live in China."

"That's not Myrtle, that's Sylvie."

"Does Myrtle have children?"

"Doesn't she have a sister?"

"Yes. And a nephew whom she dislikes."

"I think she might not get along with the sister, either."

Suddenly, I was sad for Myrtle. Had she alienated everyone?

Dave raised his eyebrows at me. I knew just what he meant. It should be a lesson to us all.

The tragic conversation continued, naming people with whom Myrtle no longer spoke. A scream brought it to an abrupt halt.

# Thirty

Sylvie screamed a second time and jumped toward me.

"What is it?"

The light from the fire wasn't the best but I couldn't see anything wrong.

Dave flicked on his flashlight. The beam landed like a spotlight on a mouse. A tiny little nervous mouse sat next to a pair of shoes. And right beside the mouse was none other than Leo, once again looking thoroughly perplexed about the commotion.

"It's that cat again! With another mouse!" Sylvie backed toward the fire and climbed on a chair. "It ran over my foot! Why do you have mice in this inn? It's revolting. You really need an exterminator. Where is it? Where is it?"

I didn't bother explaining that Leo had probably brought the mouse inside. Who knew where he was getting them? Leo's fascination with Sylvie was a mystery to me as well. But I knew what was going to happen if I didn't catch the mouse very, very fast. I looked around for something to throw over it, like a bowl or a box.

It was too late.

Twinkletoes saw the mouse. She pounced. The mouse ran. Twinkletoes leaped after him. The two cats on leashes bounded after her. Ella Mae couldn't resist the chase, and in two seconds, Puddin', Trixie, and Gingersnap were in on the fun. Like a ridiculous conga line, they raced through the inn. I didn't think it would end well for the poor little mouse.

Oddly enough, Leo stayed behind. When I helped Sylvie off the chair, Leo rubbed his face against her legs. "I think there's something wrong with this cat. What's he doing now? Is he going to bite me?"

"Sylvie, you dope," said Weegie. "He's being affectionate. That's what cats do."

"The only other cat I have known did the same awful thing to me. Do I look hungry? Do I appear to need a mouse?"

That cracked her friends up. I was glad to see a little release of tension.

Dave motioned for me to follow him to the door. He jammed his feet into his boots and grabbed his jacket. "That Myrtle must be a real class act. Sounds like she doesn't like anything or anyone. I didn't want to say this in front of her friends but you need to know."

# Thirty-one

"Someone must have slammed Myrtle in the back of the head with a board or something. There's blood in her hair. It was hard to see in the dark. I don't know why it's not on her hat."

"That was my hat. I was trying to keep her warm. Do you think the blow to the head knocked her out? That would explain why she couldn't get up after she fell."

"I'd say that's a pretty good guess."

"Dave, she was trying to solve Norm's murder."

His head swiveled toward me. "That opens up all kinds of new possibilities, doesn't it? I figured one of her friends did it since no one in town really knew her. But that changes everything. Listen, if anything the slightest bit weird happens here tonight, I want you to call me. Anything. Got it?"

I hoped everyone would go to bed and sleep.

By the time I returned to the Dogwood Room, it had nearly emptied out. I could hear book club members swapping books to read upstairs, and Char calling Emma Mae.

I wondered what had happened to the poor little mouse and cringed at the thought.

The two cats on leashes had been caught and were being marched back to their rooms in the cat wing of the inn.

I sent Mr. Huckle and Aunt Birdie up to bed and put Ben and Holmes to work helping me tidy up by the light of three lanterns.

We were in Oma's kitchen when Ben said, "I keep thinking you must have a dreary little life here. No Starbucks. No museums. No Apple store. But every time I come up here, there's something wild going on."

"Trust me, Ben. There's not a murder every weekend."

"I don't mean the murders. I felt sorry for you when you moved here but it's pretty cool. It's not nearly as boring as I expected, that's all."

"Is that why you came to visit?"

He shrugged. "DC isn't the same without you, Holly. Hey, we should text more!"

I didn't know whether to laugh or to cry. Same old Ben. Maybe it was good that some things never changed and there was consistency in the world. In a way, it made me more comfortable having him around. I had made up my mind about Ben when I broke off our relationship. If he wanted to be friends, that was fine with me.

He walked through the inn with me to make sure everything was locked up, chatting about Norm's murder the whole way. Casey arrived for the night shift just when we finished.

"I don't want to scare you, Casey, but one of our guests was assaulted in Wagtail tonight. Officer Dave wants to be notified if anything strange happens. Wake me no matter how unimportant it might seem. Okay?"

"You think we're in danger? Is a madman going to try to break into the inn?"

"I think you've been watching too much TV. But keep me posted." I felt a little guilty leaving him there by himself with only lanterns and the fire for light, but we would be right upstairs if he needed us.

Holmes, Ben, and I trudged up the stairs. I spotted Leo on the second landing, handed my lantern to Holmes, and scooped Leo into my arms. "You have caused enough mischief. You're sleeping over as Twinkletoes's guest tonight, and I want you to be on your very best behavior." He had the nerve to purr.

I didn't need to call the dogs. They looked every bit as tired as I was. Twinkletoes waited for us at the door.

Holmes and Ben said good night and vanished into the guest bedroom. I locked the door to the apartment and quickly closed the pet door so Leo would not go on a mouse hunt in the middle of the night. I made a quick call to Zelda so she wouldn't worry about him, and then I fell into the rollaway bed laughing at myself for *ever* having imagined a romantic evening with Holmes. It just wasn't in my destiny.

I had put Ben's rollaway bed in the guest room with Holmes. Aunt Birdie was in my bedroom, and I was sleeping on a rollaway bed in my living room. I figured I was the one most likely to have to get up in the middle of the night if a problem arose and there was no point in waking Aunt Birdie by sleeping in the bedroom.

Only I was too tired and agitated to sleep.

I hadn't had many sleepless nights since I moved to Wagtail. But this was one of them. Twinkletoes curled up with me on the bed, but it was far narrower than my regular bed, so she decided to sleep on top of me. I loved my little puss, but she wasn't helping me sleep by rising and falling with my chest each time I took a breath.

Gingersnap and Trixie had staked out cushy spots on the sofa and a big club chair. Even Leo had finally conked out. He nestled on the end of the bed by my feet. Everyone appeared to be fast asleep except for me.

Every time I closed my eyes, I saw poor Myrtle sprawled on those cold concrete stairs. Why would she have gone there? Someone must have lured her. Someone she trusted. Did that mean she knew the killer? Or was the attack on her motivated by someone she had irritated beyond their breaking point? Maybe it had nothing to do with Norm at all.

At least I was fairly sure Shadow wouldn't be blamed for what happened to Myrtle. Not unless she caught him red-handed at something illegal. Was he conning me? Was I a big sap for wanting to believe him?

I tried to focus. What did we know for sure? Two people had confirmed that Norm had been lurking outside Randolph Hall the morning of his death. That alone shouldn't have led to his murder but it had upset two women who wanted to be rid of him, Blanche and Savannah. And one had to consider that the men who loved them might have taken action to protect them. So that put Ian and Shadow on the list of people with motives. All of them had opportunity. Killing someone with an insulin injection didn't require brute strength. In fact, it was the kind of murder someone small and bookish, like Ian, might conceive.

We also knew that Norm attended the Murder Most Howl meeting at the inn that night. And that he returned to Randolph Hall instead of going home. To confront Blanche? Did he think he would find Savannah there? Was he taking advantage of the fact that the lights were out in that part of town? Whatever his intentions, he hung around outside before entering. Getting up nerve? Waiting for something to happen? Blanche had been quite forthcoming, maybe she would tell me. On the other hand, if she, with her husband or Savannah for that matter, had killed him, she wouldn't be so open. She might even pretend she didn't know he was there.

Which led me to another thought. Had Myrtle gone ahead and paid Savannah a visit? What if Savannah was the killer? That might have prompted her to lure Myrtle to those basement stairs and take a swing at her. Was that beautiful young woman taking advantage of Shadow? Had she used him to get rid of Norm? Or could she be setting him up to take the blame? Visions of Savannah living a life of leisure while Shadow wasted away in prison for a murder she committed shook me to the core. Maybe he was an innocent rube or so infatuated that she could manipulate him.

I forced myself back to the things we knew for certain. One of them was that Norm had been married to Juliana, and she had died a terrible death. Shadow maintained his innocence. His father, Hollis, thought Norm had killed Juliana.

And then my thoughts took me where I hadn't wanted to go. Val. How did Val know so much about Norm? How could she possibly know all those details about him? She had moved to Wagtail about the same time I had. Of course, she had been related to Norm and probably heard about him from Juliana. But how did she learn all those oddball details like the fact that Blanche had to live in her car? It might not be a secret—after all, Weegie had been aware of that. But it was hardly the kind of thing Norm or Juliana would have bragged about, was it?

On the clues Val wrote, the Baron von Rottweiler poisoned his second wife. Did she think Norm had poisoned Juliana? And she had said the baron had falsely accused a man of murder. Did she think Shadow had been falsely accused of Juliana's murder? I had to talk to her. Val wasn't prone to foolishness. She probably heard a lot in the bar but it seemed to me she knew too much that wasn't just silly gossip. And she had most definitely structured the clues to make Norm very, very angry. What could she have been thinking?

Oh no. I wished I wasn't thinking straight. I liked Val so much. Was it possible that she had arranged the whole Murder Most Howl weekend as some kind of misguided plot against Norm? I couldn't imagine what she thought she would achieve.

There was one person who probably knew more than anyone else: Savannah. I would think of a reason to have a chat with her in the morning.

With a heavy heart, and a heavy chest since Twinkletoes was still on top of me, I drifted off to sleep.

* * *

I woke up to the most glorious blue sky. The sun shone on the snow that blanketed the mountains. The sound of a key turning in the door lock roused Gingersnap and Trixie. They lifted their heads and perked their ears.

Mr. Huckle rolled a room service cart into my living room, and for the first time in my entire life, I was served tea in bed before I rose.

"This must be how the other half lives. Thank you, Mr. Huckle!" I drank from a lovely china breakfast cup. It was going to be a very good day. I felt thoroughly spoiled. "Is the electricity back?"

"Indeed it is. It returned about four this morning."

"Thank goodness. Hot water for the guests. Any word about the roads?"

"Not yet. I'll see you at breakfast, Miss Holly." He left the cart, which was loaded with delicious-looking breakfast breads. I fed Trixie and Gingersnap breakfast cookies. Twinkletoes pawed at my leg.

I knew what that meant. In my little kitchen, I opened a container marked Seashore Supper. I assumed it was just as good for breakfast. I spooned chunks of the fish and shrimp into two bowls and set them down for Twinkletoes and Leo. I watched them eat to be sure Trixie and Gingersnap didn't help them.

Leo ate every last morsel. Twinkletoes ate half of her food. I set the remainder on the counter so she could finish it at her leisure.

After a quick shower, I wrapped up in my Sugar Maple Inn bathrobe and tiptoed into my bedroom for clothes.

Aunt Birdie slept with a mask over her eyes and snored softly. I chose a cheerful deep pink sweater with a V-neck, comfortable khaki trousers, and hoop earrings. I carried them out, quieter than the mouse, whom I hoped had escaped last night.

When I was dressed, I opened the pet door for Twinkletoes,

grabbed a jacket, and headed downstairs. The dogs and cats all beat me to the bottom.

A handful of members of The Thursday Night Cloak and Dagger Club had already eaten breakfast. One of them called me over.

"I was packing my belongings this morning, and I simply cannot find my reading glasses. Could you make a note and ship them back to me if you find them?"

"Absolutely. We'll keep an eye out for them." And for Geof's money clip.

"I wouldn't make a fuss but they're prescription and so expensive to replace."

"Of course."

I hurried through the lobby before anyone else could catch me. The poor doggys needed to go out!

Zelda hadn't arrived yet for work.

I let the dogs out and noted that Shadow had already cleaned the walk. He was a hard worker. He must have started before dawn.

The dogs sniffed around for a few minutes but soon returned to me, ready for breakfast.

But they would have to wait. I scooted behind the reception desk to make sure Casey had been able to run off the bills. Unless the roads were still closed, I suspected we would see a mass exodus today.

Happily, they were all sitting exactly where they should be. I leafed through them. Everything seemed to be in order. I picked up the phone and called Dave. He sounded alert when he answered.

"Any news on Myrtle?"

"They're still looking for her next of kin. Even if she's not speaking to her sister, maybe one of her friends knows how to get in touch with her?"

"I'll ask. How's she doing? Did she come around yet?"

"Still unconscious. They're worried about frostbite on her fingers and toes."

"Keep me posted. What's the story with the roads?"

"They have a few more cars, including Ben's, to get out of the way but they anticipate opening the road around noon."

I thanked him and considered calling Val. Her place stayed open late, though. She might not be up yet.

Trixie and Gingersnap watched me hopefully. "Breakfast."

They took off for the dining area, and I followed.

Holmes was up, eating a stack of pancakes that made my mouth water. Trixie was already making sad eyes at him. Holmes grinned at me. "I knew you couldn't be too far away."

Shelley swung by and filled my mug with coffee. "I heard about Myrtle. Is it true that one of her book club members shoved her down some stairs?"

"Where did you hear that?"

"Here. I pick up bits of conversation when I'm serving."

"Her friends think someone in The Thursday Night Cloak and Dagger Club did it?"

"I heard some people betting on Weegie."

"That's nonsense," I scoffed, but quickly added, "unless they know something I don't."

"Pancakes?" asked Shelley. "I think Trixie and Gingersnap have their hearts set on them."

I thought the same thing. "Yes, please." To the dogs, I said, "Tomorrow we're back to healthier food."

"You realize that they're laughing at you," Holmes pointed out.

Their tails swished on the floor. Their mouths were open, and they seemed to be smiling. They probably *were* laughing at me.

"After breakfast, I'm heading home to my parents' house to pack. Maybe I ought to spend a few minutes with them, too."

"They'd probably appreciate that. Tell them I apologize for stealing you this weekend." I knew he had to go home to Chicago but that didn't stop me from feeling a little melancholy about it.

"Aww, you can steal me anytime."

I wished that were true.

"If the airport is open, I'll head back to Chicago tonight, but I'll be at Hair of the Dog at noon to see who won Murder Most Howl. Now that Myrtle is out of the running, I bet it's Ian and Geof."

My pancakes arrived. A mixture of fresh strawberries, blueberries, and blackberries adorned the top. Maple syrup flowed over the sides of the stack. I checked the bowls that Shelley had brought for the dogs. Their pancakes were smaller. A dollop of mashed pumpkin sat on top, adorned with berries, which Trixie probably wouldn't touch but Gingersnap would eat for her. They even had a drizzle of maple syrup.

They snarfed their pancakes and gave me the I-love-you-and-your-pancakes look that I knew all too well.

After breakfast, Gingersnap took up her position in the lobby, greeting everyone who passed through. I popped into the inn's commercial kitchen.

"Need something?" asked Shelley.

"An excuse to visit Savannah."

"How about an apple Bundt cake with caramel drizzle?"

"That sounds good."

"Help yourself. We probably won't have as many people for tea today anyway. A lot of them will leave right after the meeting at Hair of the Dog."

"Good point." The cake wasn't a lightweight. Thick caramel coated the top and it smelled heavenly. I set up a box and lowered the cake into it. Once closed, I wrapped it with an elastic gold band to secure it.

When I emerged from the kitchen, Aunt Birdie pounced on me. She wore a rust turtleneck with a navy blue boiled wool cardigan and trousers in the same shade. Large silver earrings and a chunky silver bracelet completed her ensemble. Her outfit was actually quite chic. "You look nice."

She cast a critical eye on my apparel. "*Hmm.* You'd do well to take my advice on your wardrobe."

Suddenly I was very glad I had someplace to go.

"Holly, dear, your grandmother's absence provides the perfect opportunity to make some much-needed improvements here at the inn. For starters, the towels I used this morning were an adequate quality but they really should be imprinted with the name of the inn."

It took me a moment to recover from my surprise. "Aunt Birdie, I'm just on my way out. Maybe you could have breakfast, and we'll talk when I return? I recommend the pancakes."

In a rush, I pulled on my jacket, dressed Trixie in hers, and told Mr. Huckle to call me if I was needed. Trixie and I headed out the door into the glorious after-snow day. The air had warmed a little. Between the sun and the snow, the glare forced me to dig into a pocket for sunglasses.

It was as though Wagtail had awakened. Shopkeepers smiled and waved. Everyone was glad the blizzard and wind had passed. Things were getting back to normal. But they would never be the same for Norm or for Myrtle.

I knocked on the green door.

Bingo barked twice, and Trixie barked back at him.

Savannah opened the door and pulled me inside. She closed it fast and locked it.

# Thirty-two

"What's going on?"

Savannah stood with her back to the door. She held a finger up to her lips indicating that I should be quiet.

Nothing happened. I didn't hear a thing. I held up my free hand in question.

She escorted me into the living room. All the curtains were drawn. Half-packed boxes cluttered the floor. "Are you moving?"

Savannah burst into tears.

I held her while she sobbed. "Where's the kitchen?"

Sniffling, she led me to a cheerful yellow kitchen with white cabinets. A kitchen table occupied a sweet bay window that probably overlooked the backyard. But all the shades had been drawn.

I told her to sit down, put the kettle on, and looked around the kitchen for tea. I found it in a cupboard. Mugs hung on a little stand on the counter. I slid tea bags into two mugs.

Savannah jumped up. "We can't have tea! We can't eat anything in this house! It's all such a mess. I thought it was my fault that Norm died. But—" her eyes grew big "—they know I'm here."

"Honey, what is going on?"

Bingo started barking, which sent Savannah into a new frenzy.

"There's a guy outside watching me. I need to go someplace private."

"Come to the inn, and we'll talk this out. Okay?"

She nodded. "Give me just a second."

I returned to the living room and peeked out from behind the curtain. Looked pretty peaceful to me.

Savannah returned with her hair tucked under a knit hat. It was pulled down so low that she was barely recognizable. She wore what had to be one of Norm's coats. It was too long and totally shapeless. If I had passed her on the street, I wouldn't have recognized her. "Ready?"

"When we leave, act like I'm some old lady, okay?"

Bingo would give her away to anyone who knew her, but she was already so agitated that I didn't think I should mention that.

She locked the door and closed it behind us.

A block later, I spotted a guy in a blue ski jacket. On any other day, I wouldn't have paid much attention to him. But given Savannah's fear, I tried to watch him surreptitiously while being cheerful to Savannah so she wouldn't notice. I could tell she was scared out of her wits even without knowing he was behind us.

Instead of walking back through the residential neighborhood, I cut over to the green, where shops and restaurants lined the sidewalk.

I pointed out the cute display in the window of Shadow's mom's store, which gave me a chance to see if the guy had followed us when we turned.

He had. He wore a baseball cap that said *Yankees*. As odd as that might seem in the South, the Yankees had recently brought an affiliate team to a town about an hour away, so the caps were turning up everywhere. It no longer marked him as an out-of-towner.

We continued on our way and entered the inn through the main lobby. Mr. Huckle greeted us, and took Savannah's coat, which gave me the opportunity to see if the guy was outside.

Sure enough, he lingered on the plaza, looking up at the inn.

I excused myself and told Savannah I needed a word with Mr. Huckle. She wandered into the Dogwood Room for a look at the view of the lake and the mountains.

"We were followed," I blurted out.

Mr. Huckle's forehead furrowed with concern.

I motioned him to the window. "Blue jacket, Yankees cap."

"Shall I call Officer Dave?"

"Please. I'm taking her down to the office."

I collected Savannah, who raved over the view. At least it had taken her mind off her problems. I took her straight into the office.

Zelda flashed me a curious look. "Lock the outside door," I whispered.

I had carried the cake back. I set it on the coffee table. "Are you hungry? You probably haven't eaten much."

Gingersnap appeared out of nowhere, as though she knew someone needed comforting. I would have expected Bingo to cozy up to Savannah, but it was Gingersnap who sat beside her and placed her head in Savannah's lap.

She stroked Gingersnap's head, and I finally saw the glimmer of a smile.

I made idle chitchat for a few minutes to calm her nerves.

Mr. Huckle surprised me by bringing tea in a silver tea service. When he handed me a floral tea cup, I asked, "Who's watching the door?"

He whispered back, "Ben. We're still trying to reach Officer Dave." And then he served the cake. I felt a little bit guilty. I wasn't used to being waited on like this. Oddly enough, his presence appeared to calm Savannah.

When he left, I closed the door and said, "Tell me what's going on." I no longer thought she was overreacting or being dramatic.

"Do you remember that day on the green when Trixie came to play with Bingo?"

I nodded.

"I had made up my mind to leave Norm. Things weren't working out at all between us. And then this girl came by to thank Norm for the puppy he gave her."

"That was nice."

"No! It wasn't! That was when I realized that I was Juliana."

I wasn't following her at all. "You're not making sense."

"Don't you see? Norm gave me Bingo. And then Juliana died. It was the same thing all over again. Except this time, he gave another girl the puppy, and I was the one he wanted to get rid of."

"Maybe not." It was a bit of a leap.

"Blanche was the only one who made it out alive. Norm mentioned that she was coming to town and staying in Randolph Hall. So I went over there to talk with her. He was such a jerk. He followed me and waited outside. When Blanche's husband came home, Norm finally walked away. The coward! He had no problems frightening two women, but as soon as a tiny eighty-pound weakling guy showed up, Norm took off. I couldn't call my dad. My parents thought Norm walked on water. He was always right in their eyes. They never would have supported my decision to leave him. So I called Shadow, who said to take Bingo and go to his cabin. He met me there and let us in. I stayed with him that night. When Dave called my cell phone and said Norm was dead, I couldn't believe it. And then I realized that if I had been home that night, I would have known Norm didn't come home. I could have looked for him or called Dave and reported him missing. I felt so guilty. I wanted to leave him. I didn't want him to die!"

A soft scratching on the door alarmed Savannah. But I knew exactly who it was. I opened the door and Twinkletoes walked in. She leaped onto the sofa and rubbed her head against Savannah's arm.

Savannah cooed at her. "What a pretty kitty you are. Honestly, I'm jumping at everything now. First all kinds of nice people came by the house, offering sympathy. Even Shadow's parents. I think they always hoped Shadow and I would end up together. Anyway, the next morning I answered the door and this man was standing there. I had never seen him before. He demanded that I pay him money. And a couple of hours later another one showed up. I guess they were loan sharks or something. They made all kinds of threats. So I figured I better pay them, but when I checked with the bank this morning, I found out that we're dead broke. Norm borrowed against everything. Our house, Randolph Hall, everything we have. Only he didn't do it through the bank, he did it through people that break your legs when you don't pay them back. There's about four hundred dollars in our bank account."

I wasn't particularly surprised to hear that Norm was involved with scuzzy people. "Did you call Dave?"

"No. I called my dad. He said Norm had to have his money stashed somewhere. That a man like him surely had investments. I just had to go through Norm's papers and find them."

"So that's what you were doing today when I came by?"

"Yes. But there's one more thing. Dave called me this morning. When Norm died, they found a little vial in his pocket. At the time no one was very concerned about it but they had it analyzed anyway. It was rat poison."

"Eww. Why would he be carrying around rat poison?"

"Did you know that stores in Wagtail won't even carry rat poison? It's because it's so dangerous for cats and dogs."

"I did not know that."

"He must have bought it over on Snowball. So I've been thinking and thinking on it, and I realized that he was planning to kill me."

"What?"

"Don't you see? I'm the new Juliana. He slips rat poison

into something I'm eating or drinking and then he sues the company that made the food—the ketchup company or the soup company or a restaurant where we got takeout. He gets a new wife and an infusion of money."

I absolutely hated that she was making sense. "So Shadow didn't poison Juliana."

"I don't think so. I never thought Shadow did it on purpose. It wouldn't be like him to do that. He's kind and gentle. But anyone can make a mistake. Now I know it wasn't an accident either. I'm sure of it."

"That's why you didn't want to drink tea in your house."

"Exactly. I don't know what Norm might have tampered with."

"I'm so sorry, Savannah."

"I feel like such an idiot."

"Did you tell Dave about the men who came to collect money? Maybe one of them killed Norm."

"Dave said they probably wanted him alive so they would get their money, and that hitting someone with a syringe full of insulin probably wasn't the way they would dispatch somebody."

Maybe that was true, but I had a hunch one of them was responsible for the guy who was following her. Hoping she would lead him to Norm's money? "Savannah, did Norm ever say anything about Val?"

She clanked her tea cup against the saucer. "I don't know what she ever did to him, but he hated her. I mean *hated.* From the day she set foot in town, he had nothing but contempt for her. He was so mad when she outbid him for Hair of the Dog. You know those auctions are for cash. She just went really high. I never understood why it was so important to him. If he had wanted to run a bar, he could have started a new one."

"Val was Juliana's cousin."

Savannah blinked at me. She wrapped her hand over her mouth. "That explains so much. She's lucky she's alive."

"Why would you say that?"

"She was a daily reminder that he murdered Juliana. I bet she knew or suspected." She reflected a moment. "I can't believe I married him." She shuddered. "He was a low-life scum. Blanche was right. He had to keep marrying naive women who were taken in by him. Once married, we all saw a different side of Norm."

"Did you know about Blanche before you married him?"

"Oh, sure. But he spun it so that it sounded cool that he had been married to a supermodel. I had no idea that he was so awful to her." She paused and stroked Twinkletoes. "Norm spent his life trying to acquire things. That's all we were. His latest acquisition, like a fancy vase."

"Savannah, do you know who killed Norm?"

"Not a clue. I had no idea so many people hated him. As awful as it is that he was murdered, I think the killer did us all a favor. Especially me. If he hadn't killed Norm, I might be the one who was dead right now."

Savannah dug into a slice of apple cake like she was hungry. Poor thing. She had fallen into the clutches of a truly unscrupulous man. Everything she said rang true, but I was no closer to understanding who had killed Norm or injured Myrtle.

"Did a petite woman with dark hair and silver streaks come by to see you yesterday?"

"No. Who are you talking about?"

"Myrtle. The woman who was attacked."

Savannah frowned at me. "Was she supposed to?" She gasped. "Was she on her way to see me when she was attacked?"

"It's possible. She went off by herself but no one knows why."

Someone knocked on the door.

Savannah gasped and gazed around as though she was searching for a place to hide.

I understood her fear but seriously doubted that her stalker waited on the other side of the door. Nevertheless, I opened it cautiously.

Trixie and Gingersnap bounded past Dave as he strode inside.

"I hear Dwight scared you."

"Dwight?" asked Savannah.

"He's a cop. We thought it might be a good idea to have someone watching you. There aren't too many loan sharks around here. None in Wagtail, actually, so we think we know who your visitors were, but Norm was, uh, well, he might have had connections we aren't aware of."

"You really ought to tell a person," I protested. "She was scared half out of her mind." I could hear a dog barking.

"It cuts both ways. If she knew, she might act differently, not be as careful or even take a soda out to him or something and give him away."

Zelda stepped to the doorway. "One of the guests called. There's a little commotion of some sort upstairs."

Someone was barking frantically in the distance. Ella Mae? Puddin'?

"Excuse me."

I dashed up the back stairs. Now two dogs were barking. *Oh swell.*

A little crowd had formed in the hallway outside Catch. I wedged past them into the room where Robin was staying. I recognized Trixie's rump sticking up in the air. Her head was under the bed. Puddin' lay on her stomach with her head under the bed. What was going on under there?

"The dogs are all wild about something," said Robin.

I dashed to the housekeeping closet where we kept flashlights just for this kind of emergency and was back in less than a minute. There was no choice but to lie down and look for myself. I suspected the mouse from last night's little drama may have found its way to Catch.

Sure enough, the cute little devil was under the bed, frozen with fear. An odd assortment of items was underneath the bed with him.

I considered my options. Maybe I could whisk him out of there with a wide flat janitor's broom. But then he would run, and the dogs would give chase, and we'd go through this in some other area of the inn.

Ben crouched next to me. "What is it?"

"The mouse Leo brought in last night."

"Really? How do you know it's the same one? Do you recognize him?"

I banged my arm against his leg lightly. This was no time for silly jokes. I backed up and sat on my legs. "If I get a broom and manage to pull him out, could you be ready to pop a little wastebasket over him?"

"Sure. How hard could that be?"

Ben clearly had no experience with mice.

I returned to the housekeeping closet and fetched a wide broom. I didn't know if my plan would work but I didn't know what else to do. When I returned, a little crowd had gathered at the door. I made my way through them to find Ben holding the wastebasket from the bathroom, and Robin questioning him about what was happening.

"Ready?" I asked. I knelt on the floor, lay down next to the broom, and slid it under the bed slowly so it wouldn't alarm the mouse. His beady little eyes seemed to stay focused on me. I scooted it past him, then tried to get it behind him.

With the broom in position, I backed away from the bed and knelt again, ready to pull the broom out, and hopefully, the mouse with it.

Unfortunately, at the exact moment that I pulled the broom, Leo came to see what was going on and wedged himself under the bed.

I pulled, Leo hissed, and Ben plunged the wastebasket over—a tissue box. We didn't get the mouse.

I had to assume the mouse had taken shelter in the other things under the bed. It struck me as more than a little bit odd that Robin had lost so many items under her bed. Had she kicked them all there? Why would anyone do that?

This time the broom brought out a treasure trove of items.

"Hey, that's my wallet." Ben bent down and plucked it from the pile.

"Be careful," I warned. "The mouse is in there somewhere."

Ben looked in his wallet. His eyes met mine. "Nothing's missing."

This was definitely weird. Was Robin a thief who had been caught by a mouse? "I didn't know you had lost it," I whispered.

"Me, either. I thought it was up in your apartment in the guest room where I left it." He shoved it into his back pocket.

Ben lifted the wastebasket off the tissue box and held it at the ready.

I picked up a T-shirt and shook it gently. A pair of glasses lay under it. The missing reading glasses? I placed them on the bed along with an eyebrow pencil, one glove, two mismatched socks, and a traveler's sewing kit. A bunch of tissues lay in a bundle. I shook them out, one at a time. No mouse.

I looked under the bed one more time. No mouse. No other items. Either he had made a clean break, or Leo had nabbed him.

"Thank goodness everyone stopped barking." Char barged into the room carrying Ella Mae in her arms. "My glove! I've been looking everywhere for that." She leaned over to take it. "What's it doing in here?"

Robin had flushed redder than a cranberry. "I don't know. I truly don't know how any of that stuff got under my bed."

I didn't say anything in the hope that she would keep talking. They were odd things to take from people, which made it all the more sad that she felt the need to swipe them. Except of course, for Ben's wallet, which was a very serious matter.

Robin was totally flustered. "You have to believe me. Ask anyone. This isn't something I would do. I'm not a kleptomaniac. Really."

She sniffled and leaned over to grab a tissue out of the box, touching it with one hand and pulling with the other. When she did, the mouse flew out and scrambled for safety. Leo and the dogs chased after him, out the door and down the hall.

"Holly," said Ben, "aren't you going after them?"

I focused on something else. Something I'd thought we would never find. In the tissue box lay a multiple-dose insulin pen.

As calmly as I could, I said to Ben, "Dave is downstairs in the office. Would you please ask him to come here now?"

He looked in the box. His expression told me that he had recognized the item as an insulin pen, too. He left immediately.

I stood up. Pretending that everything was normal, I said, "All right. Everyone out, please."

Char evidently thought everyone did not include her. She thrust the glove toward Robin. "You knew I was looking for this. You even suggested that I must have lost it and that I should buy a new pair. Which I did!"

Robin seemed at a loss. I wasn't surprised. How do you explain to your friends that you took something of theirs? Or that you have a murder weapon hidden in a tissue box underneath your bed?

"Really, Char. Why would I want your glove? Or two socks that don't match? And that eyebrow pencil isn't even my color."

Dave strode in with Ben.

Robin recoiled at the sight of him.

I pointed to the tissue box.

Dave knew what he was looking at immediately. "Has anyone touched it?"

"It was under the bed." I gestured toward the broom. "I pulled it out with that." And then I gasped. "Robin grabbed a tissue."

She glared at me.

She was either brilliant or stupid. If she knew that was where she had hidden the insulin pen used to kill Norm, then it was stupid to pull a tissue from the box. On the other hand, it was a good way to explain any fingerprints of hers that they might find on the box.

"It was in the box under the bed? Or did you put it in the box?" he asked.

"It was in the box. Seems kind of odd, doesn't it? If this is the murder weapon, you'd think the killer would have hidden it better."

"I agree. But no one would keep an insulin pen under the bed."

I nodded. "Not very sanitary."

"But isn't that what makes it a great hiding place?" asked Ben.

"Could it have been left by a previous occupant?"

"I guess so. Marisol is pretty good about cleaning, though. I think she would have found it."

"Which one is Robin?" asked Dave.

To her credit, Robin stepped toward him and held out her hand. "Robin Jarvis."

"This is your room?" he asked.

"Yes. But I have never seen this stuff before. Maybe the tissue box but they all look alike."

"Everyone wait in the hallway, please. Especially you, Ms. Jarvis."

I followed along, but Dave grabbed my arm. "Not you!"

He pulled out a camera. "Tell me exactly where and how you found this."

I explained in detail from the barking to the mouse to the insulin pen. "You think it's the one that was used to murder Norm?"

He didn't answer me. He put on gloves and pulled a paper bag out of his jacket.

"Do you always carry evidence bags?"

"I do when I'm looking for evidence. I didn't think we'd find this. What do you know about Robin?"

"Not much. She arrived late the night of the Murder Most Howl introduction meeting. She's friends with Geof and Charlotte Tredwell, who are staying here, and with Blanche and Ian Tredwell, who are staying at Randolph Hall." I switched to a whisper. "There's been some idle gossip that something might be going on between Geof and Robin."

"Like what?"

"They've just been seen together. It might not be anything. She likes to hike, and he likes to run, so maybe they just share a love of the outdoors."

Dave was clearly sarcastic when he said, "Yeah, sure."

His sarcasm aside, I realized the importance of that information. Robin might have hidden the pen for Geof. Or Geof might have hidden it in Robin's room for Blanche or Ian. There was a host of possibilities.

"Mind if I use your office again?"

"Not at all."

"How soon will we know if this is the pen that killed Norm?"

"I'll have to send it to the lab. Could be weeks."

"You're joking, right? I thought they could test for fingerprints right away."

Dave lay on the floor and peered under the bed. He pulled out his flashlight and made a slow careful sweep. "I have a hunch, given the season and the preplanning that this murder probably involved, that our killer was wearing gloves."

"Then how can you prove it's the one that killed Norm?"

"It's my understanding that the pens will have a very minor amount of cells in them from the injection. They call it backflow. But it will take time for the lab to test it."

"What are you looking for under there?"

He stood up. "The cap. Don't these things come with caps? Otherwise they'd get germs on them. Right?"

A cap? Where had I seen a cap recently? "Let me see that pen again."

Dave pulled it out of the bag far enough for me to look at it. "What's up?"

"I'm not sure. I could be way off. But it's possible that I saw the cap at Randolph Hall."

"Randolph Hall? Where Blanche and her husband are staying?" It was more of a statement than a question.

"Right. Blanche and I were going to Hair of the Dog, and she stopped at Randolph Hall to change clothes. Apparently Leo likes to hang out there. He was playing with Trixie and batted something out from under a pie safe in the kitchen. I picked it up and set it on the counter. I remember thinking that it was a plastic cap. I couldn't swear to it, but it could be the cap for the pen."

Dave took a deep breath.

I interpreted it to mean, *The plot thickens.* At least, that was how I felt. It appeared that the Tredwells were knee deep in this mess and one or more of them was Norm's killer. But which ones?

"I need a favor. We'll keep Savannah here with Mr. Huckle, just as a precaution. You take the cop who has been watching her, and go to Randolph Hall. Show him where the cap is and let him collect it as evidence. Meanwhile, I'll be having a chat with Robin and the Tredwells."

He checked the lock on the door. "Do you have a way of securing this so no one can enter?"

"No."

"Lock it when we leave, okay? I'll get Robin's key from her."

I nodded.

He walked into the hallway and, sounding very authoritative, instructed the Tredwells and Robin to accompany him downstairs. I locked the door and watched him follow them. I headed in the other direction, to the grand staircase and the main lobby.

I hadn't even made it all the way down the stairs when Aunt Birdie flew toward me. Tapping her fingernail on the banister, she waited as I descended. "The cook will not make changes to the lunch menu without your approval. Would you *please* tell him that I have authority? And Shelley laughed at my request that she crack a raw egg and put it into the coffee grounds with the shell. It makes for superior coffee."

On the other side of the dining area, Shelley, Mr. Huckle, and the cook watched us. Uh-oh. A standoff! I did *not* have time for this nonsense right now.

"Excuse me, Aunt Birdie, but I have a little emergency to take care of at the moment. We'll talk as soon as I return."

I could hear her gasp as I fled to Oma's kitchen for our jackets. Mr. Huckle, Shelley, and the cook followed me. Shelley and the cook threatened to quit unless I did something about Aunt Birdie.

"Don't quit. I just have to think of a way to get rid of her."

Mr. Huckle smiled. "Oh, children. Watch and learn."

He walked out to the dining area with the three of us behind him, trying not to be too obvious.

Mr. Huckle sidled up to an irate Aunt Birdie. "Miss Birdie, may I bring you a cup of tea and a pastry? You've had such a busy morning."

Aunt Birdie drew herself completely erect and held her chin high. "Thank you. I would like that very much."

But before she could sit down, Mr. Huckle said, "I'm

surprised that you're not at Tall Tails. I understand Max is hosting an author chat this morning."

Aunt Birdie stopped dead. "He might need help."

"Indeed," said Mr. Huckle.

"I believe I will take a rain check on that tea. Excuse me, Mr. Huckle."

She hurried up the stairs faster than I thought she could move.

Mr. Huckle returned to us, all smiles. "And that, my dears, is how it's done."

"Is Max hosting an author chat?" I asked.

Mr. Huckle shrugged. "Perhaps. Or perhaps an elderly gent got his days confused."

I explained the insulin pen situation to Mr. Huckle, who seemed a little bit too delighted to be part of the plan. I slid on my jacket, bundled up Trixie and Gingersnap, and headed out to the plaza in front of the inn to pick up Dave's cop buddy.

He was even more thrilled than Mr. Huckle. Dave had informed him that he was going to collect evidence but he didn't know the whole story. I explained it all while we walked.

He was a young guy and obviously excited to be released from his boring post at the entrance to the inn.

When we reached Randolph Hall, I rang the bell.

Ian answered the door. "Yes?"

I was pretty sure that he recognized me from the inn. Maybe he didn't know my name.

The cop made quick work of identifying himself. He whipped out his badge lickity-split and asked if we could come in.

"No." That was all Ian said.

I hadn't expected that.

From the look on his face, neither had the cop. "I can come back with a search warrant."

Ian gave a curt nod. "Fine. You do that." He closed the door!

I was stunned. It never occurred to me that they wouldn't cooperate. "What now?"

"It's up to Dave, but I suspect he'll send me back to Snowball to get a search warrant."

"That could take hours."

"Yup."

"They'll be gone by then."

"Probably."

I looked toward the side yard. "What if I sneaked in through the back?"

"Don't do that. It would be tainted evidence. We have to go by the book."

I heard him but I walked around the side of the house anyway. There was a tiny screened porch in the back. More of a stoop, really. Four steps up, and I would be able to see inside the kitchen door. My heart hammered but I tiptoed up the wooden stairs and dared to step inside the screened area. I cupped my hands around my eyes to see inside the window of the door that led to the kitchen.

There was the cap, still sitting exactly where I had left it. I scrambled to leave the screened porch before Ian caught me. Breathless, I hurried back to the cop, who said, "Are you deaf? I wish you hadn't done that."

"Good news. It's still there."

He stared at me with a stony face and put away his radio. "Dave is sending me over to Snowball for the search warrant. Will you be okay walking back to the inn by yourself?"

"Of course. No loan sharks are after me."

He walked away, and I looked up at Randolph Hall. Ian watched me from a front window.

Back at the inn, the reception lobby seemed like a train station. Luggage was piled in heaps along the wall. Robin and Geof waited on the love seat, looking miserable, and Zelda was in the process of checking out members of The Thursday Night Cloak and Dagger Club.

I squeezed past them and slipped behind the counter to talk to Zelda. "How's it going?"

"So far no problems."

Weegie waved at me.

I moved over, out of Zelda's way.

Weegie walked up to the counter. "Two of the other book club members and I would like to stay on for a few days to be here for Myrtle. She's a pest and annoying, but she doesn't have anyone, and we wouldn't feel right leaving her in the hospital all alone. Would you have a room for three? I'm not sure how long we'd need it. At least until her sister arrives."

"Of course. Given the circumstances, we'll give you a special rate. You're probably tired of that rollaway bed, too." I checked the schedule, and blocked two connecting rooms for them. "I'll let you know when your rooms are ready."

She leaned over the counter. "Is it true that one of the Tredwells murdered Norm?"

"Honestly, we don't know anything yet." Sheesh. Now I was starting to sound like the police. I hated it when they sidestepped questions. On the other hand, it was remotely possible that the insulin pen in question was not the one used to kill Norm. And that the cap I had seen at Randolph Hall was meant for something else entirely. "I'm sorry. I don't mean to dodge your question. I've actually been out so I don't know what has happened."

The door to the office opened, and Char marched out, her face flaming. She still carried Ella Mae, but she avoided my eyes entirely.

Dave called me. I waved to Weegie and hurried over. "They're protecting each other. Didn't get a thing out of them. Is it okay if Savannah hangs out here today with Shadow?"

"Sure."

"I'm going over to Randolph Hall to question Ian and Blanche."

"Good luck. What if they shut the door in your face?"

"Then they will be taken to Snowball for questioning at headquarters."

He watched something behind me. "My guess is that the Tredwell clan will be departing Wagtail shortly."

I turned around and saw Geof and Robin walk out the door. The Thursday Night Cloak and Dagger Club rushed off right behind them to Hair of the Dog for the awarding of prizes.

"Can't you detain them? On TV they're always telling people not to leave town."

"I can tell them that. But I can't enforce it. If they have a lawyer they can call, I bet they leave ASAP."

"I don't know about that. Ian and Geof were heavily invested in the game."

Dave coughed. "You're joking, right? Let's see, what would be preferable? Avoiding being arrested for murder or winning a game?"

"Well, when you put it that way . . . What about Robin and her room? She'll want to pack."

"Stall. Stall as long as you can."

"You're not going to arrest her? Don't you think she killed Norm?" asked Zelda.

Dave winced. "At this point, all I have is an insulin pen. I don't even know if it was the one used in Norm's murder. I've got no fingerprints and no confession. I'll know more after I get this over to the lab."

I looked over at Zelda. "Our job is to stall Robin."

She nodded. "Gotcha. Holly is the only one who can let Robin into her room, and by gosh, I just won't be able to find Holly."

Dave shot her a thumbs-up and took off. In a matter of minutes, the rush had ended and the reception lobby was so quiet I could have heard kitten feet.

I had promised Val I would attend the prize ceremony. Given everything that had happened, I debated the wisdom of going. But the inn was quiet with everyone out at the final meeting of Murder Most Howl.

I walked out on the front porch.

Mr. Huckle followed me. "We had quite a morning here at the Sugar Maple Inn."

"Yes, we did."

"Your grandmother would be proud of the way you're handling these crises."

I smiled at him. "Thank you, Mr. Huckle. I fear we're not done yet, though."

"Dave appears to have it in hand. He'll take it from here." He looked at his watch. "Aren't you supposed to be at the ceremony where the prizes are awarded?"

"I wonder if I should stick around here."

Mr. Huckle toddled inside and returned with my jacket. "I shall call you if anything untoward happens."

Maybe he was right. "Okay. Thanks, Mr. Huckle."

By the time I walked over to Hair of the Dog with Trixie and Gingersnap, the presentations were almost over. Val was in her element, handing out prizes for all kinds of amusing things like *Silliest Motive* and *Most Dog Clues Eaten*. I watched from the back, laughing along with the participants. To my surprise, Holmes and Ben had made it on time and assisted Val in handing out gift certificates and fun prizes.

Ian and Blanche were notably absent. Robin and Geof had come, but not Charlotte or Ella Mae. I watched them, wondering if I would have attended in their shoes. If I had murdered someone, would I go to an unimportant presentation? I thought not. Maybe that spoke to their innocence. Or maybe that's what they hoped for—to appear unconcerned.

As I looked around, I realized that most of the participants were smiling. Maybe they hadn't been impacted by Norm's death. Maybe some of them hadn't even heard about it.

When it ended, a lot of people stayed for lunch. Some filtered out clutching gift certificates for local stores. The chatter I heard was all positive but I had arrived too late to hear who killed the baron.

I made my way through the tables to Val, Holmes, and Ben. In spite of the din, I could hear burgers sizzling on the grill.

"Congratulations, Val. Looks like you pulled it off after all."

"I heard a bunch of people say they're coming back to play again with friends." Holmes high-fived Val.

But Val flinched. "I think the merchants will be the judge of whether there's a next time. Half the town isn't speaking to me. I keep telling them it was Norm who wrote the scandalous clues, but some of them remain unconvinced."

"Do you have a minute?" I asked.

She gazed around. "Lunch rush has started. Can you make it quick?"

"Why didn't you tell me about Norm?"

"What about him?"

I stared at her in surprise. Why was she acting this way? What was she hiding?

She closed her eyes for a moment. "Okay, okay, okay. Come into my office."

Holmes, Ben, and I followed her. She closed the door.

After a deep sigh she said, "Where to begin? I was surprised when Juliana and Norm moved to Wagtail. But then she started sending me gorgeous pictures. Juliana and her dog on a mountain peak. Juliana and her dog swimming in the lake. You get the idea. Fabulous pictures. She kept inviting me to come to Wagtail but I was always too busy at work. And then she was dead. It hit me hard."

She stopped talking and looked away. "Last year, one of my work friends who was exactly my age died in an accident. When I came back to work after the funeral, they already had someone else in her cubicle, and I kept thinking—is that all there is? I come to work every day, and when I die, they plug someone else into my place like I never existed?" She blew out a breath.

"So I came to Wagtail on vacation. This will sound stupid, but I felt Juliana here. I felt at home. I loved that dogs and cats could go everywhere. Juliana would have liked that, too. I was out walking and saw that Hair of the Dog was up for auction. I did a little calculating, and with a loan from my parents, I thought I might be able to swing it. A couple of days before the auction, I went by Norm's house to say hi and introduce myself. The minute I met him, I knew something wasn't right. He fooled a lot of people by being charming but I saw through him right away. Imagine my shock when he showed up at the auction and bid against me!"

"He didn't want you here," said Ben.

"Exactly. That became obvious very fast," said Val. "So I did some checking up on him. The man was a worm, and he didn't like that I was asking people about Juliana's death. Shadow's dad, Hollis, didn't like that I was stirring things up again so he came into the pub one day and confronted me. Why was I asking questions about Shadow's involvement in Juliana's death? He came in to yell at me, but suddenly I had an ally because he also thought Norm murdered Juliana. The only downside to Norm's death is that now we'll never be able to prove what he did."

"If it's any comfort to you, Savannah also thinks Norm killed Juliana." I explained about the rat poison. "There's no way of knowing what he intended to do with it, but if one wife died from poison in her food, and he got away with it—"

"Why not do it again?" Holmes finished my thought.

"That's why you were trying to yank Norm's chain by making the clues in Murder Most Howl match his life." I looked to her for confirmation.

"I hoped that they would push him to the edge when he found out. That he would slip up and confess in anger. I even bought a little recorder that I carried around, just in case he showed up to berate me and incriminated himself."

I gave her a big hug. "I'm so sorry. But you went about it pretty stupidly. He could have killed you, too."

"It's over now. Whoever knocked him off gets my respect."

Ben raised his eyebrows. "I'm not sure I'd go around saying that, even if I did think it."

Val shooed us out of her office. "Go on now. I have work to do!"

On the walk back to the inn, Trixie and Gingersnap played with other dogs they met along the way.

In the lobby, Weegie hustled over to me. "Did you hear? I won! I can't believe it. Of course, I feel a little bit guilty for stealing those clues from Myrtle, especially now that she's in the hospital, but that's the way the game is played. Right?"

I gave her a little hug. "Congratulations. Well played."

"I thought for sure Ian and Geof would win but they were off by one very important little item. It was a clue that I found on the back of the cow at the ice cream place. They had weapons but I guess they didn't think I was worth questioning." She giggled with delight.

A number of her friends gathered around.

"So what was the solution?" I asked. "Who killed the Baron von Rottweiler?"

"As you know," said Weegie, "I was his third wife. And I was quite afraid of him. I confided that to my brother, Max, who owns the local bookstore. Our mom had an upper respiratory infection. She was taking acetaminophen with codeine for it. When my brother cooked dinner at our mother's house, he took some of Mom's pills and put them into the baron's flask to get rid of the baron to protect me."

Her friends groaned and laughed, all talking at once. Some

of them had half the clues, but none of them had figured out the full story.

Mr. Huckle came over and announced, “Your victory table is ready, ladies.”

He had pushed together a number of tables in the dining area so they could all sit together. I spied Leo on the grand staircase watching them.

Walking calmly so I wouldn’t frighten him away, I approached Leo and scooped him up in my arms. “No more mouse gifts, please.”

I carried the big cat, who purred, to the reception desk. “Zelda, I don’t mean to be cruel, but do you think Leo would mind terribly if I shut him in the office until Sylvie has left? They’re having lunch now, so it would only be a couple of hours. She clearly doesn’t appreciate his attention.”

“He knows her. That’s why he’s acting this way.”

“Zelda!” I didn’t want to insult her but I doubted that Leo was telling her that. “Are you . . . reading his mind?”

“No. I’ve been thinking about this. He never came over to the inn before Sylvie arrived in town. Didn’t you notice that? I walk to work all the time but he never follows me here. And giving gifts of mice, that’s something he does to the people he likes. He’s always bringing me little presents. He takes them to my neighbor, who is very sweet. But he never brought anything to my good-for-nothing ex-husband. His previous owner told me about his gift-giving habit. She warned me because her mother was appalled when he brought her gifts.” Zelda stroked Leo’s back. “He knows Sylvie from somewhere.”

I walked into the office and placed him on the sofa. “I’m sure you don’t like being cooped up, Leo. But it won’t be too long.”

I closed the door behind me. “Sylvie lives in North Carolina. Unless Leo has been there, I’d think it highly unlikely that he knows her.”

“He’s not the youngest cat. Maybe he’s getting senile, and she reminds him of someone.”

"Where did the previous owner live?"

"Here in Wagtail. In Randolph Hall. She loved Leo so much. She cried and cried when she gave him to me. She was moving to Shanghai and didn't think he would like living in a cramped apartment after years of roaming free in Wagtail."

I looked down at Trixie, who gazed up at me as though she was smiling. "I don't know if I could do that. It was probably the right thing to do for Leo but . . ." No question about it. I couldn't leave my little sweethearts. I picked up Trixie and held her close at the mere thought.

"It was complicated. Her husband found a job there. I had just moved here when they were leaving. Leo sort of latched on to me, and she asked if I would take him. It was my lucky day. He's such a cool cat."

"Shanghai. That's awfully far away. Didn't someone say that Sylvie's kids live in China?"

"Really? I can't imagine there's any connection."

The sound of footsteps racing on the back stairs drew our attention.

"Holly! Holly!" shouted Robin. "We figured it out. We know how those items came to be under my bed." Robin beamed and hurried toward me with a phone in her hand. "Look!"

She showed me the phone, which displayed a picture of Ella Mae, her ears pinned back, carrying a man's money clip. Robin pressed a button and a video played as the camera followed Ella Mae, who disappeared under a bed and emerged without the money clip.

"She stole it?"

"Exactly. She's Klepto Dog! That's why it's such a weird collection of items. Do you know how to reach Officer Dave? We have to show him."

I had seen Ella Mae dragging the mock candlestick. She had darted out of Weegie's room right in front of me. "Of course. Zelda, would you call Dave?"

"Can I go in my room and pack now?" asked Robin.

"I think we had better wait until Dave gives the okay." I

excused myself and skedaddled to the main lobby so she wouldn't keep pressing me. While Robin might be off the hook, there was still the issue of the pen cap at Randolph Hall. Not to mention the fact that Ella Mae must have found the insulin pen somewhere in the inn. Would she have put it inside the box? Or had someone else hidden it there and Ella Mae thought she was just stealing the tissue box? Instead of narrowing the list of potential murderers, everyone who had stayed at the inn was now suspect.

I watched the members of The Thursday Night Cloak and Dagger Club eat lunch. They were a noisy and happy bunch. The unlikeliest group of killers that I could imagine.

But I was reminded that Myrtle wasn't with them, and that I had to pack up her belongings.

Ben walked toward me, putting his phone away. "My car is now at the parking lot outside of Wagtail. I'm going to take a Wagtail taxi over to see the damage. I'll be back soon, though, if that's okay."

I assured him it was.

He headed out, and I walked upstairs to Myrtle's room.

I left the door wide open, as was our practice when working in an occupied guest room. It wasn't as though Myrtle would come running in and be shocked to find me there, but it also indicated that I wasn't doing anything that I needed to hide.

It was eerily still. Like a life interrupted. I told myself that was only my imagination because Myrtle had been attacked. I pulled open the drapes. Sun flooded in, dispelling some of the creepiness in the pretty room. Myrtle hadn't been the tidiest of guests. Her luggage lay on the floor, half-open. Clothes were strewn around, hanging on chairs and covering the bed previously occupied by Weegie. I set her suitcase on a luggage rack and lay sweaters, blouses, and pants inside as I folded them. I collected three books she had brought along and inserted them along the sides of the suitcase.

I scooted into the bathroom and collected her toiletries. There weren't many. She wasn't heavily into makeup. I placed them in the suitcase and noticed a thick gray sweater tucked behind an armchair. When I picked it up, a cell phone fell out.

Aha! Maybe she had contact information for her sister on the phone. I examined it. It wasn't quite like mine. I managed to turn it on and an e-mail came up. On the chance that it was from her sister, I read it.

> You're going to Wagtail? I'm so jealous. Mike and I dream of moving back there. I wonder if the stigma will ever go away? If people will ever forget? I can't forget. It will haunt me to the day I die. I still cry when I think of my wonderful Leo. He would hate it here, though. Look up Shadow for me? I hope life turned out okay for him and that he didn't have to flee, too.
>
> Hugs and kisses,
> Michelle

I sat on the edge of the bed, trying to put everything together. Michelle and Mike. Hadn't Shadow said they owned The Doggy Bag? That made sense since she was asking about Shadow. Zelda would know if Leo's previous owner was named Michelle.

But how were they connected to Myrtle? Was Michelle her daughter? Her sister? A friend? I scrolled back and found the addressee, *SylvieP*.

Sylvie Porter's phone? Had Myrtle swiped it from her or was it more of Ella Mae the Klepto Dog's handiwork? I had some trouble imagining that Ella Mae could have wrapped it in the sweater and stuck it behind the chair, but then who'd have thought she would steal things and hide them under the bed? So Sylvie knew the people who had owned Randolph Hall and The Doggy Bag. I'd thought Zelda was being silly when she said Leo recognized Sylvie and that was why he brought her gifts of mice. Hadn't Zelda said that Leo had brought them to the mother of his previous owner? Could Sylvie be Mike or Michelle's mother?

I heard a scuffle and looked around but I didn't see anyone. An impatient whine came from under the bed. The voice Trixie used when she wanted something from me.

Not again. I placed the phone on the bed and looked under it. The frame holding the mattress must have been higher than in the other room because Trixie had managed to wedge herself underneath it, squashed flat on her belly. There was another broom in the housekeeping closet. I retrieved it along with a flashlight, lay on the floor, and aimed the beam under the bed.

Trixie didn't take her eyes off—Leo? "How did you get up here?" Someone must have opened the door to the office. Leo's tail twitched back and forth, and sure enough, in the far corner was the poor mouse.

The door to the room closed, and I heard footsteps.

I raised myself up to see who it was. Sylvie! I debated hiding or saying something. She would see me in a minute. At that moment, she was looking at the top of the dresser. She swung around.

"Hi." I stood up.

Sylvie gasped and clutched her chest. "You scared me! I, uh, lent Myrtle a book and wanted it back."

I played along, even though I suspected she really wanted her phone. "I've been packing her things. There are a few books in her suitcase." I pointed at it, hoping she would look in it, and I could open the door.

We heard a commotion under the bed.

"What was that?" she asked.

The mouse! She hated mice. Perfect timing. My heart pounded but I tried to sound casual. "I'm so sorry, but it seems Leo has trapped another mouse."

She winced and stepped back, but then her gaze fell on the bed, and her phone. Her eyes met mine. "Nice try, Holly."

The sweet dimples were gone. Her eyes seemed to change in front of me, to a viciousness born of desperation.

She pulled a hunting knife from her pocket and flicked the wicked blade open. "I brought this along thinking I might need it if Norm didn't succumb to the insulin fast enough. I'm sorry to do this to you, Holly. You were a lovely hostess, and you remind me a little bit of my daughter. I don't know how you managed to put up with Myrtle. Honestly, it felt good to swing that board at her."

She flew around the bed at me. Was she kidding? I had played this game with Holmes and my cousin for years. She didn't know she was dealing with a pro at dodge-the-bed. I climbed on top of the bed, vaguely aware of more scrambling underneath it. Leo shot out from under the bed with Trixie right behind him. But in the moment that I spied them, Sylvie grasped my ankle and yanked.

I let out a shriek as I fell to the bed. "Help!" I tried screaming louder but it wasn't easy what with kicking at her face.

She pulled herself forward, almost over top of me. Where did she get so much strength? I saw the knife in her hand, raised and ready to plunge. With all my might, I shoved her toward the pillows and rolled away in the other direction.

I leaped off the bed and opened the door.

Sylvie was faster than she looked. She raced toward me, holding up the pillow. All I could see were her wild eyes, the mouse clinging to the pillow for dear life, and the savage blade that had pierced the pillow.

I stepped into the hallway, out of her path. "Help! Dave! Zelda!"

Gingersnap, Puddin', and Rooster, the adoptable yellow dog that Char hadn't wanted, barreled down the corridor.

Sylvie dashed through the doorway, tripped over Rooster, and landed flat on her face. The mouse climbed into her hair. She moaned and rose slightly. It appeared her shoulder had landed on the handle of the knife. *Ouch!*

"Game over, Sylvie," I said.

"Not by a long shot." She tried to dislodge the blade of the knife but it had wedged in the hardwood floor. She twisted, grabbed my ankle, and pulled.

I bent over slightly. "There's a mouse in your hair." I said it as calmly as I could.

The mouse took that moment to crawl on her forehead and between her eyes. Sylvie passed out cold.

Dave, Zelda, Shadow, and the Tredwells bounded toward me from the back stairs.

The rest of The Thursday Night Cloak and Dagger Club ran toward me from the grand staircase.

Dave kneeled beside Sylvie and brought her around.

Shadow said, "Mrs. Porter?"

The two of them helped her to her feet. "Where's the mouse?" she asked.

They assisted her down the stairs to the office and the rest of us followed. Zelda closed the door.

Sylvie's book club friends gathered in the reception lobby, buzzing with speculation.

Charlotte Tredwell glared at Geof. "What is that yellow dog doing here?"

I jumped to Rooster's aid. "Thank goodness he was here. Sylvie fell over him."

Geof ran his hand over Rooster's head. "Did you hear that, Char? He's a hero. He literally tripped up a murderer."

"Geof," she warned.

"We're adopting him. Robin and I have been running with him and taking him for walks."

Robin flushed. "He's such a great dog. You know I can't have a dog with all the traveling I do. And Geof loves him."

"*Your* dog stole my money clip," said Geof. "And she cost Ian and me the Murder Most Howl game. She hoarded all the weapons under our bed."

Char clutched Ella Mae tighter as if she feared he might take her away. "Well, *your* dog has . . . a stupid name and a really cute face." She smiled at her husband.

Geof high-fived Robin. "Hey, Zelda," he called. "How does Rooster feel about the name *Duke*?"

Zelda raised her chin and rotated her hand underneath it. "He loves it. He says he always suspected he was royalty. Um, and he wants you to know that he's particularly partial to big crunchy peanut butter cookies and pig's ears."

Duke wagged his tail and licked Geof's hand. Duke was going to have a ball living with Ella Mae the Klepto Dog.

Dave emerged from the office. "She'd like a word with Shadow and Holly."

Geof asked, "Are we free to go then? You have your killer, right?"

"Not so fast. It seems there are a few contradictions and unanswered questions. Why don't you folks have a cup of coffee in the dining area?" He raised his voice. "All of you!"

Shadow and I ventured into the office.

Shadow tilted his head like a puppy. "You are Mrs. Porter. Right? Michelle's mom?"

Sylvie sat on the sofa, her hair a mess, and her hands on her lap in handcuffs. "Michelle wanted to know how you're doing, Shadow. She still thinks of you."

"I'll never forget her or Mike. I wish everything had worked out for them. You tell Michelle that I'll be okay."

Sylvie stared down at her hands. "I'm the one who stole the shamrock necklace." She looked up. "I'm so sorry, Shadow. I knew you would recognize me."

Shadow scowled at her. "I don't understand."

"I didn't want you here. I . . . I was trying to get you fired so I wouldn't have to dodge you around the inn."

"So that's how the necklace got across town," I said. "You took the necklace to his house to incriminate him."

She nodded. "I didn't come here to hurt Shadow. It was Norm who had to be killed. Shadow will tell you that. He ruined our lives. If it wasn't for him, my daughter and her husband would be living the high life in that big mansion with a huge national business. Instead, they're stuck in a tiny apartment a world away."

As she spoke, her sweet dimpled face twisted with rage. "Norm sued The Doggy Bag corporation. They had to close. The publicity about Juliana dying as a result of eating their food sealed that deal. They had taken personal loans to expand the business. My husband and I co-signed some of the loans. The Doggy Bag was going to be a really big thing. But when Juliana died, no one wanted to eat there anymore and the money dried up fast. None of us had the funds to repay all the debts and the massive attorney's fees."

Sylvie covered her face with her hands and sobbed. "My husband and I had to sell our house, and the kids lost Randolph Hall. We all filed for bankruptcy. The stress caused my husband to have a massive heart attack. And the kids couldn't get jobs. Juliana's ghost followed them everywhere they went. It was all Norm's fault. I knew he murdered his beautiful wife. For five years, I have lain in my bed every night and thought about how I could get revenge on him."

"But Sylvie," I protested, "the police didn't suspect Norm. Shadow was convicted."

The dimples had disappeared and Sylvie looked like a despondent old woman. "Don't you think we talked about that? Don't you imagine that the kids, my husband, and I examined every little detail inside out and upside down to consider all the possibilities? Shadow, Norm stopped by The Doggy Bag that day to pick up Juliana's order, didn't he?"

Shadow nodded. "Yes, ma'am. But Juliana had already picked it up."

"My husband and I think Norm spied the package of laundry detergent on the counter and recognized an opportunity. He probably distracted Shadow, stole some of the laundry packets, and slid them into his pocket. No one would have been the wiser."

"But he went to a football game that night," said Shadow.

"There wasn't a thing in the world to prevent him from stopping by his house to poison Juliana's dinner on the way to the game. He left her there to die. My family lost everything they worked so hard to attain. Everything! All because that jerk Norm got away with murdering his wife and pinning it on Shadow. He didn't care about them. I figured if he could get away with murder, so could I."

"You almost did. But why did you leave him on the bench with the poison bottle? Were you trying to point the finger at someone else?"

Her eyes grew large. "I didn't. I don't know how he got there."

"I don't understand."

"I left him at Randolph Hall and figured his wife would find him dead."

Shadow looked at me. "I don't get it."

"I knew he bought the place with the money he got from suing my daughter! I thought he was living there. The idiot never changed the lock to the back door, so I just let myself in. The power was out, which was a stroke of good luck. I waited for him, and when he showed up creeping into the kitchen—" she raised her hands and brought them down "—BAM!"

"Where did you get the insulin?" I asked.

She shrugged. "No biggie. It was my husband's. He's diabetic and has plenty. It didn't take long for Norm to succumb. He was so weak. I had expected to have to stab him but he couldn't stand. I sat him down in a chair and told him what I thought of him. Said I knew he murdered Juliana."

I thought Shadow might have stopped breathing. "Did he confess?"

"Not at first. I wanted him to know why he was dying. He begged me to call for help. I asked him how he thought his lovely Juliana felt all alone and dying. And that was when he broke down and confessed that he was the one who poisoned her. When I thought he was dead, I left."

"Then how did he get to the park bench?" asked Shadow.

"Beats me!"

Was she lying? Did she think that little detail would somehow save her?

"What about Myrtle? I thought she was your friend."

"That wicked malcontent? Hah. I had to stick to her like glue to be sure she didn't figure out who killed Norm. And then I realized she stole my phone. She read the e-mail from my daughter just like you did. She had put it all together."

"Why did you leave the gun with her?"

Sylvie cringed. "It's not as easy as you'd think to kill someone. It was icy and slippery. The gun must have fallen out of my pocket when I hit her. I didn't realize it until I got back to the inn."

Dave appeared in the doorway. "The cruiser is here." He walked over to Sylvie and helped her stand.

I expected her to look beaten and tired, but she held her head high and walked through the empty lobby like she was proud of herself. It scared me. The woman looked so sweet with those dimples, but underneath, something wasn't right in her head.

Dave returned. "Did she tell you she left Norm at Randolph Hall?"

"She did. That's so weird," I said. "Do you think Blanche and Ian moved him?"

"That's my guess."

At that exact moment, Shadow opened the door, and Blanche rushed past him into the inn. "Was that Robin in the squad car? She didn't kill Norm. I won't let her take the blame."

Without looking at me, Dave reached sideways and held his palm toward me as if he didn't want me to speak.

"I can't let Robin go to jail over this." Blanche smoothed her hair and caught her breath. "I found Norm in the kitchen at Randolph Hall. He was already dead. I thought he came to kill me and had a coronary. Ian had been out walking the dog, and when he came home, bless that sweet man, he thought I murdered Norm. He called Geof and the two of them put Norm on a sled and pulled him to the bench where he was found. Honest. Robin had nothing to do with it."

Dave scratched his ear but didn't say a word.

"You believe me, don't you?" Blanche breathed in giant shudders.

"How did the poison bottle get there?" asked Dave.

"Geof had it. They hoped it would distract anyone from thinking I murdered Norm. They were just trying to protect me."

Dave's cheek twitched a little. "It's a felony to move a corpse."

Blanche blinked rapidly. "But they didn't hurt him. They

didn't mean any harm. And Robin had nothing to do with any of it."

"We have the murderer in custody. But I'd like to speak with Ian and Geof. Would you mind stepping into the office? I'll be right with you."

Zelda showed Blanche where to go.

Dave patted Shadow on the back. "I hear Savannah is going to be staying with you."

Shadow beamed. "Now we just need to get those loan sharks off her back."

"We'll help you with that. Don't go doing anything stupid."

"Yessir!"

"I'm going to interview the Tredwells, then I'll talk with the book club members."

"Fine. You know where to find me," I said.

Shadow looked at his watch. "Would you mind if I took a little break? I'll come back and shave down that door that sticks. Assuming I'm still hired."

I nodded at him. "You sure are."

Ben and Holmes clattered down the stairs. Ben carried his suitcase.

"Are you taking off?"

Ben nodded. "The car's okay. Not as pretty as it used to be but it's running fine."

"He's giving me a lift to the airport. Mr. Huckle told us about Sylvie. Who'd have thought it? She seemed so sweet." Holmes reached down for a hug and kissed me on the cheek. "No more getting into trouble."

"I promise. Ben, if Ian and Geof Tredwell moved Norm's body, will they go to prison?"

"Probably not. They're squeaky clean, and they'll hire an ace attorney. Most likely they'll get a couple of years of probation."

Ben reached over for a hug and kissed my other cheek. "Tell Twinkletoes I'll miss her hissing."

Trixie looked up at me and whined when they walked out the door. "Me too, Trixie. Me too."

I was bringing Dave coffee when Shadow returned. "Some folks around Wagtail take their dogs to work. Like you!" Shadow scratched behind Trixie's ears. "So I was wonderin' if it would be okay—"

"You got a dog!"

"Yeah. He was put up for adoption in the If the Dog Fits program. I'm just lucky those folks found another dog they liked better." He walked over and opened the door. "C'mon, boy."

A little red bloodhound puppy walked inside. I had a hunch he was the one the Tredwells had ignored when Charlotte choose Ella Mae. He was adorable. His long ears flapped when he walked. If his paws were any indication, he was going to be a big fellow. He looked around curiously and trotted over to Trixie and me.

"Does he have a name yet?" I set the tray on the reception desk.

"Elvis."

I reached for the little guy and swung him up in my arms. "Welcome to the Sugar Maple Inn family, Elvis!"

# Thirty-nine

The next day, Weegie and I left Puddin' and Trixie at the inn with Zelda and paid Myrtle a visit at the hospital.

"The food here is lousy and the nurses don't know what they're doing. They might finish the job of killing me for Sylvie."

Weegie whispered, "I think she's feeling better."

I placed a vase of flowers near the window. "We're all wondering how you knew Sylvie murdered Norm."

"I didn't," she grumbled. "When we were eating at The Blue Boar, she left her phone on the table while she went to the ladies' room. I read her e-mail." Myrtle shrugged, which I took to mean she knew it was wrong of her. "I slipped the phone into my purse and hid it in my room because I wanted to see if I could find any other interesting e-mail. She pretended she had never been to Wagtail before, which I thought very peculiar. She must have followed me when I left the inn to pay a visit to Norm's widow. Sylvie caught up to me, placed a gun in my back, and led me to those stairs. I knew I was a goner."

I wondered if I should tell her that the gun was the fake one used for Murder Most Howl but decided against it. "None of you ever knew of Sylvie's connection to Wagtail? She never mentioned that her daughter lived here once?"

Weegie shook her head. "All the girls have been talking about this. Sylvie had only been a member of The Thursday Night Cloak and Dagger Club for a few months. She complained bitterly about her daughter living so far away. And we knew about her husband's health issues, but she never mentioned Wagtail to any of us."

"Myrtle, is there anything I can do for you?" I handed Myrtle a gift certificate for a weeklong stay at the inn.

Myrtle tore it into shreds and threw them in the air. "You couldn't pay me to go back to that dump." She clenched her teeth and refused to look at me.

After that little tantrum, I thought it best to wait for Weegie out in the hall.

When she left Myrtle's room, she said, "Wouldn't you think a brush with death would make a person appreciate life?"

I would have thought so.

The following week, a letter came in the mail from Blanche.

*Dear Holly,*

*I don't know if you will remember me, but we recently met in Wagtail.*

Was she kidding? Who would forget Blanche Wimmer Tredwell?

*You took me to a cute pub called Hair of the Dog, where I made my favorite hamburgers. Turns out that one of the people who was watching videotaped the whole thing and posted it on the web. It went viral and found its way to an executive for a TV cooking channel. They have just hired me to host my own cooking show, "Brunch with Blanche." Funny how things turn out sometimes.*

*All best,*
*Blanche*

The snow had melted by the time Oma and Rose returned from their vacation. They brimmed with tales of their adventure. We settled back into a normal routine. No one missed Norm.

Over a breakfast of French toast and strawberries one morning, Mr. Huckle and I told Oma what had happened, omitting the more worrisome details. She was appalled, but took it in stride, until a month later when she called me into the office.

Oma slid a magazine in front of me. It was open to a beautiful photo of the Sugar Maple Inn after a snowfall. And the byline read *Robin Jarvis.*

*Oh no!* She was a travel writer! My heart sank right down to my toes. She described the If the Dog Fits program in glowing terms, complete with a picture of Duke and Ella Mae posing by a fireplace in their new forever home.

She went on to describe Murder Most Howl as a funtastic weekend.

*The mountains were majestic, the inn romantic, and the service sublime. In spite of a blizzard, power outages, and other unexpected calamities, Holly Miller and her staff kept their guests comfortable and entertained. Five stars.*

I hadn't realized I was holding my breath. I sucked some air in.

"Good work, *liebchen*!" Oma smiled proudly.

If she only knew.

# Author's Note

I have home-cooked for my dogs for many years. Consult your veterinarian if you want to switch your dog over to home-cooked food. It's not as difficult as one might think. Keep in mind that, like children, dogs need a balanced diet, not just a hamburger. Any changes to your dog's diet should be made gradually so your dog's stomach can adjust.

Chocolate, alcohol, caffeine, fatty foods, grapes, raisins, macadamia nuts, onions and garlic, salt, xylitol, and unbaked dough can be toxic to dogs. For more information about foods your dog should not eat, consult the Pet Poison Helpline at petpoisonhelpline.com/pet-owners.

# Recipes

***For People, for Dogs, and a Few the Two May Share***

## Caramel Apple Bundt Cake

For people.

### Cake

*1½ cups flour*
*1 cup pecans*
*2 teaspoons baking powder*
*½ teaspoon baking soda*
*1½ teaspoons cinnamon*
*¾ teaspoon nutmeg*
*¾ teaspoon cloves*
*¼ teaspoon salt*
*2 medium apples, peeled and cored*

*½ cup sugar + extra*
*1¼ sticks (10 tablespoons) butter at room temperature + extra for greasing the pan*
*1 cup packed dark brown sugar*
*2 large eggs at room temperature*
*1 cup applesauce*

Preheat oven to 350°F.

Place the flour, pecans, baking powder, baking soda, cinnamon, nutmeg, cloves, and salt in a food processor and pulse until the pecans are fine. Transfer the flour mixture to a bowl. Insert the grating disk and grate the apples.

Take 1 tablespoon of sugar out of the plain sugar and set it aside. Cream the butter with the sugars. Beat in the eggs. Alternate adding the applesauce and the flour mixture until completely combined. Stir in the grated apples.

Grease the Bundt pan liberally. Sprinkle the extra sugar on the butter. You may need another tablespoon of sugar for full coverage. Use a cooking spoon to ladle the batter into the Bundt pan and smooth the top. Bake 40 minutes or until it begins to pull away from the sides and a cake tester comes out clean.

Allow to rest on a baking rack about 5 to 10 minutes. Loosen the edges, and flip onto the rack. When cool, top with caramel.

## Caramel

*4 tablespoons unsalted butter*
*1 cup packed dark brown sugar*
*¼ cup heavy cream*

Place the ingredients in a deep microwave-safe dish (I used a 4-cup Pyrex measuring cup). Microwave in short bursts, stirring occasionally, until it bubbles up and the sugar melts. (You may find that you even like it if the sugar doesn't melt!)

## Swedish Tea Ring

For people.

### Dough

*½ cup milk*
*½ cup water*
*2 packages instant yeast*
*3½ to 4 cups all-purpose flour*
*¼ cup butter, softened*
*¼ teaspoon salt*
*¼ cup sugar*
*1 egg*
*1 teaspoon cardamom*

### Filling

*¼ cup butter, softened*
*¼ cup dark brown sugar*
*1 tablespoon cinnamon*
*½ cup walnuts, chopped*
*½ cup dried cherries*

### Glaze

*1 cup powdered sugar, sifted*
*2 tablespoons milk*
*¼ teaspoon vanilla extract*
*maraschino cherries*

Warm the milk and water to 105°F to 110°F. Sprinkle the yeast on it and stir with a fork. Let stand until foamy, about 10 minutes. Pour into a mixing bowl and use the dough hook of your mixer. Add 3 cups flour, butter, salt, sugar, egg, and cardamom. Mix until a soft ball forms. If it's too sticky, add a bit more flour about ½ cup at a time. Let the mixer knead the dough about five minutes. Turn it out onto a lightly floured surface and knead a couple more times until smooth.

Lightly oil a large bowl, place the dough in the bowl, and turn to coat with oil. Cover with plastic wrap or a kitchen towel and let rise in a warm place until doubled in volume, about 1 hour.

Line a baking sheet with parchment paper. Punch down the dough and turn out onto a lightly floured surface. Roll the dough out to a 12-by-18-inch rectangle.

To make the filling, spread the softened butter on top of the rectangle. In another bowl, mix the cinnamon, sugar, walnuts, and dried cherries. Sprinkle across the dough. Roll the dough into a long, tight roll and press the seam closed. With the seam turned downward, seal the two ends together to make a ring.

Move the ring to the prepared parchment paper. With a sharp knife, slice the dough every inch or so, cutting only three-quarters of the way through. Cover the roll with plastic wrap or a kitchen towel and let rise in a warm place for 45 minutes.

Preheat oven to 375°F, and bake 20 to 30 minutes. Remove the ring from the oven and place on a rack to cool.

When cooled, stir together the powdered sugar, milk, and vanilla, and drizzle the glaze all over the ring. Decorate with maraschino cherries if desired.

# Sugar Maple Inn Mini Mac and Cheeselets

For people.

*3 cups cooked elbow macaroni*
*1½ tablespoons unsalted butter + more for brushing*
*4 tablespoons Parmesan cheese, divided*
*2 tablespoons all-purpose flour*
*¾ cup milk*
*1 cup sharp cheddar cheese, shredded*
*2 ounces cream cheese*
*2 slices crisp bacon, crumbled*
*1 egg yolk, lightly beaten*
*2 tablespoons panko bread crumbs*

Preheat oven to 425°F.

Use one 24-mini-cupcake pan or two 12-mini-cupcake pans. Brush each well of the pan with butter. Sprinkle the wells with 2 tablespoons Parmesan cheese. Over the sink, turn the pan to distribute, much as you would to flour a cake pan.

Melt 1½ tablespoons butter in a heavy pot and whisk in the flour. Cook about 2 minutes and whisk in the milk. Bring to a boil and simmer 5 minutes, whisking. Add the cheeses and whisk until melted. Remove from heat and whisk in the egg yolk.

Fold in the macaroni and the crumbled bacon. Use a measuring spoon to add a heaping tablespoon to each well. Mix 2 tablespoons Parmesan with the panko and sprinkle over each well. Bake for 10 minutes. Let stand for 5 minutes. Use a thin knife to loosen and remove.

# Sugar Maple Inn Chicken Stew for People

For people, *not* for dogs, because it contains onions.

*1 whole chicken*
*2 large onions, diced*
*6 carrots, peeled and sliced*
*4 stalks celery, sliced*
*1 teaspoon thyme*
*1 bay leaf*
*water*
*6 potatoes, peeled and quartered*
*2 8-ounce packages frozen yellow corn*
*1 package frozen baby lima beans*
*salt and pepper to taste*

In a large stockpot, combine the chicken, onions, carrots, celery, thyme, and bay leaf with enough water to cover everything. Put the lid on the pot, bring to a boil, then reduce heat and simmer for 1½ to 2 hours.

Remove the chicken, bay leaf, carrots, onions, and celery. Take out the fat using one of these methods:

- Refrigerate the broth overnight and skim the fat off the top;
- Skim off the top with a spoon or fine mesh skimmer;
- Pour through a fat-separating pitcher.

Add the carrots, onions, and celery back to the pot. Bring to a simmer again and add the potatoes. When they have cooked, remove 1 cup of the potatoes, mash them with a fork, and put them back in the soup to thicken it.

Meanwhile, take the meat off the chicken and dice.

Add the corn and lima beans. When they are warm, add the meat, salt and pepper to taste, and serve.

## Blanche Burger

Only for people, makes 2.

*½ medium-size sweet onion*
*1 to 2 tablespoons canola oil*
*½ pound ground beef*
*Boursin cheese*
*2 hamburger buns*

Peel the onion, and slice into rings or half rings. Heat the oil in a frying pan over medium heat. Add the onion rings and sauté slowly until translucent. Remove from the pan. Shape the ground beef into 2 hamburger patties and place in the pan. Cook to medium rare, about 3 to 4 minutes on each side. Meanwhile spread a thick layer of cheese on the tops and the bottoms of the buns. Place the hamburgers on the bottom buns, add a little more cheese on top. Add the onions and put the top bun on.

## Krista's Chocolate Chip Cookies

For people *only*.

*2 sticks butter, melted*
*2 cups flour*
*¾ teaspoon kosher salt*
*1 teaspoon baking powder*
*½ teaspoon baking soda*
*2 whole eggs*
*¼ cup sugar*

*1¼ cups dark brown sugar*
*1½ teaspoons vanilla*
*2 cups chocolate chips*

Preheat oven to 350°F.

Line a cookie sheet with parchment paper. Melt the butter in the microwave at half power in short bursts. Mix the flour, salt, baking powder, and baking soda in a bowl. Beat the eggs with the sugars. Add the cooled melted butter, alternating with the flour mixture. Add the vanilla. Stir in the chocolate chips. Drop the raw dough on the sheet in generous spoonfuls a couple of inches apart. Bake at 350°F for 10 minutes. Remove to a cooling rack when done.

## Nutella Hot Chocolate

For people only!

*3 tablespoons powdered chocolate (or use amount recommended for your brand)*
*2 tablespoons cold water*
*¼ cup sugar (omit if chocolate powder is already sweetened)*
*3 cups milk*
*¼ cup Nutella*
*¼ cup hazelnut liqueur, such as Frangelico (optional)*
*whipped cream*

Mix the chocolate with the water, then stir in the milk. Heat until the milk just starts to simmer. Or microwave until hot. Whisk in the remaining ingredients until smooth. Top with whipped cream.

## Gingerbread Cupcakes

For people, though dogs may have a bite of unfrosted cupcake. Makes 12 to 14 regular size cupcakes.

*1⅓ cups all-purpose flour*
*1 teaspoon ground cinnamon*
*½ teaspoon baking powder*
*½ teaspoon baking soda*
*½ teaspoon salt*
*1 teaspoon ground ginger*
*½ teaspoon ground nutmeg*
*¾ cup packed brown sugar*
*½ cup butter, softened*
*2 eggs, room temperature*
*½ cup warm water*
*½ cup molasses*

Preheat oven to 350°F.

Prepare a cupcake pan with cupcake liners. In a bowl, mix together the flour, cinnamon, baking powder, baking soda, salt, ginger, and nutmeg. Set aside. Cream the sugar with the butter about 2 minutes, then beat in the eggs. Mix the water with the molasses and add in thirds, alternating with the flour mixture. Beat well. Fill cupcake liners one-half full. Bake 16 to 20 minutes. Cool on a rack. Dust with powdered sugar or frost with your favorite frosting.

## Maple Syrup Bacon Slices

For people, but dogs may have a *small* taste.

*bacon*
*maple syrup*

Preheat oven to 400°F.

Drape the bacon slices on a rack set in a pan. Cook 15 to 20 minutes. Brush with maple syrup and cook another 3 to 4 minutes. Remove to a plate covered with a paper towel to catch the drips.

## Mac and Tease

For dogs. Makes 2 Gingersnap-size servings or several Trixie-size servings.

*2 cups cooked elbow macaroni*
*1 cup cooked cauliflower (steamed or roasted)*
*½ pound cooked ground beef*
*¼ cup shredded white goat gouda cheese*

Preheat oven to 350°F.

Chop the cauliflower and mix with the macaroni in an 8-by-8-inch baking pan. Crumble in the beef and mix. Sprinkle the cheese over top. Bake 4 to 5 minutes, until the cheese has melted on top. Let stand for 5 minutes or until cool enough to eat. Spoon into bowls.

# Sugar Maple Inn Chicken Stew for Dogs

For dogs, do *not* add onions or garlic! People can eat this dish, too, but will likely find it bland. Please note: *Never* use commercial chicken broth for dog recipes because it contains onions. This recipe makes a large amount. Freeze the remainder without the barley, then thaw and warm to serve.

*1 whole chicken*
*1 large turnip (optional)*
*6 carrots, peeled*
*4 stalks celery*
*1 teaspoon thyme*
*1 bay leaf*
*7 cups water*
*6 potatoes, peeled and quartered*
*1 8-ounce package frozen yellow corn*
*1 package frozen baby lima beans*
*cooked barley or rice*

In a large stockpot, combine the chicken, turnip, carrots, celery, thyme, and bay leaf with enough water to cover everything. Put the lid on the pot, bring to a boil, then reduce heat and simmer for 1½ to 2 hours.

Remove the chicken, bay leaf, carrots, turnip, and celery.

Take out the fat using one of these methods. *Do not skip this step*—too much fat can make your dog sick:

- Refrigerate the broth overnight and skim the fat off the top;
- Skim off the top with a spoon or fine mesh skimmer;
- Pour through a fat-separating pitcher.

Add the carrots, turnip, and celery back to the pot. Bring to a simmer again and add the potatoes. When they have cooked, remove 1 cup of the potatoes, mash them with a fork, and put them back in the soup to thicken it.

Meanwhile, take the meat off the chicken and dice.

Add the corn and lima beans. When they are warm, add the meat and serve over cooked barley or rice. (Do not add salt or pepper to the stew for dogs.)

## Sugar Maple Inn Rodeo Roundup

For dogs. Makes 2 to 3 Gingersnap-size portions or 5 to 6 Trixie-size portions.

*1 to 2 tablespoons olive oil*
*1 pound very lean ground beef*
*½ 8-ounce package frozen corn*
*3 cups cooked brown rice*
*½ 15-ounce can kidney beans*

Heat the olive oil and cook the ground beef as you would hamburgers. Meanwhile, cook the corn according to the package. When slightly pink inside, remove the ground beef from the pan and set aside. Add a splash of water to the pan and deglaze, scraping up any bits stuck to the bottom. Add the rice to the pan and stir to coat with the flavor of the beef. Add the beans and corn, and crumble the beef into the pan. (If your dog likes to pick out the meat, crumble very fine.) Mix and serve mildly warm but not hot.

Keep reading for a special preview of Krista Davis's next Domestic Diva Mystery . . .

*The Diva Serves High Tea*

Coming June 2016 from Berkley Prime Crime!

*Dear Natasha,*

*My new boyfriend's mother loves to garden. She keeps offering me cups of home-grown comfrey tea but I'm a little nervous about drinking tea made from some weed. Do you think her herbal teas are safe to drink?*

*Uneasy in Tea Kettle Junction, Maine*

*Dear Uneasy,*

*Many herbal teas, like chamomile, have been safely consumed for centuries. However, comfrey tea is not one of them. It sounds like she wants you to find a new boyfriend.*

*Natasha*

At three in the morning the world is simultaneously peaceful and a little bit spooky. No cars rumbled by on my street. No warm yellow glow shone in the windows of my neighbors' homes. Of course, it didn't help that Natasha had woken me from a deep sleep by texting the word *Intruder!*

Who sends a message like that? I had phoned her to ask if she had called 911, but she didn't answer. She didn't respond to my return text either.

My ex-husband, Mars, who now happened to be Natasha's significant other, was out of town at a political event. I had known Natasha since we were kids in tiny Berryville, Virginia, and competed at everything except the beauty pageants she loved so much. Familiar with her predilection for drama, I hadn't hurried. I slid my feet into sandals and threw on a fluffy long white bathrobe, attached a leash to my hound mix, Daisy, and crossed the street at a leisurely pace in the warm full night.

Nevertheless, I shrieked when a cat streaked out of the shadows and across the sidewalk right in front of us. Daisy barked once at the inconsiderate cat.

Natasha's front door was locked. I rapped on it, and called, "Natasha!" I banged the knocker, which sounded unbelievably loud in the night. No response at all. I was beginning to get worried. Why wasn't she answering the door? I tried the handle again but the door was definitely locked.

"Let's go around back," I said to Daisy.

I opened the gate to the passage that ran along the side of the house. In Old Town Alexandria, Virginia, the historic houses were situated close together, often with only a narrow service passage between buildings. Daisy led the way in the darkness. In the back yard, I pulled the handle of the sliding glass door to Mars's man cave, but it didn't budge.

We hurried up the stairs to the deck, where I pounded on the kitchen door. "Natasha?"

Still nothing. There were no lights on in the house, either.

Daisy pulled on her leash.

"Not now, Daisy." Why hadn't I brought the key to Natasha's house? I considered smashing a window. Should I go home and look for the key or break the glass to save time?

Daisy yelped, startling me. She tugged toward the side of the deck.

I heard a soft whoosh. Following Daisy's lead, I tiptoed over to the railing and looked down just in time to see a person in black, wearing a hood, close the sliding glass door and sneak around the side of the house.

"Hey! Stop!"

I scrambled down the stairs but he or she had already vanished. I stopped short of following the person into the dark passage. That would be incredibly stupid. The intruder could be lurking there. Besides, Natasha might be hurt and need help.

"C'mon, Daisy," I whispered. We ran to the basement door. I slid it open. Where were the light switches? "Natasha?" I yelled.

Walking cautiously, and looking around in case another intruder remained behind, I made my way to the back of the room, where stairs led to the main floor. I found a panel of light switches. I flicked them all on, and the room blazed. I took a quick look to be sure no one hid behind the bar before racing upstairs calling Natasha's name. I turned on the lights in the foyer and the stairwell. Nothing seemed out of place. "Natasha!"

I wasn't sure where to start. She had probably been asleep when the intruder came in. I rushed up the stairs, hoping Daisy, who wasn't much of a watchdog, would alert me if she smelled someone lurking in the house. At the top of the stairs, I turned right, toward Natasha and Mars's bedroom, flicking on overhead lights as I went. "Natasha!"

In the master bedroom, decorated in shades of gray from the walls to the bedding, it was clear that her bed had been slept in. But she was nowhere to be seen. "Natasha!"

Daisy pulled me toward the bathroom door. I grabbed

the doorknob and twisted but it didn't budge. It was locked tight. I knocked, which seemed somewhat silly under the circumstances. "Natasha? Are you in there? It's Sophie."

Nothing. No response. Not a sound in the house.

I jiggled the doorknob, which accomplished nothing. I studied the lock. Who put a key lock on a bathroom door? I backed up a step and banged my shoulder into the door. Ow. It looked a lot easier in the movies.

The thud of the door knocker rumbled through the house. When I was dashing down the stairs, I heard, "Natasha? It's Officer Wong."

*Thank heaven!* I recognized Wong's voice, unlocked the door, and threw it open.

Wong enjoyed surprising people who expected an Asian officer. Her surname was the last vestige of marrying the wrong man, but she hadn't bothered to change it. Wong wasn't much taller than my five feet. Her uniform strained against her ample curves. African-American, she wore her hair short in the back with a sassy curl that fell on her forehead. "Sophie! I didn't expect to see you. Everything okay?"

"I think Natasha is locked in the bathroom upstairs. But she's not responding when I call her name."

"We had a report of an intruder."

"Someone was in the house. I saw him leave."

"Him?"

"Or her. I don't know. Someone dressed in black."

Wong frowned. "Wait here."

"What about Natasha?"

"Stay right where you are. You don't know if there's someone else in the house."

Wong had proven herself logical and reliable in the past. I followed her instruction and waited by the front door with Daisy. I could hear Wong moving through the rooms on the main floor and basement, checking them out.

Wong made her way back to the foyer. "I don't see anything unusual. How'd you get in?"

"Through the basement."

Wong started up the stairs.

I hated waiting by the door. I knew I could be in the way if I followed her and she found someone hiding in the house, but I couldn't help feeling time was of the essence. What if the intruder had hurt Natasha and locked her in the bathroom? I ran up the stairs as quietly as I could, but Daisy's paws hit the stairs like thunder.

I tried the doorknob to the bathroom again. It was still locked. "Natasha! Natasha!"

Wong walked up beside me. "What part of *wait right there* wasn't clear to you?"

"What if she's bleeding or unconscious?" I jiggled the knob in frustration.

Wong looked around, opened the drawers of a dressing table, and withdrew something.

"What are you doing?"

"Stand aside, Sophie."

She took two hair pins, pried one open, and bent the other at a slight angle. She inserted them in the lock and opened the door in a matter of seconds.

Inside, Natasha was sprawled on the floor, facedown.